·JASMINE VILLA SERIES·

ANDALEEB WAJID

One Way to Love

First published by Westland Books, a division of Nasadiya Technologies Private Limited, in 2023

No. 269/2B, First Floor, 'Irai Arul', Vimalraj Street, Nethaji Nagar, Allappakkam Main Road, Maduravoyal, Chennai 600095

Westland and the Westland logo are the trademarks of Nasadiya Technologies Private Limited, or its affiliates.

ISBN: 9789395767897

10 9 8 7 6 5 4 3 2 1

This is a work of fiction. Names, characters, organisations, places, events and incidents are either products of the author's imagination or used fictitiously.

Typeset by SÜRYA, New Delhi
Printed at Nutech Print Services-India

One Way to Love

Andaleeb Wajid is a hybrid author, having published 40 novels in the past 14 years. She enjoys writing in a number of different genres such as young adult, romance, and horror. She lives and writes in Bengaluru.

ONE

Tehzeeb Hasan's house—Jasmine Villa—was old and rundown and sat squat in the middle of a small patch of garden that was filled with the fragrance of malligai poo blossoms. Her mother Amina had planted the tree when she got married and the tender malligai poo plant had been carefully transplanted from her own mother's house in Vellore and brought here all those years ago.

When people pushed open the half-rusted pink gate as they came inside, they often stared at the strange surroundings but then the lush scent of jasmine would surprise them and take them unawares. Tehzeeb's father Yusuf had bought the house (villa in name only) decades ago when land prices were cheap and one could actually afford to buy land in Fraser Town. He had intended to demolish the house and build a fresh and sparkling new building from scratch. Three floors. Economical and clean. They would live on the topmost and rent out all the other floors.

But the land was under dispute (which was why he had got it for so cheap) and he was not allowed to touch the house until the dispute was resolved. With much money going to the lawyers and then to the hospitals for his wife's illness, Yusuf had never got around to building the house of his dreams. He continued to work for others as an accountant and never made much money. He continued to go to work on his tattered scooter even as everything around him changed.

The house was the one thing that didn't change. His daughters had been born here but his wife had not been able to see them grow into beautiful young women. She had died of cancer a few years ago. Tehzeeb had been just sixteen then and Ana and Athiya had been fifteen and fourteen respectively. But Yusuf went on, much to the dismay of his relatives, refusing to remarry like many other men did.

Tehzeeb knew her father missed her mother. She saw it on his face whenever he sat down on the steps of the house, which had become his refuge after he retired. She read it in his demeanour when he would sigh and watch the mynahs flit around the branches while he wrote Urdu poetry elegantly on a notepad. And she wished there was something she could do to ease his pain.

Tehzeeb felt everything keenly. She was observant to a fault and very good at reading emotions. She was tall and slender and had wavy dark brown hair that reached her waist. Already, aunties were chasing her father, sending rishtas for her, but he had refused. Tehzeeb had spoken to him one day, after her fifth semester concluded, telling him that she wanted to work in an NGO after her final semester in college.

Her father had merely smiled and patted her hand. 'You do what you want, beta,' he told her. His words had filled Tehzeeb with hope. Her younger sisters were still studying like her, but she knew that her father wouldn't steamroll over their dreams. She knew they were lucky to have someone like him.

As she sat in her room with the mouldy green paint—it had been advertised as moss green many years ago—she wondered what her future would bring. Her father had assured her that she could work for a couple of years at least until it would be time for her to get married.

She had just returned from work a little while back. She was working at an NGO for women and there were days when she came back filled with hope, and others when she would cry in the shower, thinking about some of the things other women endured.

She was just headed for her shower when her youngest sister Athiya walked inside, talking to someone on the phone. Athiya dropped her bag on the ground and flung her dupatta on the bed. She looked irritated.

'I said no when you asked me in college and I'm saying no now,' she said firmly. Tehzeeb frowned. What was the matter? Her youngest sister Athiya was a firebrand and known to lose her temper in seconds.

'Listen fucker, I told you I'm not interested!' she shouted suddenly.

Tehzeeb groaned. 'Athiya, language!' she told her sister in a loud whisper. 'Abbu will hear!' Athiya's nostrils were flared as she ignored her.

'Don't call me again!' Athiya told the person on the other end and switched off the call angrily. She turned to Tehzeeb with a warning look on her face. 'Api, don't start!'

'But ...'

'I've had a shitty day already. I cannot wait to say goodbye to this fucking college!' she said as she grabbed a towel and headed off to the bathroom, disrobing on the way as she went.

'Don't finish all the hot water in the geyser!' Tehzeeb called out. But Athiya didn't reply. Ana walked in then, her hands on her hips when she saw the mess that Athiya had made in the room.

'Is she being a brat again?' she asked, her lips pursed. Tehzeeb shrugged. Athiya had taken their mother's death the worst. While Tehzeeb and Ana had managed to get over their grief, it had not been that easy for their youngest sister, who had been the baby of the family. Even now, six years later, Athiya carried that hurt within her and it often manifested itself in outbursts.

'How was your day?' Tehzeeb asked Ana. Ana didn't reply immediately. She walked up to the mess that Athiya had made and gingerly picked up all the dirty clothes with her thumb and fingertip. She turned to Tehzeeb and shook her head, making a 'shh' sound with her mouth. Minutes later, they heard the shower being shut off. Athiya was probably wrapping her towel around her body. She opened the door and the steam from inside billowed out and barely had she stepped outside when Ana had flung the dirty clothes on her.

'Api!' Athiya screamed. 'I just had a bath!'

'And now you can put your clothes in the washing machine, where they belong,' Ana told her sweetly.

Tehzeeb slapped her forehead with her palm. 'Stop it you two. I'm tired,' she said as she went inside the still warm bathroom.

Their house was small. They had only two bedrooms, a hall and a kitchen. The three of them in one room was not easy to manage, especially now. Growing up too, it had been a nightmare. When her parents were younger and she was small, she had often heard her father promise her mother that he would build the new house for them. Even then she had known that it would never happen.

She heard Athiya and Ana bicker about the dirty clothes and then whose turn it was to make dinner. She shut her eyes and called out to them over the lukewarm shower that trickled over her—she would cook as long as they stopped fighting.

The lukewarm trickle then became a blast of cold water. Wincing, Tehzeeb finished her shower quickly. Ana was doing her post-graduate studies in another college and came home earlier. She could have easily made dinner already, Tehzeeb thought, annoyed with her sisters. She loved them to bits but could cheerfully have walloped the two of them every day for their antics.

Drying herself, she changed into clean clothes and took her dirty ones to the washing machine. To her surprise, she saw that Ana had already made dinner but had simply been up to her usual shenanigans, pretending that she hadn't. This was one of Ana's favourite ways of annoying her family – pretending she hadn't done something when she had done it already.

Shaking her head, Tehzeeb walked away to the tiny storage room adjacent to the kitchen where the washing machine was kept and dumped her clothes inside. She added the detergent and then switched on the machine and walked back to the small living room where Athiya and Ana were arguing over something.

'Where's Abbu?' Tehzeeb asked as she sat down on one of the sofas.

'He went out when I got home. Said he will be coming back for dinner,' Ana said. The three of them got busy with their phones, waiting for their father to return.

TWO

At eight that night, Tehzeeb was getting hungry and she dialled her father's number. He answered on the fourth ring.

'Abbu, where are you?' she asked him.

'Almost home,' he replied. She ended the call and got up, thinking it was time to make rotis now that Abbu was nearly home. She opened the fridge, pulled out the kneaded atta and kept it on the counter. Athiya followed her inside almost reluctantly.

The two sisters made the rotis while chatting about their day. Despite it being a tedious chore, Tehzeeb found that this was one of the times she actually enjoyed working in the kitchen because of the different insights she got into her sisters' lives.

'Who were you yelling at?' Tehzeeb asked as she heard the front door open and Abbu let himself inside. Athiya sighed.

'There's this annoying guy in my class, Api. He asked me if I would go with him for the class trip to Mysore,' she said.

'What class trip?' Tehzeeb asked frowning. Abbu never let any of them go on any class trips anywhere.

At this, a mutinous look settled on her sister's face.

Athiya was the opposite of her in every possible way – looks, temperament and attitude. Where Tehzeeb worried for everyone and always took into consideration everyone's feelings, Athiya often behaved like she didn't care for anyone but herself. Her size was no indicator of her temper and passion. Despite being much shorter than Tehzeeb and Ana, she often bullied them both and almost always got her way.

'It's between me and Abbu. You let it be,' she told her sister.

Ana came in to heat the gravy and she had a funny look on her face.

'What's the matter?' Tehzeeb asked her as she switched off the stove.

'Make a couple more rotis, no?' Ana told her.

'Why?' Tehzeeb asked, surprised.

'Abbu has brought a guest with him today,' she said, looking a little flustered. Tehzeeb watched as her sister washed the china plates that they used only on special occasions and kept them on one side of the sink.

'I wish he would at least tell us before doing these things,' Athiya muttered.

'Hey, it's okay. It's just a guest. We should always be …' Tehzeeb started.

'Yes, yes I know what you're going to say!' Athiya snapped at her sister as she switched on the stove.

Quickly, Tehzeeb rolled out three more rotis while Athiya cooked them. Ana pulled out the serving dish from the wooden cupboard that stood against one of the walls. Three people in the kitchen was one too many, so Tehzeeb went out, hoping her sisters would bring everything to the dining table.

Her father was seated with a middle-aged man who was talking to him earnestly in their tiny living room. He was well-dressed, in a crisp white shirt with dark trousers and was impeccably groomed. Abbu turned to her as she walked past them and beckoned her.

'This is my eldest daughter, Tehzeeb,' Abbu introduced her to the man who smiled at her. She smiled back at him. The man had warm eyes and a friendly demeanour and she nodded demurely.

As Ana and Athiya emerged from the kitchen, their faces damp from the kitchen's heat, Abbu introduced them as well, then turned to the man and smiled.

'Girls, this is my friend Bakhtiyar Ahmed. We used to study together in college, many, many years ago,' Abbu said.

The girls nodded and Athiya was rather fidgety as Abbu invited the man to join them for dinner. Bakhtiyar Ahmed stood up and looked at his watch. Tehzeeb noticed it was a flat gold watch that gleamed quietly, hinting at its expensiveness.

'No, no Yusuf! I didn't even realise the time! It's really late!' he said. Abbu too had stood up, shaking his head.

'We've met after so long! You have to eat dinner at my home today,' Abbu insisted. If only Abbu had informed them before, Tehzeeb would have cooked something else. As it was, there didn't seem to be any time to order anything from outside either.

Bakhtiyar continued making objections which Abbu kept overruling and finally, he agreed to join them for dinner.

'Cover your head with your dupatta,' Tehzeeb whispered to Athiya who turned her head to look up at her and glared.

'Why?' she asked. Tehzeeb tried to convince her with

her eyes but Athiya just stared back at her. What will this man think of us, Tehzeeb wondered. But she needn't have worried. Bakhtiyar Ahmed had warmed up to them and was in a genial mood, talking about the old days.

He had a loud, infectious laugh and they were all smiling, even giggling, as they heard the stories about how Abbu had been such a straight arrow and the one day he decided to bunk and go to a movie, he had been caught by his own father.

'You girls should have seen his face! We didn't have phone cameras back then or I would have recorded the whole thing!' Bakhtiyar related, laughing as he finished eating. Tehzeeb glanced at her father and although he was smiling, she detected a little uneasiness on his face.

Bakhtiyar pushed the chair back slightly, shaking his head.

'I can't eat any more Yusuf! You're a lucky man. Your daughters cook too well,' he said.

For some reason no one could fathom, it irked Athiya. 'Hotel se mangwaya hai,' she said. Everyone looked at her in surprise. Abbu looked confused but Ana shook her head.

'No, I made it. She's just joking, uncle,' she assured him, glaring at her sister.

'I just wanted to say that there's more to us than the food we can cook,' Athiya said. 'And Abbu isn't lucky *just* because we can cook.'

Tehzeeb's face flushed as she wondered, once again, what he would think of them. She normally never felt ashamed of their home but looking at it through Bakhtiyar's eyes, she wondered how it appeared. The broken-down wall near the gate that she had been asking Abbu to fix, the peeling paint, the various gardening tools that Abbu used which were often piled up together near the entrance to the house … since they hardly received visitors, it had never really mattered.

She wondered about Bakhtiyar's house. He probably lived in some expensive villa type of place, she mused. With security guards and a personal swimming pool. She had got a whiff of an intense cologne as he had circled around them to sit at the table. Most probably, there was a driver waiting for him in an expensive car parked in one of the lanes nearby.

'Oh, absolutely,' he agreed effusively. 'Your father is lucky because he has the three of you.'

Feeling like she needed to explain her sister's behaviour, Tehzeeb smiled at him. 'Athiya is our resident feminist, uncle,' she said.

'And you?' he asked, with a broad smile.

'Api is the pushover,' Athiya replied instead, arms crossed.

'I am not!' Tehzeeb said, but without any anger. 'They only think they can get away with everything.'

Bakhtiyar nodded and then got up. 'It's time I left,' he said with an apologetic smile to them all. Abbu got up with him and they walked outside, talking.

Tehzeeb turned to her sister, eyes flashing, but before she could reprimand her, Athiya had already pushed her chair back and walked away.

THREE

'Does Abbu ever think before he does anything?' Athiya asked when Tehzeeb followed her into their room.

'What do you mean?' Tehzeeb frowned. She had been meaning to reprimand her sister about her behaviour but Athiya's question caught her off guard.

'How could he bring someone like that man here when our house is like this!' Athiya exclaimed.

Tehzeeb had been thinking the same thoughts too but she didn't acknowledge them. She always tried to take her father's side but now she didn't know what to say.

'It's okay,' she said finally, trying to brush it off. 'What wasn't okay was the way you behaved.'

Athiya's nostrils flared. 'Don't make this about me.'

'Why not? That's no way to talk to a guest!' Tehzeeb reprimanded her.

'We don't need any guests at home. Not when our house looks like this!' Athiya snapped.

'Abbu is calling both of you outside,' Ana said, standing at the door.

Tehzeeb exhaled, walked out and Athiya followed her reluctantly. Abbu was in the living room and he asked them to sit. He had a strange expression on his face, almost dreamy, and he smiled absently.

They sat down and looked at him expectantly. The power went suddenly, plunging them into darkness. The girls fiddled around and switched on their mobile phone torches and then Ana went looking for candles.

Abbu got busy with his own phone and Tehzeeb wondered why he had asked them to come outside. When finally the candles were lit, their house looked even more eerie and gloomy but Tehzeeb didn't mind. It took a little while for everyone to settle down once more.

'What were you going to say, Abbu?' Tehzeeb reminded him. He looked at her and seemed to be on the verge of saying something but he didn't.

'I ... let's talk when the power comes,' he said. Tehzeeb frowned.

'Why? We're all here,' she said. He still seemed undecided.

'In a bit, Tehzeeb. I just want to be able to see you properly when we talk,' he said.

How strange, she thought as she glanced at her sisters. They were both busy checking their phones and the silence in the house was almost unnerving. The only sound was of the candle flame flickering.

'Someone call BESCOM,' Ana said suddenly.

'You call,' Athiya responded.

'No, *you* do it,' Ana said. Her sisters started bickering again but Tehzeeb found her father looking at her strangely once more.

'What is it, Abbu?' she asked him.

He shook his head. Since both Athiya and Ana were still fighting over who would call BESCOM, Tehzeeb dialled the number from her phone and heard the waiting tone that was so annoying it could easily drive anyone crazy if they listened to it long enough. When she finally got through, the call centre woman on the other end said that it would take at least two hours for the power to be restored.

Oh no, Tehzeeb thought. Her sisters would probably kill each other by then. Power cuts were a big pain at normal times, but when her sisters were already fighting and bickering, it could get worse.

'Let's play a game?' she asked, trying to rein in the situation.

They didn't hear her at first and she had to repeat herself over their arguments. Abbu kept looking at her in that strange sort of way.

'We'll play charades!' she announced.

'Ugh, I don't want to!' Ana said, trying to get up from there.

Tehzeeb pushed her back down with a hand on her thigh. 'No, no! Let's play. We used to play it all the time before we got mobile phones!'

'There's no point in playing because you win all the damn time!' Athiya said.

Abbu frowned and Tehzeeb wondered what he would say if he heard her more colourful speech.

'I don't win all the time!' Tehzeeb said instead.

'You do! You only look like butter wouldn't melt in your mouth. You can imitate anyone under the sun!' Ana added.

'But ...'

'It's true,' Abbu nodded. 'I've seen you do that many times. We all know you're a very good mimic!'

'So? That has nothing to do with charades. Let's play, no? It's really been years since we played anything,' Tehzeeb insisted.

Reluctantly, her sisters joined the game. Abbu didn't

join but guessed with the others and soon they were busy laughing and having fun. They were right though. Tehzeeb was indeed excellent at acting out scenes from movies which made the guessing easier but also hilariously funny.

The moment the lights came back on though, they stopped.

Abbu cleared his throat. 'Girls, I have something important to talk to you all,' he said. 'Bakhtiyar and I had a very long discussion today,' he said.

'When?' Tehzeeb asked, surprised.

'We met at the masjid today and got talking,' Abbu explained. 'It was actually surprising that he recognised me. We haven't met in so many years that I didn't even know who he was at first.'

Tehzeeb nudged Athiya but her sister didn't respond. She hoped Athiya wouldn't launch into a monologue about why it hadn't been a good idea to invite Bakhtiyar Ahmed home.

Tehzeeb and the others fell silent. She knew something was up with her father. He wasn't his usual absent-minded self from the time he had come back home with Bakhtiyar Ahmed. What could be the matter?

Abbu took a deep breath.

'Bakhtiyar has brought a proposal for us. He would like Tehzeeb to get married to his son Ayub,' Abbu said in a rush. He looked at Tehzeeb and smiled, as though hoping she would agree right away.

FOUR

'What?' Tehzeeb asked, not sure if she heard correctly.

Abbu frowned. 'Is there a problem, Tehzeeb?' he asked her.

'Abbu, you told me I could work!' she protested, feeling a hot flush creep up her face.

'And you *are* working! But when you get a proposal from a house like Bakhtiyar's, you'd be idiotic to say no. They are well-settled and …'

'You mean rich!' Ana interjected with a roll of her eyes. Abbu looked at her, annoyed.

'Yes. What's the harm in that? Bakhtiyar's family is good and I'm sure his son will be an excellent choice for you!' Abbu said, turning to Tehzeeb once more.

Tehzeeb shook her head. 'How would you know that? You haven't even met him or seen him!'

'I have,' Abbu said.

'What? When?' Athiya asked, suddenly interested.

'He was at the masjid with his father. When we met up, Bakhtiyar asked Ayub to carry on and he said he would come back later. He is a good-looking young man, well-spoken and he has a kind look in his eyes,' Abbu said.

Tehzeeb looked at her sisters for help. Athiya exhaled

loudly. 'Abbu,' she said. 'He was at the masjid. He was obviously going to look kind and good at that time.'

'That's not what I meant,' Abbu said, looking at all of them, as though he was cornered.

'But Abbu, I don't want to get married!' Tehzeeb said. Abbu frowned.

'At all or just now?' he asked.

Tehzeeb opened her mouth to say something but didn't know what to say. She hadn't given marriage a serious thought. She wanted to continue working and helping people and she had hoped she would have a few more years at least.

'Look, Tehzeeb,' Abbu went on when she didn't answer. 'I know you wanted to work for a few years and you already have done so much since you finished college. Think of the advantages you will have when you get married into a family like theirs. They will not have any issues with you working. It will be the best of all the worlds, beta.'

'But Abbu ...' she began. 'Why Bakhtiyar Ahmed's family?'

'Why not? They are surely better than the many proposals I have been fending off from your aunts all these years. Either those boys worked in Dubai or the Middle East or they were not better off than us,' Abbu replied.

Tehzeeb wondered what Bakhtiyar Ahmed must have thought of their house. How quaint and rundown it must have appeared compared to the bungalow he surely lived in.

'Whose idea was it?' she asked, finally.

'What do you mean?' Abbu asked, his eyes narrowing.

'Surely he did not just say out of the blue that he would like to get his son married to me!' Tehzeeb said. Her father's face flushed a little.

'No, we got to talking about our lives and our families. I told him I had three daughters and he said he had a son and a daughter. He was planning to get his son married first. I was taken aback too when he said that he would like to get his son married to my daughter.'

'What? He asked before he even visited our house?' she asked, surprised. At this, even Ana and Athiya looked at their father in surprise. Tehzeeb immediately thought that there was probably something wrong with his son that he wanted him to get married to any gullible girl. It made the most sense.

Apparently, her sisters had the same thought.

'Maybe he's gay,' Athiya whispered to Ana and Tehzeeb's eyes widened. That could be possible. Bakhtiyar might be using them just to stop any rumours about his own son and to give him a seal of legitimacy. Her father, her poor naïve father, had assumed that Bakhtiyar was asking for her hand out of the goodness of his heart. But how to tell this to him?

'What did you say?' he asked Athiya, frowning.

'Abbu, just think about it. You meet a man whom you haven't met in years and he asks for your daughter's hand in marriage for his son, without even seeing her. There has to be something wrong with his son, right?' Athiya explained.

'No, no, there's nothing wrong with him!' Abbu exclaimed.

How do we explain this to Abbu, Tehzeeb wondered frantically.

'Obviously, there's nothing *wrong* with him. But what if he's gay? And I don't mean that being gay is wrong, but how can you get Api married to such a man?' Athiya asked. Her father looked shocked.

'Abbu, please be realistic. It's entirely possible,' Tehzeeb said, hoping to make him understand.

Abbu was silent. He looked at all three of them and he shook his head.

'I … I didn't think about all this. I really don't think that's the case. But I don't want to ruin Tehzeeb's life either,' he said.

Tehzeeb felt a moment's relief. But then he went on speaking. 'What if I arrange a meeting with Ayub?' he asked her.

'What?'

'Yes, why don't you meet him and see him for yourself?' he asked.

'But Abbu! How will I …' Tehzeeb trailed off.

'Tehzeeb, there is no better way. It would be a good idea to see him for yourself and decide,' Abbu said.

Ana and Athiya both looked doubtful but Tehzeeb nodded slowly.

'Okay. I'll meet him but I don't want anyone else around,' she said. Abbu frowned but she shook her head.

'Abbu, I would need to speak to him honestly. It won't be possible if there's a crowd of people breathing down our necks,' she said.

'Yes, but … Bakhtiyar might …'

'You said they are rich and most rich people are progressive. They won't mind what Tehzeeb Api is asking,' Ana said.

Sighing, Abbu nodded. 'Okay, I'll talk to Bakhtiyar and see what we can do.'

FIVE

One week later

Ayub Ahmed didn't have the time for this. His father had set up this meeting last night all of a sudden, telling him he *had* to meet this girl in the coffee shop on the way to his office and that had baffled him. Why was his father acting so strange? If he wanted Ayub to hire this girl as his assistant, she would have to be qualified, it didn't matter if she was his best friend's daughter or a long-lost friend's daughter, he was not going to take her on. It was as simple as that.

He parked his car in one of the by-lanes and walked towards the coffee shop, his mind buzzing with the various activities that he had planned for the day. As one of the leading architects in the city, his day was often full and didn't include unplanned meetings with potential assistants in coffee shops. What was his father thinking? Why couldn't this girl come to the office and give an interview like others? Where was her resumé? Why had his father said that she was perfect for the role?

None of it made sense but he didn't even have time to wonder about it. He had to get away from here in thirty minutes or less. His meeting with the builders was this afternoon and he had to prep quite a bit before that. This was the only coffee shop that was open at nine in the morning and he had specifically told his father that if this girl was late, he wasn't going to wait for her.

He had been looking for an assistant for a while now, someone who would make his life easier, but most of the people who showed up were either not qualified or if they were, they happened to be plain idiots.

At twenty-eight, Ayub was a successful man in his own right and while he may have gotten a leg up thanks to his father, he had gone on to forge his own success after he had finished his education. He knew he was meeting the daughter of the man they had met in the masjid last week. What was his name? He couldn't recall it right away.

If his father hadn't had a client meeting on that side of the town, they would have never met him. Yusuf Hasan. His father had gone quite still when he recognised Yusuf and initially, when the two of them met, it was not like old friends but wary enemies. But then his father said something to Yusuf softly and the other man had smiled. It had been a startling smile, one that warmed the onlooker too. Ayub had liked Yusuf instantly. There was something old school and charismatic about the man and it was the sort of thing that you just felt. You could never really understand why.

Then, his father went away with his friend, informing Ayub that he would come home later. This surprised him even more. In fact, Ammi had not been amused that Abba had disappeared at dinner time and hadn't even answered his phone when she tried to reach him.

Anyway, Ayub may have liked Yusuf on sight but his daughter had better be good or he was not going to be pleased about this detour from his workday. He pushed open the glass door of the coffee shop and walked inside. Built in a refurbished old house, the coffee shop was very popular with startup owners and other businesses who came here to conduct their meetings, interview candidates or just work in peace. He paused for a second, looking around, inhaling the cleansing scent of coffee as it hit his nostrils.

The skylight in the middle of the room lit up the coffee shop, flooding it with natural light. They had just opened and some of the employees were refilling the trays on each table with sugar sachets and they smiled at him as he strode inside. The whirring of the coffee grinder caught him off guard but he looked around for a suitable place to sit down. Ideally, he wanted to face the door so he could see this girl when she walked inside.

If he had more time, he would have googled her to see if there were any red flags but he wasn't very concerned. He was just doing this as a favour for his father's friend. Abba had said that this girl—he only knew her name—Tehzeeb was working in an NGO and she was very committed and hard-working. How would he even know that, he wondered.

Nevertheless, he made himself comfortable on one of the tables and wondered if he would have the time to quickly look over a design on his laptop. He glanced at the Chopard watch on his wrist. He was early as usual. The girl wouldn't be here for another five minutes. The urge to tick off an item from his work sparred with his need to be alert for the moment this girl came. Finally, the urge won.

He was just unzipping his laptop case and pulling out his laptop when the door opened. He glanced up cursorily and he forgot about his laptop which slid back into the case with a thud. One of the most stunningly beautiful girls he had ever seen had just walked inside the café and he wondered if his mouth had dropped open. There was a strange sort of buzz going in the background, noises that he couldn't distinguish and the air in the café suddenly seemed warm and stifling.

The girl was tall and slender and was wearing a pastel blue salwar kameez, her dupatta slung carelessly over her shoulders. Almost as if she remembered something, she lifted the dupatta and tried to cover her head with it. But it slid down and, irritated, she let it be as she looked around. Her hair was pulled back into a braid and he could see that it was brown, a shade that was almost alluringly red. Her nose was straight, cheekbones high and flushed with colour and her lips were the most enchanting shade of pink he had seen. She was wearing silver jewellery, bangles that covered her wrist and pretty earrings which added to her charm.

Before he realised it, she had seen him and was walking up to him. *This* was Yusuf's daughter? Tehzeeb? He didn't have time to arrange his thoughts before he stood up and offered her his hand. She looked at it like it was a strange object and hesitated before offering her own. He took her hand in his and they both looked at each other in surprise. Had she also felt the same prickling jolt?

Trying hard to bring his thoughts under control, Ayub indicated that she should sit down opposite him. For some reason, she narrowed her eyes but she sat down. He got a whiff of delicate jasmine as she leaned forward and once more, his mind went to places it shouldn't. Like, did she smell of jasmine all over? There was an otherworldly sort of beauty to her face – fair skin, brown eyes, delicate bone structure, full lips and such an expressive face.

'Would you like something?' he asked, offering her the menu. She took it almost absently and he realised that she was also staring at him. An errant strand of hair had come untucked from her braid and it kept flying across her face. This was ridiculous and surreal. It was like a scene from a movie. Maybe one of his friends had set it up and they were secretly recording him. He looked around but couldn't keep his gaze away from hers long enough. How was she this beautiful? She sighed and tucked the strand behind her ear.

'I'll have a cappuccino,' she said. Her voice was firm and soft. Nodding, he beckoned a waiter and ordered two cappuccinos.

She was here for an interview with him but he could not imagine working with her without possibly falling under her spell. As it was, he was not able to think clearly just being in such close proximity to her. If he gave her this job, what would happen to his peace of mind? Maybe he could set her up with a better job somewhere else. Maybe she would feel grateful and wouldn't mind it if he asked her out. Maybe ... she was saying something and he tried to shut down the inappropriate thoughts that were running through his mind.

'I'm sorry for asking to meet like this,' she said. That was okay, he thought. It was almost like a date. He smiled and then reminded himself again that these were highly inappropriate thoughts. She was here for a job. He had to let her down gently.

'It's all right,' he said. He was glad he had come here today.

'I don't know how to say this,' she said, lifting her eyes and staring straight into his. He was lost once more. That tendril of hair had come undone again.

'Say what?' he asked.

The waiter brought their cappuccinos and placed them

on the table between them. He watched as she tore open a sachet of sugar on top of the foam and stirred it lightly. She spooned some of the foam into her mouth. The tip of her tongue came out to catch a drop that had remained on her lip and he realised something. He was hard. Aroused by just watching her sip cappuccino. Was she a witch or a fairy? Was she even real?

His mind was struggling. He should get up and leave. No, was he out of his fucking mind to get up and leave when this beautiful girl was sitting in front of him?

She placed the coffee cup back on the table and looked at him straight in the eye. Exhaling, she said the words he had never, ever expected to hear.

'Are you gay?'

SIX

'What?' Ayub asked her, his mouth dropping open. Tehzeeb was trying to understand the reason for his shock but she knew the answer already. It was too late to take back the words because they were out there now. She should have kept her mouth shut. The way he had been looking at her, the way his eyes caressed her face, that funny jolt that she had felt when he shook hands with her, the tingling in her fingers, the light fluttering in her belly – all these were indications that she was attracted to him and he possibly to her. But she had just ruined whatever prospects they'd had by asking this question.

'I … I didn't mean to offend you. I'm sorry. But I had to know,' she said, breathlessly. She had not expected him to be this good-looking. Abbu had told her that he was but she had not counted on feeling this visceral tug towards him when she walked inside the coffee shop.

The way he had looked at her when they ordered the coffee was very different from the way he was looking at her now. That time, there had been a stunned sort of expression on his face. At the moment, he just looked irritated.

'All right, tell me who put you up to this?' he asked, his voice hard and almost angry.

'What?' she asked confused. He was looking around, a little wildly as though expecting to see someone.

'This is not funny. How much are they paying you?' he asked. It was her turn to get irritated.

'What are you talking about? I have no clue,' she said.

'Why did you ask if I was gay?' he asked in a lowered voice. She was caught by the intensity of his eyes and the low tone was doing something strange to her. Swallowing, she took a deep breath.

'I ... I was ... I'm sorry if I offended you. Can we just go back and start over?' she asked. In retrospect, directly asking him had been the silliest idea that Athiya had come up with. When she told her sisters about having a conversation with him, Athiya had said that it was a waste of time to try and gauge whether or not he was gay instead of directly asking him. That was her style. Direct and to the point. No beating around the bush. But look how it had turned out for her. He was quite angry.

'Err, no. You asked me something and I want to know why. But to answer your question, I am *not* gay,' he said, his nostrils flaring.

'You don't need to get this angry, you know. It's a reasonable question,' Tehzeeb countered. She was getting annoyed now. Okay yes, it had been a shock but why couldn't he just let it be?

'A reasonable question?' he asked, leaning forward. She inhaled the sharp musky smell of his cologne and damn if it didn't do funny things to her stomach. But she refused to be cowed down by him.

She shrugged. 'People ask even more intrusive questions. I was just being outright. For this to ... to work out between us,' she blushed, quite sure that she had ruined her chances with him already but then brazened it out. 'For this to work out, I wanted there to be complete honesty.'

He looked puzzled. Cocking his head to one side, he stared at her. Then straightening up, he nodded.

'Okay fine. Where's your resumé then? Let's get this over with. I have a ton of things to do after this meeting,' he said brusquely. His eyes were no longer warm and friendly.

Resumé? Why did he want her resumé? She was confused.

'I'm sorry, I didn't know I had to bring it with me,' she said. His jaw tightened.

'Fine. Then I'm not sure we can work this out. I can't give you the job,' he said, standing up and offering her his hand once more.

Job? Did he think of his future wife as his employee? What an ass, she thought, now equally annoyed. She stood up and took his offered hand. There was that jolt once more and his eyes widened. She tried to extricate her hand out of his but he held on for a little too long. She could see the pulse beating at the base of his throat, his dark intense eyes as he stared at her.

To her shock, she found herself asking him, 'Are you sure we can't work something out?' What? Why did she ask him that? Stupid, stupid mouth. Didn't consult brain at all.

He let go of her hand abruptly then. 'I would have loved to give you a chance Ms Tehzeeb but it looks rather doubtful to me. If you're attending an interview, then you really do need to brush up on some interviewee skills. You don't ask such questions to your prospective employers,' he said.

'Employers?' she whispered, surprised. What was going on?

He glanced at his watch and then shook his head. He beckoned one of the waiters and asked for the bill. When he sat back down on the chair, looking at his phone, she realised that she had been dismissed, but Tehzeeb didn't know how to make a graceful exit after what he had just said. What did this man think of himself? Or wait. Had this been a mistake? Did he think she was someone who was applying for a job in his company? But no, he knew her correct name, so he had known who she was.

Collecting her things and straightening her shoulders, Tehzeeb knew that she had to say something before walking out. She wouldn't be cowed down by his behaviour or demeanour. He might be very rich but she had been justified in asking for this meeting too. If she was going to spend her life with someone, why shouldn't she know what he was going to be like?

She cleared her throat and he looked up at her as though surprised she was still here.

'Yes?' he asked. His tone was condescending and that annoyed her even further. Straightening up, she pushed the strand of hair away from her face, and she spoke to him evenly, trying not to show her anger.

'I'm sorry for upsetting your schedule but *my* father didn't ask for this. *Your* father asked for my hand in marriage for you before he even saw me and that obviously was a red flag for us. We wondered if there was something wrong with you and that's a fair assumption to make. I may have been a bit frank by asking you right away if you were gay but nothing else made sense to us. I had no clue that you looked at prospective b-brides as employees and I'm glad we got to the bottom of this in this first and last meeting,' she said.

To say that he looked stunned was an understatement. Why? She hadn't been overtly rude or anything. She turned around to make a grand exit when he called out to her, his voice husky. She turned and looked back at him, irritated.

'What did you just say?' he asked in a soft voice. She looked at him, exasperated.

'You want me to repeat everything?' she asked. He shook his head but stood up and came towards her. She fell back a step and then straightened her back. She was not going to get intimidated by him.

'No, I don't want you to repeat anything. My father asked for your hand in marriage for me?' he asked.

Her face paled. 'Shit. You *are* Ayub Ahmed, right? Bakhtiyar Ahmed's son?' She looked around to see if there was someone else in the coffee shop and she had mistakenly sat down at his table.

He grinned then, the smile altering the hard lines of his face into something soft and warm.

'Yes. I am Ayub. And you are Tehzeeb,' he shook his head, still smiling, and she wondered what was going on in his head.

'I better be going then,' she said, not sure she could stand this close to him. It was disturbing, to say the least. To her shock, he lifted the strand of hair and tucked it behind her ear but his hand lingered near her cheek. He brushed the pad of his finger down her cheekbone and she felt something stark and acute inside. A sort of pleasure that almost bordered on pain. His thumb swiped across her lower lip and she stepped back, breathing heavily. She had never reacted like this to anyone ever before. Her face flushed and she wanted to turn around and run but couldn't move. It felt like his proximity had paralysed her.

'There's been some confusion,' he said, dropping his hands and pushing them inside his pockets. He looked at her and smiled and this was a different sort of smile. He shook his head as though enjoying a private joke.

'There is no confusion. You made it abundantly clear that we couldn't work out,' Tehzeeb said, trying not to notice how his shirt stretched across his chest.

He shook his head and then, to her surprise, took her hand. 'For some reason, my father lied to me. He said I was meeting you here to interview you for the position of my assistant,' he said.

Tehzeeb's eyes widened. What games was his father playing? But Ayub's behaviour made sense now.

'Why?' she asked.

He shrugged. 'I don't know. I'll have to ask him.'

She tried to pull her hand away but he held it tighter. 'I have to go,' she said breathlessly, and he shook his head.

'No, don't. Let's start over again. Please?' he said. The look in his eyes as he said this was so intense that Tehzeeb couldn't look away. She found herself taking a deep breath and nodding.

SEVEN

Ayub was under her spell and he was enjoying every minute of it. Everything about her enchanted him. It was like she had stepped out of the pages of a fantasy, his fantasy—the way her skin flushed under his gaze, the warm brown eyes that were perceptive, the strand of hair that kept flying across her face, the full lips that were begging to be kissed—he blinked, shifting his gaze away from there and focused on what she was saying.

'I don't know why your father would lie to you. Is this some sort of joke to him?' she asked. She looked distraught. Well, she had reason to be. He was still confused himself regarding his father's motives.

'No, it's not a joke. But he must have had his reasons,' Ayub said. She looked at him, her gaze strong and unwavering.

'What reasons could there be? He told my father that he wanted my hand in marriage for his son and he told you I was coming here for an interview?' she shook her head.

Ayub stared at her, transfixed once more. They may have gotten off to a rocky start but he had hopes now. If his father had asked for her hand in marriage, then what was he, Ayub, waiting for? He wanted to say yes right away. He had always been a sceptical sort, shaking his head when he saw couples holding hands in college, but something had shifted in him the moment Tehzeeb had pushed open the door and walked inside.

'Maybe we should ask Abba directly,' he said. He was reluctant to call his father and put an end to this conversation he was having with Tehzeeb. But he would have to do it to appease her.

'Yes, please do it,' she said, looking down at her lap.

Sighing, he dialled Abba's number and put it on speakerphone and kept the phone at the centre of the table. Tehzeeb looked up, surprised when she heard the phone ring loudly.

'Hello,' Abba's voice sounded hopeful and Ayub wished he wasn't reading too much into it.

'Abba, you're on speakerphone,' Ayub said right away. 'Tehzeeb is sitting with me and we had the most bizarre miscommunication. Because you lied to me.'

There was silence on the other end and he noticed Tehzeeb staring at the phone intently. Abba spoke finally, after clearing his throat.

'I'm sorry, Ayub. I lied to you because every time I bring up marriage, you just brush it off, saying you're not interested.'

Ayub winced. That was true. He had never given serious thought to marriage. Until now. He glanced at Tehzeeb who was still staring at the phone, spots of colour rising on her face.

'But what were you hoping to achieve by lying?' he asked.

'Ahem,' his father cleared his throat once more. 'I thought that if you met Tehzeeb you will change your mind about getting married.'

Ayub lifted his gaze and looked at Tehzeeb. She too was looking at him, almost in a challenging manner.

It was his turn to clear his throat. 'Well, you're right. I have changed my mind about marriage,' he said, still looking at Tehzeeb. Her face flushed.

'Alhamdulillah! That's such wonderful news! I'm so happy!' his father exclaimed. 'Tehzeeb had some questions to ask you. I hope that's been sorted.'

Ayub grinned. 'Yeah, it's been sorted. I'll let you go now but at home, we're going to have a talk about you making life-changing decisions on my behalf and lying about them,' he said and ended the call.

He pocketed his phone and stood up. She stood up uncertainly as well.

'So you were willing to get married to me, provided I wasn't gay of course,' he said. Even the words sounded surreal to him.

She shook her head. 'That was part of it. I wanted to know if you had some sort of …'

'Defect?' he asked, amused.

'Yes, defect,' she replied, defiantly.

He raised both arms and looked up and down his own body. 'You can see for yourself. No defects ma'am,' he said.

'Fine. I have to go now,' she said, stepping back further.

'Not so soon,' Ayub said and she stopped. Once more, he came around the table and stood before her.

'My father wasn't too happy about this arrangement. He'll be worried,' she said, trying to move away from him.

'You mentioned 'we' earlier. Who's there at home apart from your father and you?' he asked, curious.

'I have two younger sisters – Ana and Athiya,' she replied.

'That's nice. I have a younger sister too,' he said, leaning forward and picking up her hand.

'Okay. I … I have to leave now,' she said, trying to pull her hand away.

'Wait. What are your thoughts on this … this arranged marriage?' he asked her. Surely she wasn't just doing this because her father and his father thought it would be a good idea to get them married.

She shrugged but at the same time, she also blushed. 'I need some time to think,' she muttered, tugging her soft hand out of his but he clasped her fingers, reluctant to let her go.

'Can we exchange phone numbers? Can I call you?' he asked.

She looked up at him, surprised. 'Why?' she asked.

'I'd like to get to know you better,' he said. She looked at him intently, as though gauging his motivation.

'I don't think my father will be pleased about it,' she said finally, pulling her fingers out of his grip. His hands felt bereft without hers.

He raised an eyebrow. 'He wasn't pleased about you meeting me here either, you said. So will it really matter if we talk on the phone? Or even just text each other?'

She stared back at him for a few seconds and then reeled off a number so quickly, he was glad he had near perfect memory so he could remember it. He pulled out his phone and tapped the number and saved it.

'Are you going to call me to see if it's a real number?' she asked, almost amused. He shook his head. He was fascinated by the different aspects of her. Not only was she the most beautiful girl he had ever seen, she was also frank and outspoken and there were so many more layers to her personality. He looked forward to discovering them all.

He told her his number as well but she didn't move

to save it on her phone. 'Not saving it?' he asked, wishing she didn't have to go, wondering how he had become this lovesick man in the space of an hour. He, who had meetings to attend, people to meet and plans to discuss.

She shrugged. 'I'll save it when you call me,' she said with an impish smile and walked off. He watched her leave and then, at the door of the café, she turned around and smiled again.

EIGHT

'Oh my god! And then?' Ana asked, her eyes wide. The three of them sat on the bed in their room and Tehzeeb recounted what happened earlier that day. She had been dying to tell her sisters but both of them had college and she had had to wait till they came back. As it was, she had told Abbu that she needed a little time to think before she could give her answer.

Abbu hadn't been too pleased but he had given her till morning to decide. 'Bakhtiyar has been calling me, asking me for the wedding dates and you're saying you still need to decide?' he asked her. That had annoyed her a little. Just because Ayub had said he was okay with getting married didn't mean that she was fine with it too.

'I'll give you my answer in the morning,' she said shortly and walked away to her room, waiting for her sisters. Thankfully her father hadn't asked her how the meeting went, and how she had been able to decide whether or not Ayub was gay. Ayub was definitely not gay, she thought, her face flushing when she remembered the way he had held her hand, touched her lips and even the way he had just looked at her. She felt hot just thinking about it.

But now, with her sisters, she couldn't bring herself to

tell them everything but Athiya gave her a knowing look and grinned.

'So he's very good-looking then?' she asked in a teasing manner.

'Very,' Tehzeeb admitted.

'It's SO annoying that he doesn't have any social media profiles,' Ana said. That was true. They had initially hunted for him on social media, hoping to discover more about him, but they couldn't find him.

'Maybe they're private or under a different name,' Tehzeeb said.

'But what was his reaction when you asked if he was gay?' Athiya asked.

'Oh, he was shocked. So shocked, I tell you. But he was assuming that I had come for an interview. So it was all very strange when he asked me for my resumé. I wondered what sort of family he belonged to but then thankfully he cleared it up when I got up to leave the first time.'

'So, how much do you really like him?' Ana asked.

Tehzeeb blushed, thinking of the way he had looked at her, the strange jolt she had felt when he had shaken hands with her.

'She likes him a lot!' Athiya said, getting up from there and jumping up and down in excitement.

'I don't know anything anymore!' Tehzeeb said, looking down at her hands.

'Why?' Ana asked, looking curious.

Tehzeeb shrugged. 'It's all happening too fast! I hadn't even thought of marriage for at least another two years.'

'Have you *seen* your face?' Ana asked almost derisively.

'Why? What's wrong with it?' Tehzeeb asked, touching her cheeks immediately.

'That's the thing. Nothing is wrong with it. You're the most gorgeous woman in our entire family and you've been getting rishtas from the time you were in seventh grade. If you like this Ayub, then you should just say yes or you never know the sort of proposals one of our many aunts might get,' Ana replied. Athiya was looking at the two of them and she nodded.

'I agree. None of the proposals can match this guy Ayub!' she said.

'What do you know? You haven't even met him!' Tehzeeb remarked.

'Yeah, I know I haven't. But there's a light in your eyes whenever you talk about him and that has never been there before. I was actually planning on coming with you when you met him but I couldn't miss the practical session today in college,' Athiya said ruefully.

'That would have been fun,' Tehzeeb said, grinning. 'If he thought I came for an interview with my sister.'

'So, give us more deets! You said he's good-looking. What about other factors? Is he tall? Is he built? Come on!' Ana said.

Tehzeeb looked away. There was no way she was going to describe Ayub to her sisters. He wasn't some hot eye candy they had spotted somewhere or an actor they all crushed on. If things went without a hitch, he was going to be her husband.

There were still some aspects to this whole thing which were disturbing though. Why had Ayub's father asked for her hand before even seeing her, especially since his son appeared to be perfect? And there was the question of status too.

Jasmine Villa was a joke in many ways and she was sure that Ayub lived in a huge bungalow or an actual villa somewhere. She had grown up here, in this mouldy room, surrounded by her sisters and the fleeting fragrance of malligai poo that bound them, reminding them of their mother. She was used to living on a budget, spending money only on essentials and splurging rarely. How would she fit into that larger than life world?

Her phone rang then. It was an unknown number. Could it be him? Her sisters looked at her in an inquiring manner. She shook her head and answered the phone.

'Hello,' she said, a little hesitant.

'Hello.'

It was him. His deep voice seemed to flow over her even across the phone. She got up from there, wishing her sisters would leave and give her some privacy. But knowing them, they would want to listen in on their conversation.

'One minute,' she said and then, despite protests from Ana and Athiya, she walked out of the room. In the living room, Abbu was watching TV. The kitchen was too small and stuffy. So, she opened the door, stepped into their wild garden and spoke.

'Hi!' she said.

'Busy?' he asked.

'Sort of,' she replied, and she knew he was startled at her reply. 'But I can spare some time for you,' she added loftily.

He chuckled. 'You are certainly one of the most intriguing women I've met,' he said.

'I assume you've met many women to be able to say that,' Tehzeeb said, twirling her hair around her finger.

'Um. I don't know how to answer that.'

'It's okay. I won't hold it against you,' she said. 'So? Did you talk to your father?'

'About what?' he sounded puzzled.

'You wanted to talk to him about making decisions on your behalf,' she reminded him.

'Ah. That. No, not yet. I'm on my way back home from my office. I'll meet Abba at home and talk,' he said.

That reminded her of what her father had told her. 'Err … I think our parents have already been talking to each other. My father said that your father is asking for … wedding dates.'

'What?' Ayub sounded shocked too. 'Okay, I'll talk to you once I go home and talk to Abba. Although …'

'Although?' Tehzeeb repeated. She realised she was enjoying talking to him far too much for someone she had just met. But she had read about such things, having an instant connection, a feeling that this was the right person. Was that what had happened between them?

'Although I wouldn't mind if he does hurry up with the wedding,' Ayub said softly.

She didn't know how to respond to that.

'Bye,' she said.

'No wait,' he said quickly. 'I just … I just want to say that I am really happy I met you today.'

At this, she found herself smiling. 'I'm happy too,' she said.

NINE

Ayub didn't stop his car at the huge gates to his house because they were opened by the uniformed watchman who sat there at all times. He nodded, smiled at the man and continued driving inside the driveway as he thought back to the conversation he had had with Tehzeeb just now.

Since his meeting with her, his day had been spectacular. Or rather, it had felt that way. Even when one of the builders objected to his plan, he had been able to brush it off and focus on the positives. The biggest positive, of course, was meeting Tehzeeb today. He could almost taste the moment she had walked inside the coffee shop, lighting up his life like a succession of stars exploding around the horizon.

He parked the car in the space reserved for him and stepped outside. Her firm but soft voice still remained with him as he jogged up the few steps to the humongous double doors of the house. Before he could tap the numbers on the digital lock on the door, they swung open. His mother smiled at him and he smiled back. He dropped his laptop case in the foyer and hugged her impulsively.

Surprised, she stepped back. 'What's going on?' she asked.

'I'm just very happy today!' he announced. He wondered

how much of Abba's plan she knew. He had a feeling she was unaware of it or she would have mentioned something at least. For the first time that day, he felt a moment's doubt. He knew Tehzeeb's family was not rich. He had been able to ascertain that from the moment he had met her father. When he met her though, he had been so stunned he hadn't paused to notice anything else. And it didn't even matter to him.

His mother had been trying to get him interested in one of her friend's daughters, someone called Nadia, but he had managed to evade meeting her so far. The girls who visited home, daughters of Ammi's friends, all looked the same to him. He wondered how Ammi would take the news. Abba would have to handle her, he thought. But Abba also owed him an explanation for his actions.

'Good day at work, I presume,' she said and he nodded. Yeah, she didn't know anything. He wondered what was going to happen once she heard that Abba was planning wedding dates already. There were going to be fireworks at home.

'Where's Abba? I need to talk to him,' he said, unbuttoning his cuffs.

'In the living room. Why?' she asked.

He looked at her unlined face, the result of numerous beauty treatments and extensive spa visits, and shrugged.

'Where's Maira?' he asked.

'She's gone to sleep early. She's doing a makeup video tomorrow morning and she doesn't want to look tired for it,' Ammi said. She looked up at him, as though he was challenging the credibility of Maira's work, which involved social media and Instagram. He didn't say anything and merely nodded.

He continued walking on the carpeted hallway, paused at the entrance to the living room and debated whether he should go directly talk to Abba. But he was also tired and grimy and he wanted a shower. So, he went on to his room on the first floor where he stood under the hot shower for ten minutes until he felt refreshed. He changed into comfortable track pants and a tee shirt and walked outside, a smile on his face as he thought of the phone call with Tehzeeb a while back.

In the semi-darkened living room, his father was sitting on the plush sofa, watching TV. Ammi was sitting with him too and they both looked up when he came inside. His father's expression changed the slightest bit and Ayub understood that he was not to speak about what had happened today in front of Ammi.

Wondering why this was the case, he sat down with them and they talked about this and that, until Ammi got up to ask Haleema Auntie, their cook, about dinner. As she walked away, he turned to Abba.

'What were you up to Abba? It was so embarrassing!' he said in a loud whisper, shifting closer to his father.

His father nodded. 'I already told you that if I said the truth, you wouldn't have gone to meet her. Aren't you glad you met her?' he asked.

Ayub stared at his father, at his bright eyes and trimmed beard and wondered how Abba's brain worked.

Finally, he spoke. 'Look, I met her and liked her instantly, but she told me that you had asked for her hand in marriage before you even saw her. What was that all about?'

Abba looked conflicted and then sighing, shook his head. 'Meeting Yusuf at the masjid was no coincidence, Ayub,' he said finally.

Ayub was shocked. 'What? But he looked genuinely surprised!'

Abba nodded. 'Yes. Because he didn't know that. He ... he was my classmate in college,' he said.

'Yes, I already know that. But ...'

Abba sighed. 'I was awful to him back then. Really awful. He was the class topper and I always used to come second. I hated the sight of him. I did some terrible things to him then, Ayub,' he said, looking shamefaced.

Ayub was shocked. His father was a ruthless businessman but a gentle father and loving husband. Now he understood the slight reluctance on Yusuf's face when they met in the masjid.

'What terrible things, Abba?' Ayub asked. He needed to know.

Abba looked quite distressed. 'I did some terrible things but the worst was when I planted some chits on him during an exam and he was disqualified from writing all exams that year,' he said.

'What? Why would you do such a thing? If Yusuf uncle tells Tehzeeb, she'll never want to marry me,' Ayub said. He couldn't believe his father would do something so cruel.

Bakhtiyar Ahmed shook his head. 'He won't. He's not that sort of man. Even then he didn't rat on me and I hated him even more for that. I don't know how someone could be so selfless and forgiving. Anyway, I saw him a month ago, entering one of the supermarkets and I couldn't believe it was him. Everything came rushing back to me and I wanted to go and talk to him. But he was with his daughters and I didn't want to embarrass him.'

'So you had seen Tehzeeb already then,' Ayub remarked softly.

Abba shrugged. 'I didn't know it was Tehzeeb because there were three of them and they were all pretty. It just occurred to me then that I had wronged him terribly and I had to make some sort of reparation.'

'And you threw me in front of the bus?' Ayub asked.

'You really think that? After meeting Tehzeeb?' Abba asked him. Ayub rolled his eyes and shook his head.

'If he didn't have a marriageable daughter, I would have thought of some other way to help him out. He hasn't done very well in life. His house is in shambles and the three girls certainly deserve better. I found out where he lived ...'

'You followed them?' Ayub asked, even more shocked. This was so unlike his father.

Abba didn't answer. 'And then, I engineered that meeting in the masjid when you were there so he could take a good look at you too. As we were leaving, I told him that I'd like you to get married to his daughter. He was naturally shocked and started telling me that we are not of the same status; that it would be inconceivable for him to get his daughter married to you.'

Ayub listened in silence. 'Then?' he prompted his father.

'I insisted. He said that it would be better if I visited his house first. I told him nothing would change my mind. Anyway, you know the rest,' Abba said, getting up from there and walking to one of the bookshelves.

Ayub got up too. 'Abba, this could have gone wrong in so many ways! I really wish you hadn't used me as a pawn for your own redemption.'

Abba turned around, eyes glittering. 'But it didn't go wrong, so don't you want to help your father redeem himself?'

Ayub had no answer to that.

TEN

The engagement was announced for the following month. Tehzeeb was shocked it was all happening so soon. For several days after they met, she hadn't heard from Ayub at all, but her father had heard from his. Both sides had given the go-ahead and even then, she hadn't heard from him. She wondered if he had changed his mind but the preparations were going ahead normally, so it was a little confusing.

The engagement was going to be held in a five star hotel and Tehzeeb wondered why her father was going along with everything that Ayub's father was suggesting. In fact, Bakhtiyar was paying for everything and she didn't like it one bit. Maybe that had put off Ayub as well. However, she refused to call or text him first.

Nevertheless, she was surprised when he called her a week before the engagement. After breakfast, she was reading a book, feeling restless because her father had told her that it would be a good idea for her to quit her job and stay at home now. She had argued with him but he had said she could get another job once she got married.

'What will I do till then?' she asked him. He shrugged. They had finally come to an agreement that she would take leave from work until the engagement and then she could quit just before the wedding. Her supervisor was not pleased. She had said it was better for her to quit instead of playing around like this if she wasn't serious. Tehzeeb told her that she was absolutely serious but this was also happening and she couldn't ignore it.

Anyway, she was trying to focus on a book because there was nothing else to do, when her phone rang. She looked at it, surprised to see Ayub's name on the screen.

'Hi,' she said, surprised.

'Hi. I'm sorry I haven't called,' he started off right away.

'It's okay. I understand you're a busy man,' she said. She was still irked about the engagement happening at a hotel, at how extravagant everything was going to be. Her relatives had been filled with jealous disbelief when they found out that she was getting married to him. They wondered how her meek-mannered father had managed to bag one of the most eligible bachelors in the city. Hearing their whispers when they came home to discuss the engagement annoyed her even more.

'No, that's not the case. I wanted to talk to you. But …' he trailed off. She wondered if he had spoken to his father but she wasn't going to probe. He had said he would call her and she had waited that night. She felt foolish in retrospect.

'I said it's okay,' she said softly.

He sighed. 'I can't wait to see you next week,' he said. She didn't know how to reply to that so she stayed silent.

'Tehzeeb?'

'I'm here.'

'Is something wrong?' he asked.

She couldn't quite articulate what she was feeling without sounding stupid.

'No, it's all good,' she said. But at the same time, she felt the urgent need to tell him something. She took a deep breath. 'Ayub, we're not rich like you. So, I'm not very comfortable with the engagement happening in a five star hotel.'

There was silence for a few seconds. Then he spoke quickly.

'Look, I don't care about wealth,' he said. She rolled her eyes even though he couldn't see her.

'Ayub, only rich people say that they don't care about money,' she reprimanded him. He chuckled nervously.

'You're right. I'm sorry for being patronising. But the engagement in the hotel was planned by our parents. So let's leave them to it. They know what they're doing,' he said. He sounded conciliatory but she wasn't sure she wanted consolation. But she didn't know what else to tell him either.

'Okay,' she said.

'Listen, I called you because my mother and sister want to take you shopping,' he said.

'What?'

'Um, yeah. The boy's side brings the engagement outfit for the girl if I'm not mistaken,' he said.

That was right, but …

'But why do they want to take me along? That's not the norm, right?' she said.

'It is in our family. They want to make sure that you like the outfit,' he said.

Tehzeeb bit her lip as she thought. She was nervous about meeting his mother and sister. She was surprised they hadn't asked to see her yet. Maybe they weren't okay with this proposal at all. Not maybe. She was sure they weren't okay. Or why else hadn't they come to see her?

'When do they want to meet me?' she asked him finally.

'Today, if possible? They'll be happy to pick you up from your house,' he said. Her eyes widened as she looked around at the mess her house was in. No way!

'No! I'll meet them wherever they're going for shopping,' she said.

'Um, but ...'

'Ayub, please,' she said.

'Okay,' he said, sighing. 'I'll give your number to Maira, my sister. She'll text you the address.'

'Fine.' She stood up. She had to shower and get ready if she had to be presentable for his mother and sister. She had no idea what they expected from her.

'I had a doubt,' she said, suddenly wanting to know something.

'Yes?'

'Was your mother okay with this proposal? Since your father jumped into this, and he hadn't even consulted you,' she said.

There was a moment's silence and it was enough for her. 'Ammi is very happy,' he said. His words were right but the tone was measured and insincere. She half-wished this wasn't happening. The meeting with his mother and even the engagement.

'Ayub, what if our fathers are making a big mistake? What if I don't fit into your family at all?' she asked him suddenly and then winced. She hadn't intended to say it out aloud.

'Tehzeeb, this is no mistake. I promise you. Everything will be fine,' he said. His tone was reassuring.

'If you say so,' she said.

'I'm not just saying it. I mean it,' Ayub said softly. 'And as I said before, I can't wait to see you next week.'

'I'm feeling nervous,' she told him honestly.

'Nervous?' he was surprised.

'This is all too much. It's too overwhelming,' she said.

'I … I don't know what to say,' he said. He sounded genuinely confused.

'It's okay. I'll be fine. I'll see you next week,' she said and ended the call before he could prolong the conversation. She was going to meet her future mother-in-law and her sister-in-law and she had to be ready to face them.

ELEVEN

Tehzeeb walked into the store later that day, wishing she wasn't feeling this nervous. There was no precedent for this sort of a visit in her family. Even among her cousins who had got married before her, no one's prospective in-laws had taken them shopping. Ayub's sister Maira had texted the name of a big store on Commercial Street, one that Tehzeeb often walked past, knowing she could never afford any of the clothes inside.

Being practical was one of her traits, unlike Athiya, and shopping with her youngest sister was often an exhausting affair. She would walk into the very shops they couldn't afford, even try on the clothes and then haughtily tell the attendants that she didn't like anything. Thankfully, Ana wasn't like that and the two of them would apologise to the attendants before leaving the shop. Athiya would roll her eyes whenever they apologised.

'That's where you make the mistake, Api,' she would tell Tehzeeb. 'Rich people don't apologise for other people's inconveniences.'

'And we're not rich. Try to remember that,' Tehzeeb often snapped at her.

Tehzeeb thought that her sister would be perfectly at

home with what she was about to do now. Walk into this store and pretend she bought clothes here all the time. As it was, both of them were very excited when they heard that she was going shopping with Ayub's mother and sister. Thankfully, both had college today or they might have insisted on tagging along.

She wondered why Abbu hadn't said anything. He looked the slightest bit troubled when he heard that she had been invited to go shopping. Then, shuffling a bit, he walked to his room and came outside, handing her a wad of notes.

'It's not much. But you should also keep some,' he said. She had refused but he had insisted that she take it and go, even if she didn't use it. 'Just keep it with you.'

The five thousand that her father had given nestled at the bottom of her handbag now, part of a separate zipped compartment. She had taken care with her appearance and wore the outfit from last Eid. It was a watered silk yellow salwar kameez which she had paired with her mother's gold earrings and bangles. She still felt like a fraud but she walked inside nevertheless, wondering what she would talk about with these two women.

Inside, the air conditioning hit her like a blast, chilling the skin on her arms, but it was a welcome respite from the heat outside. She looked straight ahead at first, not smiling at the attendants like she normally did. But Ayub's mother and sister were not in her line of vision. Sighing, she looked around, wondering if she was early. No. She was deliberately five minutes late, something that she had struggled with because she was a stickler for punctuality.

But there was no one inside. Feeling a little foolish, she walked around before she finally turned to one of the curious attendants and smiled.

'I'm waiting for someone,' she said. The woman nodded and let her browse through the clothes. Tehzeeb rifled through some of the clothes in the collection and winced when she saw the prices. Abbu's money wouldn't buy her even a dupatta here. Sighing, she continued to walk past the hanging clothes, some glinting with sequins, some embroidered beautifully and delicately. She wondered what she was doing here, why she had agreed to this strange expedition and knew it was because Ayub had asked her. Slightly annoyed with herself, she continued walking down the marbled floor, inhaling the smell of new, expensive clothes when suddenly there was a flurry of activity at the store's entrance.

Two women walked inside and the attendants rushed to aid them. Tehzeeb wondered if these were the ladies in question. Her heart pounded when she realised that it had to be them. One of them was a little old but just barely. The other one, however, was quite young, probably Athiya's age, she thought.

They hadn't yet seen her and she was glad of it. She observed the two women as they walked inside like they owned the store. The older woman was wearing a cream coloured outfit, the top reached her knees in a high low cut, and she had paired it with peach-coloured raw silk cigarette pants. A wispy scarf was slung across one shoulder and huge sunglasses were pushed into her hair. They were dark brown and bordered with glinting stones that Tehzeeb hoped weren't diamonds. The woman's hair was a deep chestnut brown shade and it spoke of spending hours in a salon to achieve that perfect shine.

The younger woman was wearing quite a bit of make-up. Even from afar, Tehzeeb could see that there had been some serious contouring done to her face but she had tried to pass it off like it was natural day wear. Her eyes were grey and she was stunning. Her lips were painted in a deep maroon matte shade that made her look a little older than she was.

She was just about to walk up to them when the younger woman lifted her phone high in the air, pouted at it and walked around the store, still holding the phone up. Err … what was she doing? Tehzeeb watched in wonder as she walked past her, and she realised that the young girl was taking a video. For Instagram? Tehzeeb made a mental note to check her out later.

Clearing her throat, she stepped forward and the two of them, her prospective in-laws, turned to look at her. Maira's hair had blonde highlights and she was wearing a tiger print blouse with tight black jeans. Tehzeeb had never felt so out of place in her life than she had at that moment.

'Hello,' she said softly. Maira's eyebrows went up and she smiled and came forward to hold Tehzeeb's hand.

'Bhabhi!' she said effusively. She took in Tehzeeb's clothes and her nearly free-of-makeup face but she didn't say anything. She just looked at her and shook her head.

'Beautiful. You are so beautiful!' she said.

Maira's mother was not so forthcoming. She still stood near the counter, observing the two of them and Tehzeeb looked at her. Finally, she stepped forward and stood before Tehzeeb. She inspected her – literally from top to bottom and Tehzeeb felt like hiding her plain shoes from this glamorous woman's sight. Both women were wearing heeled shoes and seemed accomplished at walking around in them without tripping and falling face forward. But even with the heels, her mother-in-law was shorter than her by a few inches.

Nodding, she walked away further into the store. Maira took Tehzeeb's hand and the two of them followed her.

'Aren't we ...' Tehzeeb looked at the clothes hanging from the hangers but Maira shook her head.

'No, no! Ammi knows the designer who works for this store. She's asked him to design a special collection for you and they're going to show it to us now. They'll do the fitting once you choose the one you like,' she said.

Wait, what? They had designed a collection *for* her? Whatever did Maira mean? Suddenly, Maira stopped and let go of her hand.

'Selfie?' she said.

'Uh, okay,' Tehzeeb didn't know what to say. Maira stepped close to her, bringing her head next to hers and Tehzeeb inhaled a sharp, expensive perfume. She lifted her phone high in the air and tapped the screen with her thumb. A camera app opened on the screen.

'Just smile,' she said. Two flowery halos appeared on their faces on the screen. Tehzeeb wondered if she looked as foolish as she felt but Maira didn't seem to notice anything as she clicked the photo, pout in place.

'Great! This is going on my Insta stories now. What's your handle? I'll tag you,' she said.

'Maira!' the older woman called out to her, sounding annoyed. She looked up in the direction of the voice.

'Coming Ammi!' she said. 'Bhabhi, handle?'

'Later? Just post it without tagging me,' Tehzeeb said, feeling the moment to be surreal.

TWELVE

Ayub stared at his laptop screen but his mind was elsewhere. He couldn't focus because he was thinking of Tehzeeb. When Abba had announced Ayub's marriage, Maira had been excited but Ammi had been appalled.

'My only son! How could you decide his wedding without even telling me?' she had asked. She had been angry, and with good reason too. Ayub wished he didn't have to choose sides, and only then he realised that Abba had been quite devious by making sure he had met Tehzeeb before anything formal could take place. If he hadn't met her, and if Abba had announced that his marriage had been fixed to some random friend's daughter, he would have been livid too.

Also, while he understood Abba's motivation for getting Tehzeeb married to him, he didn't like being a pawn in his father's games. Nevertheless, Ammi had been furious when she discovered that Tehzeeb didn't come from a family like 'theirs' and that Abba had planned to undertake all the wedding expenses.

'I don't understand why you're doing this!' she had lamented when ranting and railing had failed. Abba was firm.

'I've given my word and that's it. Just meet her once and you'll be smitten with her,' he said. That made her even angrier and it was why she hadn't bothered to meet Tehzeeb all these days. He was glad his father hadn't added 'smitten like your son'.

After his talk with Abba about Yusuf and their dubious history, Ayub hadn't wanted to talk to Tehzeeb right then. He was worried he would unwittingly reveal something and then Tehzeeb would call off the whole thing. It would have to be a secret between him and Abba and he was uneasy about it.

Every day he woke up wondering if it would be all right to talk to her that day but he kept putting it off, despite wanting to hear her voice. When finally there was just a week left for the engagement, his mother had reluctantly accepted that the wedding was happening whether she liked it or not and decided that it was time to meet her prospective daughter-in-law. That morning, she announced at breakfast that she would like to take Tehzeeb out shopping for her engagement gown.

Ayub had been startled at first and then he was happy because his mother had finally come around. He knew his mother just had to meet her once and she would change her mind. Tehzeeb wasn't just beautiful – there was something about her that changed the people she met, that drew them towards her. Maybe it was those empathetic eyes, he thought, the ones that felt like they could look into his soul.

Sensing that he could put it off no longer, he had called her to inform her about his mother's decision. The call with her hadn't gone well but that was to be expected. He had disappeared after that first phone call with her when he promised to call back and he knew she was probably wondering why. He wasn't prepared for the sucker punch he got just by listening to her voice and it was all he could do to stop himself from joining his mother and sister.

Maira had been excited – she always was when it came to shopping. His mother had been more subdued. She had been equally displeased when she found out that Ayub had already met Tehzeeb thanks to his father's machinations and she had indicated her displeasure by not talking to him for days even as his father went back and forth with Yusuf uncle, discussing the engagement and where it would take place.

Hearing Tehzeeb's voice after so long had been a revelation to him. He hadn't realised how much he had missed listening to her voice until he had spoken to her today. How could his feelings be so intense and all over the place already? He didn't know what it was but he wanted to see her more than anything else.

But after ending the call with her, he had been uneasy too. What was going to happen today? What would his mother tell her? Would she make her feel unwelcome in the family? He hoped that having Maira there would neutralise his mother's anger. He knew he wouldn't hear from Tehzeeb today. A day of shopping with her mother was going to wipe her out. He just hoped it wouldn't completely subdue her spirit.

He opened his sister's Instagram page hoping to find some insights into their day. Some of the posts she put up made him wince. But she had 800 followers and felt obliged to liven up their feeds all the time. True to his expectation, Maira had updated her stories.

There were plenty of selfies and he tapped through them quickly until he found a video of her walking through the store, pouting at the camera. His heartbeat quickened when he spotted Tehzeeb standing at one side, looking at his sister, puzzled. He checked the time stamp. It had been two hours ago.

Then, he felt a familiar jolt when he saw a photo of Tehzeeb and Maira in the next post, Maira still pouting while Tehzeeb looking like she'd rather be anywhere but there. Maira had done something to the photo to make it look like it was raining stars and they both had flower headdresses on their heads and there was an unreal quality to the photo. He realised Maira had filtered the shit out of it.

Wit ma Bhabhi!

The caption made him wince. He wondered what impression Tehzeeb had formed of his mother and sister. He knew what they were like. Should he have warned her? Tehzeeb seemed like she came from a sensible family where no one talked *lyk dis* and neither did she seem to be the sort who would post Instagram stories of what happened in her life, every single minute.

There were no more photos or videos, which was surprising. Maira was never able to resist posting things on Instagram. Maybe Ammi had asked her not to?

He was dying to talk to Tehzeeb now, to ask her what had happened, what she had selected and how much he wanted to see her wearing it. His fingers itched to send her a message. He stopped himself in case she was still with Ammi or Maira. In fact, he wanted to call Ammi and ask for an update but he knew his mother wouldn't like it. Calling Maira meant that she would get excited and screechy and everyone would know that he had been calling to find out what was happening.

The best option was to wait. Even if he hated it.

THIRTEEN

'SHUT THE FRONT DOOR!' Athiya shouted and Tehzeeb winced.

'Stop shouting! I have a headache already!' she said.

'You bought a gown for 2.3 lakhs and ...'

'*They* bought it for 2.3 lakhs,' Tehzeeb corrected her over-excited sister. Ana sat on the bed and looked bemused.

'Where is this 2.3 lakh gown?' she asked. 'How come you came back empty-handed from your shopping expedition?'

Tehzeeb pressed her fingers to her temple. Her head was still throbbing.

'Make me some ginger tea and I'll tell you everything,' she said. Both her sisters stared at her.

'I mean it!' she snapped. Making a face, Athiya went to the kitchen.

'Don't begin without me!' she called out. Tehzeeb didn't reply. She was lying down on the bed and even after she shut her eyes, her mind was crowded with images of the day. How surreal everything had been. She could still smell the sweet musky fragrance of Aafreen Ahmed's perfume. Her mother-in-law had barely glanced at her at first, but sat down beside her as they watched the parade of models dressed in one extravagant gown after the other.

Tehzeeb felt like a poor cousin at a rich relative's wedding. Obviously, even her best Eid finery couldn't hold a candle to the rich brocades and silks she had seen today. Aafreen sat with a notepad and ticked the designs she liked. Then she asked the models wearing the selected designs to sashay up and down again.

Throughout this, Maira sat sulking because her mother had forbidden her from livestreaming everything to her Instagram audience. Aafreen wanted Tehzeeb's gown to be special and she didn't want anyone to have seen it an entire week before the engagement. When they had finalised three gowns, she made Tehzeeb take the place of the models. She was soon tired from all the poking and prodding and standing like a mannequin. Aafreen said something to Maira and she frowned. She shook her head. Aafreen scowled at her and grabbed Maira's phone at which the younger woman lunged and took it back.

'Okay, okay, I'll delete it!' she said. With a mutinous set to her lips, she set about doing something. Tehzeeb presumed her mother must have asked her to delete the Instagram photo. The lilac-coloured gown that Aafreen decided on finally was gorgeous. Tehzeeb had to admit that her future mother-in-law had style. But after spending three hours with her, she wondered if that was all she had. She had barely spoken to her except to comment on the cut and the fit of the dresses they saw.

'Are you okay?' Ana asked her. Tehzeeb shook her head, still wincing in pain.

'No, not the headache. Are you okay with these people? They don't think twice before spending lakhs on clothes. Are you all right getting married into such a family?' Ana asked her softly.

Tehzeeb sat up and held her head gingerly. She was thinking the same thing. No matter how handsome or hot Ayub had been, she wasn't just marrying him. She was marrying into his family. She liked Maira but didn't think much of her. As for Aafreen, she wondered if today was a performance to intimidate her about their wealth.

'I'm back! I'm back!' Athiya chanted as she rushed inside with a tray that had three mugs of steaming tea. She nearly knocked the tray over as she kept it on the side table and handed over Tehzeeb's mug in such haste that some tea spilled over the side and scalded her hand. Tehzeeb hissed in pain and Athiya winced.

'Sorry! Sorry! I was afraid you were going to start without me. Go on now,' she said as she curled her hand around her own mug and settled on one end of the bed. 'Tell us from the beginning.'

Tehzeeb caught Ana's eye but she didn't say anything. She took a sip of the tea and then another and she knew Athiya was getting impatient. She started telling them everything – how the store attendants had treated Aafreen and Maira like royalty and how they had a special collection designed just for her.

Even the words sounded surreal to her, Tehzeeb thought. How did this happen? Someone like her who earned peanuts and had to think twice before buying a new dress, she who often tried to figure out a way to transform Ammi's old sarees into a flowy kurta – she was getting an engagement dress that cost more than two lakhs.

Everything inside her warred with the thought. Such little regard for money!

'What's this dress like? Why isn't it with you?' Athiya asked in between sips of her tea, her eyes shining with excitement.

'They have to customise it to fit me. And I told them to send the dress to Ayub's house once it's done and not here,' Tehzeeb said. Athiya frowned when she heard that.

'But …'

'But nothing. I can wear the gown at the hotel directly. At the engagement,' Tehzeeb said.

'No Api, don't be stupid. You can't go to the hotel wearing your old clothes. You have to make a grand entrance wearing that gown,' Athiya insisted.

'What did the mother and sister say when you suggested that it be sent to their house?' Ana asked. She was the shrewd one among the three of them.

'Nothing. She just nodded,' Tehzeeb said.

'Doesn't it strike you as strange?' Ana insisted.

Tehzeeb didn't reply to that. She had thought that Aafreen would say something or insist that it be sent to Tehzeeb's house.

'Maybe she doesn't trust me with their 2.3 lakh gown,' Tehzeeb said, looking into her mug.

'Why? Will you run away with it?' Athiya asked, looking incensed.

'Listen, I was the one who told them not to send it here,' Tehzeeb said, trying to be pacifying.

'Whatever. You should tell them you changed your mind. You are not going to your engagement wearing any old dress,' Athiya insisted.

Ana and Tehzeeb shared a look again. Maybe it was time she met Ayub and talked to him. Maybe she should tell him how different the two of them were. Maybe their fathers would see sense and not push for this. She better do it now before the engagement crept upon them, she thought.

'I know that look. What are you planning?' Ana asked.

Tehzeeb sighed. 'I'll talk to Ayub. I'll meet and tell him that this is all a mistake,' she said.

Athiya gasped. 'And what about the expensive gown that is being tailored to fit you?' she asked.

'He'll learn to cut his losses soon enough,' Tehzeeb said, making a face. She wondered if it was the right thing to do and how her father would take it. He would be disappointed, surely. But today had been a lesson that showed her how starkly different their lives were.

She had to meet Ayub to talk to him and to her surprise, she found herself blushing. She looked up to see a knowing look on Ana's face and Athiya crowed triumphantly. 'This is just an excuse to meet him! I know! I know!' she said.

'Whatever,' Tehzeeb said, looking away, wishing her face wasn't so transparent that her sisters could read every emotion that passed over it.

FOURTEEN

That evening, Ayub parked the car where Tehzeeb had suggested. He was waiting for her to show up so he could allay her worries and tell her it was going to be all right. He had sensed that the day with his mother and sister had not gone well. He hadn't yet gone home so he didn't know what Ammi and Maira thought of her. But apart from the anxiousness that had lodged deep inside of him when he heard her voice an hour ago, he was anticipating this meeting.

He wondered if she was as beautiful as he remembered or if his mind had just played tricks on him that day. Or maybe his memory had made her out to be more beautiful than she was. Maybe it had been that first impression of her, walking inside the café. Whatever it was, he realised he was thrilled to be seeing her again. He wanted to experience that feeling once more, to hold it for a moment and focus on why she made him feel that way.

He had never believed in love at first sight. Through high school and college, there had been several crushes and girls who had crushed on him, and if he liked the girl enough, he didn't mind being a boyfriend for a short period of time. There had been no one who made him feel that this should be forever. But now …

He tapped the edge of the steering wheel anxiously, trying to shush the doubts that were growing in his mind. Was this a good idea? They were getting engaged next Sunday anyway. How bad had today been that she wanted to meet him and discuss? What would they talk about?

He picked up his water bottle that he kept in the car and took a sip from it as he waited. He glanced at his watch and saw that she was five minutes late. Should he call her? Would it look desperate? Of course it would look desperate. What was even wrong with him?

'Nice car,' she said as she opened the door and stepped inside. He stared. He couldn't help it. His mind had not been playing tricks on him. His memory was working just fine. Because she was still the most beautiful woman he had ever seen. She turned to look at him, a slight smile on her face.

Her hair was open and to his disappointment, she quickly tied it up into a bun at the nape of her neck.

'Sorry!' she said, sheepishly. 'I tie the worse buns. They keep opening up all the time.'

He still stared at her, unable to articulate a single thought that came to his mind. The jasmine fragrance was intense because of their proximity and it was doing all sorts of things to him. She was wearing a short pink kurta paired with a flaring sort of white shalwar and her wispy white dupatta kept sliding off her shoulders. Her arms were bare, none of that clunky silver jewellery from last time.

'Ayub?' she said softly, leaning in closer and he shook his head to get out of the stupor he had been engulfed in for the past two minutes.

'Sorry,' he breathed out. 'I forgot how beautiful you

were. Or maybe I was thinking you couldn't possibly be that beautiful, but I was mistaken.'

'It's just a face,' she said, looking down at her hands.

'A very beautiful face,' he added. She looked up at him and then shook her head.

'I don't think this is a good idea,' she said softly.

'Meeting here? I know, but you were the one who didn't want to meet in a coffee shop,' Ayub said. She shook her head.

'No, I mean us. This engagement. I think we should call it off,' she said.

Ayub was shocked. 'What? Are you crazy?' he asked. Her eyes flared in anger but she tamped it down.

She shook her head impatiently. 'No, I'm not crazy. I wanted to meet you because I wanted to tell you ... we should call this off.'

'But why?' he asked, baffled. Her face was suffused with colour.

'Surely your mother and sister would have told you something,' she said, looking at him intently.

He shook his head. 'No, they haven't said anything. And I doubt they will. I'm sure they liked you,' he said.

She shook her head and her hair came undone once more. She looked annoyed but didn't tie it up again. 'Look, we come from very different societies. I don't think I can fit in yours,' she said.

'And you got that from meeting my mother and sister?' he asked. 'How?'

She looked impatient. 'Ayub, they bought a gown for 2.3 lakhs. I have *never* seen that kind of money in my life, let alone spend it on one thing.'

Ayub was silent for a moment as he processed this. He

hadn't realised how overboard his mother would go. But surely, she needn't have announced to Tehzeeb how much the gown had cost? That was tasteless and very unlike his mother. Had she done it deliberately? To elicit this reaction from Tehzeeb?

'Look. I told you before, money doesn't mean anything and you rightly told me that only someone with money would say that,' he added quickly before she could interrupt him.

'Money does matter Ayub,' she said softly.

'When you are my wife, my money will be yours. So what's the problem?' he asked.

She laughed then, and Ayub realised that she was laughing at him. He didn't like it.

'How can you be so naïve?' she asked him. Naïve? Him? Never.

'Look ...' he started but she stopped him with her outstretched palm.

'My father is retired and we barely subsist on his pension. I have a job at an NGO which doesn't pay much. Both my younger sisters are studying and they do part-time jobs so we can buy the things that we want without having to make our father worry over it. I've grown up in a house where half the time something or the other isn't working. I've learned to adjust and manage and ...'

'And I'm giving you the chance to never have to worry about anything!' Ayub snapped.

'Why? Because I'm beautiful?' she scoffed. 'I still don't know why your father set this in motion. We were both happily unaware of each other until a few days ago and ...'

Ayub knew he couldn't tell her what Abba had said. As it was, she was talking about calling this off. His mind raced with ideas, trying to think of something that he could tell her to change her mind. But what?

'Okay, look,' he said softly but firmly. She looked at him and it was hard not to be distracted by the perfect beauty of her features.

'Go on,' she said softly, crossing her arms over her chest.

'I personally think we would make a fantastic couple,' he said. She raised an eyebrow sceptically.

Ignoring it, he went on. 'None of our differences will matter when we get married. And I have a feeling you're the sort of kickass person who won't listen to anything anyone says about your family and let them live to see another day.'

Her lips straightened in a tight line but he went on without letting her interrupt. 'So why not get married to me and see what happens?' He wanted to add that he had never envisioned that he would have to *convince* someone to marry him, but he knew that wouldn't go down well with her.

'Based on what, Ayub?' she asked finally. Her voice was soft but there was an undertone of panic in it.

'Chemistry?' he asked, hoping she wouldn't flare up at the joke. She rolled her eyes.

'Come on! Don't tell me you're not feeling this,' he said, waving his hand between them. Her face flushed and he felt elated. He moved closer to her, wishing modern cars didn't have bucket seats. She stared at him, as though unable to look away.

'Other couples get married based on nothing, Tehzeeb,' he said softly, picking up her hand and holding it. She inhaled and looked at him, wetting her lips. His gaze was drawn there and he knew then, that he had to taste her.

He leaned even closer but she didn't move back. He looked up at her flushed face, at her eyes that were wide, but not in panic. In desire, he realised triumphantly. He dropped a kiss on her delectable collar bone and she shut her eyes as he kissed her neck and then slowly, her jaw.

'Ayub,' she whispered and held his arm, but didn't stop him. He kissed her chin.

'Look at me,' he whispered. He could see her chest rising up and down as she opened her eyes slowly. He nodded, wordlessly asking for her consent. She nodded too. He held her face and kissed her.

FIFTEEN

Tehzeeb knew she should stop this but her brain was foggy with desire and wasn't complying. They were sitting in a car, kissing each other hungrily, and she knew that she had wanted this as much as he had. It was why she couldn't bring herself to stop him as his hands roamed over her body, even touching her breasts lightly. She groaned into his mouth and his tongue pushed inside, making her nipples bead into hard points, and her belly flip over and over again, there was an ache lower down, which made her wonder what would possibly ease it.

'Ayub, I …' she gasped as his mouth left hers. He was breathing heavily too, his face flushed and skin stretched tight around his eyes. He suckled the skin on the base of her neck, grazing it with his teeth and she arched towards him. But she sensed him slowing down and he lifted his head away.

He rubbed his hand over his face even as he brought his breathing under control. 'Stupid,' he muttered.

'What?'

'I'm stupid. To have started something that we can't possibly … that we can't finish,' he said, looking at her steadily. She felt a blush rise up in her cheeks and she bit her lower lip anxiously. Her body thrummed, wanting more of what she couldn't have yet.

He was still breathing heavily and she saw that his hands were holding the steering wheel in a death grip. He turned to her. 'There is so much more that I want to do to you,' he said in a low voice and she squirmed in her seat, knowing that her own desire was evident on her face.

'You feel this, right? What's between us? Let's not worry about our families. It's fate that we've been brought together like this. Don't you think?' he said, reaching out and holding her hand.

She didn't know what to say. She'd come here with the intent to break off but now … all she could think of was the way his lips had moulded over hers, at those strong hands that had held her, hands that she wanted to feel on other parts of her body too. She didn't trust her voice at the moment, afraid that only a squeak would emerge.

She looked at him, thinking that it was indeed fate that had brought them together. His voice alone was doing a lot of things to her, especially that low sexy voice. And then his eyes – warm brown and so intense, like they could see right through her. And those biceps she'd felt when she held his arm. There was so much more she wanted to see and touch and taste. Her mouth was dry as she looked at him intently.

'Do you know that your face is like an open book?' he asked her hoarsely. His throat seemed to be working and she knew that what she felt was right there on her face but she wasn't embarrassed. They both knew that they wanted each other.

'This was a terrible idea,' she said finally, dropping her gaze from his and touching her brow with her shaky fingers.

'Actually, it was the best idea,' he said, grinning. She looked up, puzzled.

'I doubt I could have done any of this if we'd met in a café,' he explained.

Maybe she had subconsciously wanted this, she thought in alarm. Or why would she suggest a private meeting? She knew now that this had been an excuse to see him, to see if the chemistry that had been there between them that day was real. A chance to explore it further. She also wanted him to convince her to get married to him when she presented her very real problems and he had done that too.

'Tehzeeb, are we good now?' Ayub asked her softly. She looked at him and nodded slowly. He looked relieved.

'I … I better be going,' she said. She had to get out of this car now, she thought. His nearness was making her want him again. She wanted his lips on hers once more and she didn't want him to stop.

'Wait,' he said.

'Ayub, don't,' she said in a low voice, without looking at him.

'Don't what?' he asked.

'Don't start something you can't finish,' she said, looking at him. He looked abashed.

'I'll see you next week,' he said.

She nodded. But at the same time, she was feeling the strangest desire to continue sitting with him here, in his car in this darkened lane. She didn't want to go back home and she made no move to leave.

'Can we talk?' she asked him suddenly.

'Err … of course. But I thought we were talking all this while,' he said, looking puzzled.

She nodded. 'We are practically strangers who … who have this great chemistry between us. I'd like to know a little more about you,' she said.

He smiled. 'What do you want to know?' he asked.

'Just stuff, you know. Things you like to do, movies you enjoy, if you watch TV, if you watch sports,' Tehzeeb said.

He looked at her shrewdly but she continued before he could speak. 'Let's talk like two friends who are getting to know each other,' she said.

'Only talk?' he asked.

She nodded. 'Only talk,' she repeated. He sighed, but he also smiled at her.

*

When Tehzeeb let herself inside her house, she rushed straight to her bathroom. She looked at her face in the small mirror above the wash basin – her face was still flushed and her lips were slightly swollen. She hoped her sisters wouldn't notice but that was a bit too much to expect. The two of them were experts at noticing things they shouldn't.

She touched her lips slightly, tracing the outline with her finger, thinking of how his lips had felt against hers and she could still feel them tingle. She enjoyed the time she and Ayub had spent talking to each other. They discovered numerous things in common but also things they didn't have in common, which made the other more intriguing and interesting, nevertheless. He had suggested driving for a bit while they talked.

'Why?' she asked, puzzled.

'Because I want to have a genuine reason to not have my hands on you,' he replied, looking at her directly.

Her stupid fair face blushed so easily and just remembering those words, and the way he had said it made her blush once more. Oh, it was useless trying to hide all this from her sisters. They had been in the kitchen making dinner but they knew she had returned. She had to face their inquisition and maybe it was better if she came right out and said what had happened.

They had kissed. That's all. She covered her face with her palms. It wasn't just a 'that's all' moment. It was so much more than that. She splashed cold water on her face and tried to slow down her breathing and look calm.

Then she gave up. She stepped outside the bathroom, only to be ambushed by her sisters.

'What happened?' Ana asked as Tehzeeb wiped her face with a towel. She paused long enough to hope that they wouldn't know anything right away but she knew it was a futile hope.

Deciding to pretend like everything was okay, she dropped the towel and shrugged.

'We talked,' she said.

'And? That's it?' Athiya said, shaking her head, not believing her words for one moment.

'Obviously. I told him my problems and he said we could eventually figure it out,' she said. It was the truth.

'But do you *want* to?' Ana asked.

Not meeting her sisters' gaze, she nodded. 'Yeah,' she said softly.

'I should have insisted on coming with you,' Ana said suddenly.

'Why?' Tehzeeb asked surprised.

'At least you would have got some real talking done and not come back home with a hickey on your neck!' Ana snapped. Tehzeeb gasped and felt around for it. But she straightened up and looked at her sisters finally.

'Stop judging me. It's going to be fine,' she said.

'Yeah, we'll see,' Ana said grimly.

'Stop being such a party pooper!' Athiya said suddenly and Tehzeeb looked at her in surprise.

'What?' Ana was outraged.

'Yeah. She looks happy, no? Let things be! After all, how many of us can say we're getting married into a rich family which buys lavish gowns and has hotshot sons like Ayub Ahmed?'

Tehzeeb shook her head and walked away, knowing now the real reason why she had said yes to him.

Ayub had said he felt something when she walked inside the café that day. It wasn't just physical attraction, although that was very strong too. It was something more and she had felt it as well. There was some indefinable tug that had surprised and annoyed her when she had walked up to him. But there had been nothing annoying about his kisses, she thought. Her phone pinged as she walked towards the kitchen to get dinner ready, ignoring Ana and Athiya's arguments with each other.

It was a kiss-face emoji from Ayub. She saw that he was typing something. Before he could finish typing it, she swiftly typed and hit enter.

'Waiting to do this again!' she had sent.

He paused in his typing.

And sent her a grinning emoji.

SIXTEEN

On the day of the engagement, Tehzeeb was surprisingly calm while her sisters flew around the house in a chaotic mess. Aunts, uncles and relatives whom her father had invited had come and were filling up their already tiny house. Her father had asked everyone to assemble at Jasmine Villa and they would leave for the hotel together. But that meant that someone or the other always wanted tea and Ana and Athiya were fed up of being on tea-making duty. They had to get ready too.

The gown had been delivered home in the morning, thus refuting all the arguments that Tehzeeb's sisters had made. She slipped into it and Ana zipped it from behind. There was a gauzy dupatta that was paired with the gown that she would have to wear once she figured out what to do to her hair. She turned around to see Ana staring at her.

'Too much,' she said. Tehzeeb looked down self-consciously.

'What? What's too much?' she asked.

'Everything. You. This dress. The jewellery that came with it!' she said, referring to the tastefully sparkling diamond necklace that had been sent with the dress. Tehzeeb had decided to no longer be embarrassed about her house, if this was indeed going to be her life and she had tried hard not to make a big deal when the driver dropped off the clothes in the morning.

'I'm still the same me,' she said, sitting down before the dressing table mirror. But the truth was that she was terribly nervous inside. The clothes were befitting of their family. But what if she didn't live up to their expectations?

Outside, the aunts and uncles were making a lot of noise and Athiya walked inside in a huff. 'I swear if one more person asks me for tea, I'm going to … oh!'

She spotted Tehzeeb just then and her mouth dropped open. Shaking her head, she said, 'Oh my god, this is amazing! You look …'

'Stuck. I'm stuck,' Tehzeeb said. Her sisters frowned.

'Stuck where?' Ana asked, looking over her and shaking her head.

'I don't know what to do about my hair or my makeup. What if they're expecting me to be like them?' Tehzeeb asked.

'Oh please. Let's not get into this. You know how amazing you look,' Athiya said almost furiously.

'Let's keep your makeup and hair simple. I think the gown is spectacular on its own and you look nothing short of amazing,' Ana said.

Nodding, Tehzeeb went to work on her face. She did her usual makeup routine but deepened her eyeliner and used more mascara than she had ever before. Ana tied her hair in a simple French braid and Tehzeeb stood up, exhaling deeply.

'It's going to be fine,' Athiya assured her. 'Imagine us. We're going to look like beggars, standing next to you.'

'Shut up, Athiya,' Ana said, angrily. 'We didn't ask for

this. Ayub's family wanted Tehzeeb Api. We are what we are.'

Ana, true to her name, had a big ego. It was often enough for all of them together.

*

Two hours later, in the hotel reception hall, Tehzeeb felt panicky. Her father looked even more worried. Where was the engagement being held? Had they come to the wrong hotel? There was no sign of any big engagement party and Tehzeeb felt foolish as people stared at her. She was dressed dramatically and the huge group of people with her, relatives who had never been inside a hotel such as this, were looking around at everything, awed.

This was a mistake. Her heart thundered in her chest. Where was everybody? Her father walked to the reception and asked, and the man standing behind the desk pointed at a sign that had been kept on one side, leading towards a corridor.

'We have to go there,' Abbu said as he led everyone towards the corridor.

Tehzeeb wished she could make a regal entrance instead of looking anxious and worried but she kept pace with her father who walked ahead. The corridor led to the poolside space and her father looked relieved upon spotting Ayub's father there. Bakhtiyar Ahmed saw them coming and his eyes widened.

'Wasn't anybody there to receive you all?' he said, walking up to them quickly. Her father shook his head.

'I can't believe this. I'm so sorry. Come, let's get you all settled down,' he said warmly, leading the party towards the many tables and chairs that were spread across the lawn. The water in the pool glittered and Tehzeeb wondered what she should do and where she should go. In engagement events in her family, the bride never mingled with everyone like this. She turned around to speak to her sisters when Maira came bounding towards her.

'Bhabhi!' she said, and hugged her gingerly, air-kissing both her cheeks. Maira was wearing a deep blue ghagra and a blouse that fit her snugly. Her dupatta was there, trailing after her somewhere. Tehzeeb noticed the shiny blue glitter on her eyelids and inch-long fake eyelashes and felt terribly underdressed despite wearing the gown.

'Come with me,' she said, even as Tehzeeb tried to introduce Ana and Athiya to her. They followed her nevertheless and they walked towards another door that led them back inside the hotel.

'Where are we going?' Tehzeeb asked, trying to quicken her footsteps to match Maira's pace. How she managed to walk so fast in those heels was astounding, Tehzeeb thought, as she spotted the four-inch heels that Maira was wearing like they were sneakers.

'To get your makeup and hair done. I feel like an idiot. I should have told you about it before only, no?' she said.

'But … I don't want anything done,' Tehzeeb protested. Maira stopped in her tracks.

'I already have makeup on and my hair is just fine,' she insisted.

Maira looked over at her and only then noticed Ana and Athiya.

'These are my sisters, Ana and Athiya,' Tehzeeb introduced them.

'Lovely. But why don't you want makeup and hair done?'

Maira asked, ignoring the two of them almost immediately.

Tehzeeb shook her head. 'I'm fine as I am,' she insisted.

Maira looked at her up and down and made a face. She inspected her face from all angles, muttering something to herself.

'Fine. But at least let's get your hair done,' she said.

Tehzeeb shook her head. 'I just need to settle down for a bit and relax. If you can show me to a room ...' she trailed off.

'Sure,' Maira said, walking once more at a brisk pace. She walked past a restaurant and then came to a room where she pushed open the door and led her inside.

Ana and Athiya followed her inside. The room was furnished simply and there was a bed with a couple of chairs and a dressing table. The mirror on top was surrounded by glowing bulbs.

'Bhabhi, are you sure about this? I would have loved to work on your face,' she said, pouting a little.

'It's okay, Maira. Maybe some other time,' Tehzeeb said uneasily. Maira's shoulders drooped.

'I was hoping to post the makeup video on my Instagram page,' she said but straightened up. 'It's okay, I guess. Once you get married, I'm going to shoot a makeup tutorial video with you.'

Tehzeeb didn't know what to say to that. She saw Athiya standing behind Maira and making faces.

'Okay, I'll come and get you when Bhai is on stage and you're needed for the ring exchanging ceremony,' she said and flounced off.

'Yeh kya item thi?' Athiya asked. Tehzeeb giggled and Ana rolled her eyes.

'She's Ayub's sister and she's actually quite sweet,'

Tehzeeb said. 'I'm surprised she didn't post any updates about the walk from the poolside to this room.'

Ana gaped at her. 'Updates?' she asked.

'Really. She's always on Instagram. I kept meaning to check out her profile,' Tehzeeb said. Athiya pulled out her phone and tapped open Instagram.

Tehzeeb felt a flutter of nervousness inside as she thought of the upcoming ceremony. She would be seeing Ayub again. The thought of holding his hand in front of everyone made her blush.

'She's got some 800 followers,' Athiya said, as she scrolled through her feed. 'No wonder she was after you to do your makeup. She's a little obsessed with it. There are at least thirteen tutorials here that she's done herself.' Ana took Athiya's phone from her and they were both perusing Maira's account.

Dreamily, Tehzeeb stared at her reflection in the mirror, hoping Ayub would like her without the excessive makeup. She had a feeling he would.

SEVENTEEN

The noise that flowed around Ayub was an unintelligible buzz because his eyes were searching out Tehzeeb. He knew she was here – he had already spotted her father and her relatives. He could see his father talking to Yusuf uncle who was sitting at one of the tables and he smiled. He was waiting for the big moment when Tehzeeb would make her entrance. Where was she anyway? He held a glass of juice in his hand and when someone suggested he sit on the stage, he refused. It would look ridiculous to sit there without her. So he remained standing, lingering near the tables and trying to see if he could spot Tehzeeb.

His mother glided around the tables, a gracious hostess in a maroon saree with gold zari work. More gold flashed on her body discreetly as she spoke to their guests, smiling at them, telling them to enjoy the appetisers that the uniformed waiters were taking around on trays.

Two very pretty women walked in then from inside the hotel and made a beeline for Yusuf uncle. He wondered if they were Tehzeeb's sisters.

'Nice party,' someone said and he turned around and smiled. It was his best friend, Luqman, who thankfully happened to be in the city during his engagement. Luqman often travelled for work for days on end and could barely be seen in Bangalore. They clapped each other on the back and Luqman stepped back to look at Ayub.

'Nice. Are you sure you're not getting *married* today?' he asked as he looked at Ayub's elaborate cream and gold sherwani and gold jootis.

'I wish,' Ayub muttered. Luqman's eyes widened.

'What?' he asked, stepping up closer to his friend. 'I can't believe you're saying that. I thought the two of us were going to hold out until we were thirty.'

Ayub smiled and shrugged. 'When it's the right girl, why wait?' he said.

'Oh please. How do you even know it's the right girl? Yours is an arranged marriage like everyone else's,' Luqman scoffed. He cast a glance at the many people sitting around, some of them looking restless. It was like they were waiting for a movie to begin.

'See these people here? All these relatives and friends? Look how bored they are with their lives! You want that sort of existence for yourself too?'

Ayub shook his head. 'Mine isn't exactly an arranged marriage,' he said absently. His eyes were still searching out Tehzeeb. If her sisters were here, then where was she? He glanced at his watch impatiently. He didn't think she would change her mind now. Not after last Saturday or the many texts they had sent each other.

Luqman looked bewildered when Ayub turned back to face his friend. 'What do you mean? When did this happen? I thought I knew everything that was happening in your life!'

'It's a long story. I wouldn't say it's a love ...' his words faltered. He had just seen Tehzeeb emerge from the other end of the poolside garden from inside the hotel. He couldn't see her face yet but he knew it was her. She was dressed in a lilac-coloured gown and a transparent net dupatta in silver was covering her slightly bent head which obscured her face partially. She was walking gracefully towards him, helped by Maira.

There was a hush when everyone realised that she was walking towards him. He held his breath too. People turned to look at her. Out of the corner of his eye, he saw the two young girls he'd seen earlier get up and join Tehzeeb on either side. Maira didn't look too pleased at this addition but she didn't say anything. The four women walked slowly and the crowd fell silent. He saw Ammi walking towards them in a stately manner and join them.

Just before Tehzeeb reached him, his mother stopped and turned around. She lifted the dupatta and pushed it back until Tehzeeb's face could clearly be seen. Tehzeeb had to bend a little more for her mother to be able to do that. Ammi looked at Tehzeeb's face for a moment and Ayub had to quell the urge to push aside everyone and go to her.

Then, Ammi led Tehzeeb towards him. By his side, he could sense Luqman straightening. But instead of stopping, Ammi led Tehzeeb up the small stage and seated her on the chair on the left. She whispered something to Tehzeeb who straightened up and the crowd finally let go of their breath. She was indeed looking breathtaking, Ayub thought, his heart feeling full.

'Um, okaaaay,' Luqman said, nudging him slightly. 'Does she have sisters?'

Grinning, Ayub nodded. 'Those two young ladies,' he said, indicating the girls who were now heading back to their father's table while Maira stepped up on stage.

'I'm surprised Maira hasn't seen me yet,' Luqman muttered softly.

'Oh, she has. She's ignoring you,' Ayub said, suppressing a grin.

'What? Really? How did this happen?' Luqman said, shaking his head in relief.

'Don't know. You think I actually sit down and talk with her about why my best friend refuses to fall in love with her?' Ayub said. He was impatient to go and sit with Tehzeeb now, be near her, look at her.

Luqman made an exaggerated sound that sounded like 'aaargh' but Ayub had tuned him out. He was wondering if someone would come and lead him onto the stage or if he had to just do it himself. Thankfully, Maira stepped forward. With a bright smile on her face, she placed her hand on his wrist and tugged him.

'Come on, Bhai,' she said. She ignored Luqman who turned away and went to sit at one of the tables. Ayub felt the stares of all the guests who were waiting for him to join her. He wished their engagement had been a small affair, something just for the families, maybe even at his house. This seemed like a big production and if he was feeling exhausted already, he couldn't imagine what Tehzeeb must be going through.

His legs felt heavy as he walked towards her and then Maira indicated that he should sit down. Even though he was sitting next to Tehzeeb, he knew he couldn't turn to her and look at her directly. Everyone was looking at them. Even though they were sitting quite close together, he still felt like he was miles away from her. This sucked. But he would talk to her later tonight, he promised himself.

He looked out at the numerous people milling around

and wondered what his mother was waiting for. Then, thankfully, she walked up on the stage slowly and came towards them. Maira and some of his cousins came up on the stage as well. His sister was holding a tray and they all converged around them. Ignoring him, Ammi lifted Tehzeeb's face and looked at her. This sort of scrutiny was agonising for her, he knew, because he could sense her stiffen in her chair.

He leaned forward and looked too. He couldn't help it. It was an awkward position but he wanted to see everything instead of staring forward like a mannequin. He caught his mother's disapproving glance but he continued to look at his future wife.

Tehzeeb's skin glowed – it was almost pearlescent. To be sitting so close to her and to not even touch her while the rest of his family looked at her ... it was torture. Ammi took a string of jasmine from the tray and tied it to each of Tehzeeb's wrists. She applied ittar to her wrists, touched her face, and kissed her brow.

Someone nudged him and he turned, almost annoyed. But it was Maira who held the tray with the engagement rings on it. *Now,* she mouthed to him. Nodding, he picked up the delicate ring with a large diamond on top and turned towards Tehzeeb.

He saw her fully then, up close, and he wished everyone else was gone so he could savour this moment fully. In the lilac gown with the transparent sleeves, with the simple diamond jewellery, she looked radiant. She looked up at him shyly and there was a shadow of a smile on her face.

He didn't know who, but someone cleared their throat and he realised that they were all waiting for him. She held out her hand and he held the very edge of her fingers and slipped the ring on. Everyone clapped politely. This monkey show had gone on too long, he thought irritably, but then it was his turn and she took his hand and pushed a gold band on his finger shyly. People clapped once more. His mother bent close to him, hugging him and then she went to Tehzeeb and did the same.

So much anticipation for this anti-climactic moment, he thought, irritated when others started crowding them, congratulating them and leaving the stage. He realised that he would be led away soon and so would she. He wanted to see more of her, and he knew he didn't have much time. In the few seconds they were alone on the stage, he quickly leaned close to her and whispered, 'Meet me inside the hotel.' He had no idea if she had heard him or if she would even do anything about it.

To his utmost surprise, she whispered back, 'Where?'

EIGHTEEN

How much longer was this going to go on, Ana thought as she tapped the table lightly with her fingertips. Athiya was lost in her phone, scrolling, and it was up to her to pacify the relatives who hadn't expected such a brief engagement.

The engagements that they were used to were vastly different. First, there were no meagre jasmine strings that were tied on the wrists. There would be heavy garlands involved. And more jasmine flower thingies to tie around the head. If things had gone the way of her family, Tehzeeb would have been looking like a jasmine-covered onion. Layers and layers of flowers. Ana was actually glad Tehzeeb had escaped all that.

Imagine covering that gorgeous gown completely with flowers? But the aunts were shocked when they saw that Tehzeeb and Ayub were sitting together on the stage.

'Why aren't they doing the boy's engagement and girl's engagement separately?' an aunt whispered harshly into her father's ear. 'That's how things are done in our families! And why are all the men and women sitting together?' Both these things had shocked them.

Thankfully, her father told her that this was being done differently and they had to respect Ayub's family's wishes.

'But what about our wishes?' the same aunt insisted. 'How can you completely give in to them like this?'

'Stop screeching Taskeen!' Abbu had told her, annoyed. 'It is what it is. Don't make a scene here.'

Taskeen Auntie kept tsking away much to Ana's amusement. She was one of the most annoying aunts who had been sending rishtas for Tehzeeb for the past five years. She must have been quite miffed to hear of this proposal, especially because of the sudden elevation in status.

Relatives, Ana thought, rolling her eyes. Can't live with them and can't live with them. No question of 'without'. The ceremony on stage had just concluded. Ana was done speaking to everyone reasonably. She was tired and hungry and she wanted to go home.

Her relatives had occupied three big tables and they were the ones making the most noise. She was a little embarrassed but she kept her eyes on the stage. Tehzeeb was being led down from there and Ayub seemed to be confused before he too got up and left.

'That's it? Hogayi mangni?' another aunt asked.

Abbu ignored her. Then, to her dismay, Ana realised that the food was being served buffet style which was to be expected, since this was a fancy-ass hotel. Her relatives preferred being seated at a table and having their food served to them. What was worse was that no one was going to ask them to 'come and eat' which was the custom in her family. Unless they were specifically invited, they would even leave the venue without eating. So she got up and nudged Athiya too.

'What?' she asked, barely looking up.

'Come, let's go and see what we're supposed to do for dinner,' Ana said.

'Why?'

'Because it's a buffet and we'll have to herd everyone to the line there and then ... aaargh, it's going to get messy. Come and help me!' Ana snapped at her. Scowling, her sister put away her phone and the two of them walked towards the buffet station. Great. People were standing in lines here. No way would Taskeen Auntie and some of the others stand in line to get food. They hated buffets.

'Now what,' Ana muttered, wondering if she and Athiya should pile up a few plates to take to the tables where they were seated. Just how many times would she have to do this?

It was at moments like these when she really missed her mother. Ammi would have said just the right thing to everyone and known how to mollify them. Abbu was too much of a loner to worry about what the relatives were going to say.

She stepped back a little and realized she had stepped on someone's toe.

'Ouch!' he said.

'I'm sorry!' she said, as she turned around to see who it was. He was tall and good-looking and he frowned at her.

'I said I'm sorry,' she snapped and walked away from there. At the buffet line, she told Athiya that they would have to fill up plates and take it to the tables. Athiya looked horrified at the prospect.

'Why can't they come here like everyone else?' she hissed.

'Because you know what they're like! They'll say everyone here is a paisewala bhikari to be dressed up to the nines and holding out a plate for food!' Ana whispered.

There was a chuckle behind her and she turned around. It was the same man and he had probably heard her. She frowned at him and turned around to pick up two plates which she handed to her sister. They filled up the plates and then took them back to the tables. She did this one more time and was already dreading the prospect of going there a third time when Maira tapped her shoulder.

'What are you doing?' she asked her, puzzled.

Ana didn't know if she could explain it to her. But Maira looked at her as though it was all very obvious.

'Just tell the waiter to bring some of the dishes to the tables directly!' Maira said. 'Why are you running around like this?'

Ana felt her face heat up when she realised that Maira was right. She could have just done that. She straightened her shoulders and nodded.

Athiya, who hadn't heard the interaction, tapped her elbow. 'How many more times do we have to do this?' she asked.

'Um, no more. We'll ask the waiters,' Ana said, feeling foolish. Athiya's eyes widened.

'We could have done that from the beginning and yet you made us ...'

'Shut up,' Ana said, her eyes drawn to that tall good-looking guy who had snickered at her a while ago. Maira had spotted him and she almost tripped in her haste to go to him. He looked pained but he was talking to her earnestly. She, on the other hand, was turning this way and that way, acting like a drama queen.

Ana beckoned one of the waiters and explained the situation to him. He looked over at the tables that needed to be served and smiled at her knowingly. Annoyed at everything and everyone, Ana made her way back to the table where an uncle was waiting expectantly for her to bring a plate of food for him.

'The waiter's bringing it,' she explained. For some reason, he was affronted.

'But you got a plate for everyone else!' he said, his nose flaring.

Tehzeeb would have handled everyone easily, Ana thought with desperation. She was an old hand at putting out flames and mollifying everyone. Or maybe people just liked looking at her and forgave her easily, Ana thought. It was hard not to feel jealous of her perfect sister—so beautiful to look at that sometimes it ached to see her, a heart that was gentle and kind and wanted to help others, excellent in studies and well-read—there was nothing she wasn't good at.

Well, maybe cooking. She wasn't so great at cooking, but with those looks—and she had seen how Ayub had been looking at her—her cooking skills were not really going to matter. The only time Tehzeeb broke out of the perfection mould was when she was mimicking someone. She did it so perfectly that for a few moments you forgot that it was her.

Some people had all the luck with everything, she thought as a waiter finally brought over the plates and kept them on the table. Her father was talking to Ayub's father, along with some other men. Probably discussing the wedding date, she realised. That's what happened at engagements anyway.

But where was Tehzeeb? She looked around for her sister and couldn't spot her anywhere. For that matter, she couldn't see Ayub either. Oh shit.

NINETEEN

This wasn't funny anymore. Luqman knew he had to get away from there before Maira decided to throw herself at him again. From ignoring him to sidling up to him and now, back to her usual shenanigans, his best friend's younger sister was embarrassing herself more than anything else. He looked around, hoping to spot Ayub so he could tell him that he was leaving. He'd have a kathi roll somewhere instead of suffering through dinner here.

But he couldn't see Ayub anywhere. That was strange, because Ayub had been on the stage just a few moments ago, sliding a ring onto the finger of his bride-to-be. It was easy to see why Ayub was so besotted with Tehzeeb. There was something about her face, the features that were beyond beautiful. Shaking his head ruefully, he neared the exit, thinking he would text Ayub and tell him that he had to leave when he bumped into the same pretty girl from before. Ayub had said that she was Tehzeeb's sister.

Both of them reached the doors that led inside the hotel at the same time and ended up bumping each other's shoulders rather hard. She stumbled a little and he held out a hand to steady her. She knocked his hand out of the way, rather irritably. There were high spots of colour on her face and despite her worried expression, he realised she was rather pretty herself.

'Sorry,' he said, putting his hands out in a conciliatory manner.

She shook her head and looked this way and that. Then she turned to look at him again. 'I saw you talking with Ayub earlier. You're his friend, right? Do you know where he is?'

He narrowed his eyes and shook his head. 'Why?'

She sighed and then seemed to be caught in some sort of internal struggle. But instead of answering him, she started striding purposefully towards a corridor. He instantly got the feeling that something was wrong, so he followed her.

'Where are you going?' he asked her. She turned around swiftly.

'Don't make a scene! I can't find my sister either. This is not going to look good!' she whispered fiercely. Luqman's eyes widened. Oh man. Ayub was in serious trouble if he was up to some hanky-panky. This sort of thing was seriously frowned upon by everyone, not to mention the scandal that would erupt if they were found together.

He pulled out his phone and dialled Ayub's number. But it just kept ringing.

The girl kept walking towards the corridor and he followed her. 'Do you know where you're going?' he asked her, catching up with her swiftly.

She nodded. 'There's a room where Maira had taken my sister to get her makeup done. Maybe she's here. I don't know where else to look,' she said and then rounding the corridor, she stopped in front of a closed door.

She lifted her hand and knocked loudly and then, to his surprise, she rested one ear against the door. Then she knocked loudly again.

'Api! Are you mad?' she asked in a fierce tone.

He stepped up closer and leaned in to hear as well. She smelled nice, he thought vaguely. There was a shuffling sound from inside, and then a rustling sound as well. Oh great.

'Hurry up, you idiots,' he said a little loudly, and she jumped.

'Who's there?'

'Ayub, you idiot, it's me!' he said. The door opened the slightest bit and the girl pushed against it and went inside with a determined stride. He admired the way she just took charge of the situation.

He went inside too and shut the door behind him. Ayub and Tehzeeb were standing by the bed, close together. The four of them stood staring at each other.

'You are clearly out of your fucking mind!' he said to Ayub. Ayub looked back at him defiantly and that was when Luqman noticed that he was holding Tehzeeb's hand. Tehzeeb looked away and extricated her hand from his.

'I should leave,' she said softly.

'We didn't do anything wrong!' Ayub said, turning to Luqman, annoyed.

'Err … no one is going to be bothered about right or wrong if the two of you are found in a room like this just minutes after your engagement!' Luqman said, exasperated.

'Api, what were you thinking!' the girl said to her sister, holding her wrist. 'Come, let's go!' Saying so, she dragged Tehzeeb away from there but stopped before the mirror with the bulbs around it.

'Shit. Fix your makeup first,' she muttered.

Without wasting any time, Luqman tugged Ayub's hand. 'Let's leave before anyone else walks in. If only Tehzeeb is here with her sister, it's fine. If *you're* here …'

Ayub shook his hand away and walked away from there reluctantly. He paused before Tehzeeb, his face softening and he whispered something in her ear. Tehzeeb blushed and nodded. Her sister gave the evil eye to Ayub and indicated to Luqman that he should take him away as soon as possible.

He knew that was the best course of action and they could tell anyone who chanced upon them that Ayub had just visited the restroom inside the hotel. Nodding to her, he walked away from there, grabbing hold of his friend's hand once more and tugging him along.

'Come on!' he said, gritting his teeth.

'Fine, fine,' Ayub muttered and walked with him. Luqman looked around carefully to see if he could spot anyone nearby but thankfully, no one from the wedding party was around. They were all probably busy eating, he thought. Only other hotel guests were there, and not that many of them too.

Grateful for that, he took Ayub with him and led him outside.

'What were you thinking?' Luqman demanded.

Ayub didn't say anything but had the grace to look slightly shamefaced. 'Okay, fine. I got a little carried away but nothing happened and no one saw us. So stop making a big deal out of this or I'll just punch you,' he said.

Shaking his head, Luqman sighed.

'I'm not getting into this futile discussion. I'm off now,' he said.

'What? No! You can't leave yet!' Ayub said, shaking his head.

'Dude, Maira ignored me for like five minutes. That's all. She's been after me ever since then,' he said.

'That's because she knows you're single,' Ayub said.

Luqman shook his head. 'Whatever. I'm leaving. I don't want your mother to get on my case too,' he said.

Ayub sighed. 'Fine. I'll try talking to her. It might help if you just got married to someone, you know?' he said.

Luqman rolled his eyes. 'Yeah, right. I have two older brothers who haven't yet gotten married. You think *my* wedding is going to happen any time soon?'

Ayub shrugged. 'At least get a girlfriend so I can dissuade her more easily,' Ayub said.

Luqman shook his head. 'My mother will kill me. You know that. They're not like your parents,' he said.

'And how old did you say you were again?' Ayub teased him. Luqman just shook his head and walked away from there. He was glad he hadn't bumped into Maira again. It would have been hard explaining to her why he was back here when he had said he was leaving fifteen minutes ago. He saw Tehzeeb being led from inside the hotel by her sister and there was an odd sort of feeling running through him. He realised he hadn't even asked her name.

TWENTY

Tehzeeb couldn't sleep that night. She couldn't believe what had almost happened in the hotel. How could she have been so irresponsible? How could Ayub's honeyed words whispered in her ears make her forget everything that she had been taught?

She shut her eyes in embarrassment when she thought of the moment Ana had barged inside with someone who had to have been Ayub's friend. Ana had been merciless with her and even though she was sleeping right next to her, Tehzeeb felt like she was still yelling at her.

'You stupid foolish girl, Api!' she had ranted as she fixed her makeup. Her lipstick had got smudged when Ayub kissed her.

'N-nothing happened,' Tehzeeb said, trying to make her voice firm and strong and not back down. Ana glared at her.

'I can see the evidence of what happened. So don't give me this bakwas!' Ana snapped.

Tehzeeb decided to shut up but she hadn't expected Ana to just go on and on. 'You know why Abbu named you Tehzeeb? Because he hadn't dreamed that twenty-three years later, his daughter would not show any tehzeeb on the day of her engagement,' she said.

Arrey, Tehzeeb thought, getting annoyed. Ana was being so sanctimonious and self-righteous. But she couldn't speak because Ana was touching up her makeup. Her lips were still tingling though, as was the rest of her body.

'Imagine if it hadn't been me, but Abbu who opened this door and found you inside with Ayub?' Ana said. The thought was mortifying indeed. 'Or what if someone came looking for him and found you inside with him? Think of the scandal, Api! Think of others also for a change, will you?'

As they walked back outside, Ana's words had finally sunk in and she realised that this had been a terrible idea. Just as Ana had found her absence to be suspicious, anyone else could have also discovered her and Ayub missing. This could have gone a lot worse if it hadn't been for her sister and that gentleman.

'Who was the man with you?' she asked her, hoping that Ana would drop the subject and let her be.

'I don't know,' Ana snapped back at her. Tehzeeb frowned. Ana was right in getting angry but was it just her who was the source of her anger?

'Why are you so pissed?' Tehzeeb asked as she led her to one of the tables.

'Because not all of us will get married to rich tycoons like Ayub Ahmed and what you do reflects on us too. Who will marry me or Athiya if any scandal erupted now?' Ana said softly. Her tone was fierce though and it struck Tehzeeb that her sister was right after all. Her stomach contracted painfully and she wanted to leave and go home right away.

She couldn't bring herself to face her sister. 'I'm sorry,' she mumbled, realising that her throat was thick with tears. Ana noticed it immediately but her face didn't soften even for a second. She still looked furious.

'Where were the two of you?' Athiya asked as she joined them at the table. Other people were looking at them because she, the bride-to-be, was seated there.

'She needed to use the restroom,' Ana answered.

Athiya nodded and started talking about a dessert that was being served there which was so luscious that she wondered if they could steal a couple for later. Ana didn't reply.

'Have you eaten?' Tehzeeb asked her. She shook her head. 'Why don't you go with Athiya and have something?'

'Can't leave you alone and go,' Ana replied curtly. Blushing, Tehzeeb shook her head.

'I won't be alone,' she said because just then, Ayub's mother Aafreen was walking towards them, bringing over her friends and relatives who wanted to see her.

Reluctantly, Ana got up and went away with Athiya. The rest of the evening, Tehzeeb played the role of a demure bride who nodded and answered in monosyllables while people around her talked as if she didn't exist. They commented on her beauty and how fair she was and how lucky Aafreen was to get such a beautiful daughter-in-law. One didn't need to be a genius to figure out that Aafreen didn't think she was lucky because all she gave were tight smiles as she barely nodded.

Someone brought a plate for her to eat but Tehzeeb shook her head. She couldn't stomach the idea of eating anything. She didn't want to lift her head and look around for Ayub in a very obvious manner even though she was wondering what he was doing.

So she sat there surrounded by people she didn't know, feeling alone, a little miserable and very ashamed. She hadn't been thinking at all when she had agreed to meet

Ayub inside the hotel. She had just been focusing on how handsome he looked, how delicious he smelled and it was all she could do to stop herself from leaning close to him during their ceremony. To think that he had felt the same way had been exciting and affirming.

Even as she had walked into the hotel with the excuse of visiting the restroom, her heart had thundered loudly. Her mouth felt dry with fear and the thrill of doing something like this so openly. She had hurried to the room and found that it was unlocked. She went inside, waiting for him anxiously. If anyone asked her, she would say that she had just come here to rest a little. She was just going to sit on the bed when he pushed open the door and came inside.

The two of them looked at each other for a few seconds – she realised they hadn't been able to do it openly outside.

'You are so beautiful!' he whispered and stepped forward. He looked dashing, she thought, in the sherwani. She moved towards him hesitantly and he pulled her into his arms, inhaling deeply and kissing her neck. He lifted his head and looked at her and their lips touched, igniting a fire inside both of them. She couldn't speak or think. She was only focused on his lips as they did wicked things to hers. They kissed for a long moment and he held her face like she was something precious.

Her knees shook and Ayub pushed her until she reached the bed and fell backwards on it. On her back, she felt vulnerable and exposed as he watched her. They were both breathing hard. He had just lowered himself to the bed when Ana came knocking on the door. Tehzeeb covered her face in remembered shame. How much further would they have gone if they hadn't been interrupted?

She was glad it was so dark. Her body throbbed and her face flamed when she remembered how his strong, masculine hands had felt on her body as they touched her. The tortuous night finally ended when guests started leaving. Her own relatives had surrounded her a little later, some of them commenting on how lucky she was while others made snide remarks about how 'things were not done like this in our families'.

Her father had been quiet all along and when they reached home, most of the relatives had dispersed. Tehzeeb was happy to get out of the gown. She wondered if she should return it along with the jewellery that had come with it. When she broached the topic with Ana and Athiya, they both thought she was out of her mind.

'Why? It's yours. You weren't their rented bride!' Athiya said.

'I don't see why you would think of returning these things. They are yours,' Ana said. Ana was still not talking to her properly. She wished things between them were not strained because she knew that Athiya would notice soon enough.

Abbu was talking to some of the relatives who hadn't yet left and when they finally did, he called out to them. The three of them went to the hall where Abbu was sitting on the sofa. He removed his glasses and wiped them on the hem of his kurta. Tehzeeb watched him apprehensively. She had been reckless today, completely forgetting herself and her family and she couldn't repeat the same mistake, no matter how much Ayub tempted her.

'So, the wedding date has been fixed,' Abbu said.

Tehzeeb felt a thud inside her chest. She knew it was from excitement and suddenly, the weight of the ring on her finger now felt more real.

'I spoke to Bakhtiyar today at the engagement. We have decided to have the wedding in three months. I told him that he had his way with the engagement but we will have our way for the wedding,' Abbu said. Clearly, some of the aunts and uncles must have gotten to Abbu as well.

'No more fancy hotels. We will be doing this in a proper wedding hall, the way we have always been having weddings,' he said.

Tehzeeb didn't respond. She knew she wasn't expected to. But as she got up to leave, Abbu held her hand lightly, stopping her.

'What is it Abbu?' she asked him. He smiled at her.

'You looked so beautiful today, beti,' he said. She realised there were tears in his eyes. 'I wish your mother had been there to see you too.'

Athiya cleared her throat suddenly and got up from there and left without any explanation. Tehzeeb nodded, realising that there were tears in her eyes too. She missed Ammi so acutely sometimes.

'I'm just so happy everything has turned out so perfectly,' Abbu said. Tehzeeb caught a sharp glance from Ana then and she knew why. She had nearly jeopardised everything and the thought made her tremble inside.

'I'm glad,' she said.

Now, lying in her bed in the dark, she allowed herself to briefly think about Ayub's kisses. As if tuned to her mind, that very moment her phone buzzed. She picked it up, knowing it had to be him. Squinting in the dark, she read his message.

'Still thinking of you,' it said.

Her finger hovered over her phone screen as she wondered what to reply. Then she remembered Ana's disapproving stare and her father's words. Exhaling deeply, she exited the messaging app and put the phone face down before she went to sleep.

TWENTY-ONE

Three months later

The Nikah had been just as messy as she knew it would be. People surrounded her, crying and hugging each other, once more forgetting that she was seated there on the dais. When she lifted her head, she saw her mother-in-law give her a disapproving look. She returned the stare for a few seconds and then looked down. Aafreen Ahmed was sitting in the front row of the audience. The hall was full of relatives who were chattering and jabbering and it was a far cry from the elegant and restrained atmosphere of the engagement.

Tehzeeb was feeling a little claustrophobic as people surrounded her on the stage and she wondered if they would even notice if she fainted. Thankfully, some people stepped away and she inhaled deeply. The necklaces adorning her were heavy and her head spun a little with the thought of all the jewellery she was wearing.

Ayub's Nikah would be done in the mosque. Hers had been performed here on stage in front of everyone. She thought of Ayub—now her husband—and wondered what he had made of her silence these past three months.

After nearly being caught together during their engagement, and after the dressing down she had received from her younger sister, Tehzeeb had decided that she was going to stay away from him until the wedding. She knew her silence would confuse him but she also knew that the moment she launched into an explanation of her actions, Ayub would overrule it and she would let him. She wanted him too badly.

Her stomach coiled nervously at the thought of the approaching night. They would be spending it as a married couple and ... she changed the direction of her thoughts. Not now. Not yet. She didn't want to go there just yet. When she lifted her head slightly, she saw that the hall was half empty and only then realised that lunch had been served and people had left to eat.

Maira came and sat down beside her.

'Weddings in your family are like this?' she asked her. Tehzeeb nodded as slowly as she could without entangling the jewellery or the flowers.

'So interesting! My Instagram is blowing up with comments and reactions!' she said. Tehzeeb knew she wasn't expected to answer so she kept quiet. She wondered how much of her family had been featured on her Instagram account. She'd have to tell Athiya to check.

Where were her sisters? She looked up and around and spotted them sitting in a corner, talking quietly. She felt a tinge of jealousy then. The three of them had been a team, always sitting together at weddings, gossiping, laughing, while she quietly mimicked some of the people she saw, and now the two of them were chatting away without her.

She beckoned them with a nod of her head and Ana smiled. Understanding, she got up and pulled her sister along and they approached the stage. Maira was sitting beside her and she fidgeted a little but her sisters came up on the stage and hovered near her. There wasn't place for them to sit, so Athiya pulled a couple of chairs from nearby and they sat down near her.

'Congratulations, Mrs Ayub Ahmed,' Ana whispered. Tehzeeb looked at her sister and smiled. The two of them were no longer at loggerheads and she knew the decision to stay away from Ayub had been the right one. The past three months had brought them even closer together when they had realised that Tehzeeb would be going away.

Athiya looked a little downcast but before Tehzeeb could ask her what the matter was, an older lady climbed the stage and walked up to her. Tehzeeb and the girls fell silent. To her surprise, Maira stiffened.

'Hello Salma Auntie!' she said effusively, getting up from there. Tehzeeb could see her hug the woman, who stepped back and then bent in front of her to see her face clearly.

Then she straightened up and talked to Maira as though Tehzeeb and her sisters were not present at all.

'I *had* heard that your mother had found a beautiful bride for your brother. Does she have any sisters?' the woman asked softly.

'Yes, those two are her sisters,' Maira said, indicating to Ana and Athiya. Tehzeeb's eyes widened. Was someone actually checking out her sisters as prospective brides? She knew these sorts of things happened at weddings, which was why she and her sisters had often stayed away from the limelight but then she had idiotically asked them to come on stage.

'How's Luqman, Auntie? Why hasn't he come for Bhai's wedding?' Maira asked.

'Oh, you know him. He had to travel to the US for some work. He'll only be back after a few months now,' the woman replied.

Tehzeeb didn't know what this exchange was all about and she wished the woman would go so she could breathe a little easier. Thankfully, she left soon and Maira went with her, leading her to the dining hall, talking effusively.

'Who was that?' Ana whispered in her ear. She turned to her sisters and shook her head.

'How would I know?' Tehzeeb said.

'She looked at both of us like she was examining mithai at a shop!' Ana said.

'No, like she was checking meat at a butcher's,' Athiya countered.

'Yuck. Never mind her,' Tehzeeb said. 'Look, before things get chaotic here again, I just wanted to tell you two to take care of Abbu. Of course, I'll visit every other day but …'

Ana stopped her. 'You're just going to be a few kilometers away. You're not going away to some other country. So chill. And anyway, it's not like only you were taking care of Abbu all these days,' she said.

Tehzeeb rolled her eyes. Trust her sister to shut her up right away. She wanted to just be there with them, talk to them, but other women came on the stage to see the bride and her sisters got up from there and left. This was going to be a long day, she thought. The strangest thing was that her Nikah was over and she hadn't even seen Ayub yet.

It was another hour or so until the guests had left and only relatives remained. She was tired – her head was aching and so was her back. She wanted to lie down and sleep and for a short period of time, someone took her to the room at the back of the hall where she sat down on the bed and winced. But it wasn't possible to lie down because of the jewellery. It would only poke her, she thought, annoyed.

The deep rose ghagra was embellished with Swarovski crystals – she had heard Maira repeat that about ten times already. It was elegant and royal and the makeup people Maira had sent over to her house had worked on her face for an hour, just to make it look like she wasn't wearing any makeup. She knew Maira was going to be disappointed but the fresh dewy look was what she told them she wanted.

Before she could relax a little while longer, someone came to touch up her makeup and take her outside once more. She was once again seated on the dais and she couldn't even spot her sisters this time. Some women from her family came up to the stage and started talking amongst themselves. She ignored them, wondering if it would be all right if she took a nap while sitting on stage when suddenly there was a hush.

She lifted her head to see what was happening. The hall was mostly empty now but the voices had fallen silent because Ayub had appeared at the entrance with some other men.

Her heart started beating quickly. She hadn't met him since their engagement. She knew he was probably angry with her because she had gone incommunicado. Her lips parted slightly. Even from so far away, she could feel his gaze on her. She lowered her head, although the way he looked was imprinted on her mind. He was wearing a navy blue sherwani and he looked regal as he walked towards the stage. She knew there was some ceremony involved here and that her family members were expecting him to come up on stage.

She sensed him walking towards her and the blazing

lights of the videographer accompanied him. They were about to see each other after three months and it was in full view of everyone. She tried to keep her thoughts from getting scattered, but it wasn't easy. He was at the dais now, climbing the steps on the side. Then he was moving past her and sitting down next to her. Her chest contracted and felt like it was folding in on itself. Was she having a panic attack, she wondered. But then she took a few deep breaths and became calm. Ayub, her husband, was sitting next to her. Finally.

TWENTY-TWO

Finally. They were married. Ayub didn't know if he was relieved or anxious. Tehzeeb's complete silence over the past few months had been disturbing. After what happened at their engagement, he hadn't expected her to disappear. He had messaged, called her but everything had remained unanswered. On the other hand, communication between their fathers had proceeded as they made plans for the wedding, where it would be held, who would pay for it, etc.

Ayub wondered if she had become wary because they had almost been caught together. But she could have explained, at least? They could have continued to text. The only photos he had of her were of their engagement. There had been no communication since then. He had been hurt and angry and had immersed himself in his work, treating the impending wedding as a task, and nothing else.

His father and Tehzeeb's had argued over everything for the wedding genially. The Nikah would take place according to Yusuf uncle's wishes while the Valima or the reception would be hosted at a hotel because that's what his father wanted.

The Valima was the day after tomorrow. As he walked up to the dais where Tehzeeb sat waiting for him, making a pretty picture in pink, he wondered what would happen in these two days. His annoyance towards her was tempered by anticipation and the unmistakable attraction that he had felt for her the minute he had seen her.

As he sat down beside her for some ceremony that her family wanted to conduct, he heard her intake of breath. Since he was looking straight ahead, he couldn't see her face properly but soon the dais got crowded with people from her family coming up, women who were covering their faces and giggling away.

He frowned slightly. What was going on? He had never seen anything of this sort happen at the weddings he'd been to all his life. To his surprise, a couple of young men shifted the chair that he was sitting in, while he was still in it. He was startled and almost stood up when they said it was all right, and insisted he continue sitting. He realised that even Tehzeeb's chair had been shifted so they now faced each other.

He tried hard not to look at her but her head was lowered anyhow. He lowered his too because he didn't want others to see him ogling his own wife. Wife. Wow. That word still felt strange. He almost smiled but stopped himself in time. Everyone was looking at him. At them. More people came up on stage and it felt like he was farther away from her, despite sitting so near her.

The next half an hour was surreal. They had kept a table between them and there was a large gilded mirror on it. Both of them were asked to lean forward and that was when he realised that this quaint custom was when the bride and groom probably saw each other for the first time. He wondered what his mother was making of all this. He hadn't seen her after the Nikah in the masjid when he had come here briefly to meet her.

Tehzeeb's face in the mirror looked back at him. She smiled tremulously. He didn't smile back. The whole world was watching them look at each other when he'd rather gaze at her in the privacy of their room.

They removed the mirror and then proceeded with other customs where both of them had to drink milk from the same cup – first him, then her. Tehzeeb refused politely but firmly. Despite himself, he was amused. After that, he was presented with a number of gifts from various in-laws. What was happening, he wondered. But he continued smiling and nodding lightly. This had been a long day. He couldn't wait to go home now.

The atmosphere changed subtly as the gifts were cleared and the chairs were rearranged. Her father and sisters came up on the dais and hugged her, one by one. Her father then hugged him too, and Ayub was uncomfortable when he realised that there were tears in Yusuf uncle's eyes.

Yusuf uncle opened his mouth to say something but couldn't seem to find the words. He gave a watery smile instead and hugged Ayub once more. The girls were hugging and crying and then it was all over. Tehzeeb was coming away with him to his house.

The enormity of getting married finally sunk into his head. She was going to be there in his house, his room, his bed.

Someone came forward and took her hand and put it in his. He held her hand in a comfortable grip as he led her away from the hall, followed by everyone who had been seated there. Someone had driven his car out from the basement and brought it up front and one of his cousins leaned forward and opened the passenger door for them to sit inside. Ayub let go of her hand and they seated themselves inside.

His father's driver was in the driver's seat. Ayub was aware of all the people outside the car who were waving at Tehzeeb but just as they were about to drive away, someone came and sat down on the other side, pushing him to the middle. Maira. He frowned. What was she doing here?

Maira sighed. 'Chalo, Bhaiya,' she told the driver, leaning back in the seat and shutting her eyes.

Ayub looked straight ahead even though his thigh was now pressed against Tehzeeb's. The ride home was thankfully not too long, he thought. He allowed himself to sink back into the seat and shut his eyes for a minute. It had been such a tiring day and it wasn't yet over. He was glad there was nothing planned for tomorrow.

He was tempted to turn to her, to make small talk, but he didn't want to do it here. Not with Maira sitting next to him. To his surprise, he felt her hand slip into his. He was still looking ahead, but he smiled and pressed her hand lightly.

She pressed back.

TWENTY-THREE

Tehzeeb felt alone and isolated in the big house. Ayub had let go of her hand when they reached his house and she felt bereft without that connection. Maira escorted her out of the car and led her inside. She couldn't quite take in the surroundings right away but she knew that the house was indeed very big.

A number of steps led up to the doors and she was grateful to have Maira by her side as they climbed them carefully. Ayub followed them at a distance and the doors were opened by someone. There were more people inside and she sensed their stares but she didn't lift her head to look at them. Maira took her to the living room and helped her sit on the sofa.

There was a buzz around her as various women came up to her and started talking to her. She finally looked up into their faces and smiled. Everyone was talking together, introducing themselves to her and she struggled to remember their names or how they were related to Ayub.

All of these women were also very similar – they all had blondish streaked hair, their faces were made-up perfectly and they looked very sophisticated. Maira joined them and Tehzeeb wondered where Ayub was. The moment he walked inside the living room, she knew it. The atmosphere changed, contracted and made it difficult for her to breathe. He sat down beside her on the sofa and all the chattering stopped.

This was embarrassing, Tehzeeb thought. She wished all these people weren't here.

'What are *you* doing here?' a woman asked Ayub. She sensed his shrug.

'Who's in charge of decorating my room?' Ayub asked. Oh shit. The room. Decoration. Rose petals. Bed. Hindi film wali suhaagraat, Tehzeeb thought wildly.

'Why?' the same woman asked.

'It's not been done. They're doing it now. Shouldn't they have done it earlier?' he asked. Tehzeeb was looking down and the dupatta covered her face slightly. She smiled at the imperious tone he used.

'We all came back from the wedding hall just now. When did you think it was going to happen?' his mother asked, coming inside.

'I'm tired. I want to sleep,' Ayub said. The living room fell silent for a few seconds and she realised everyone was looking at the two of them.

'Sleep?' a woman asked finally, in disbelief. That was enough to get everyone cackling. Ayub muttered a 'shit' under his breath. Would he turn to her and address her in front of everyone? But that wasn't required because one of the ladies came up to her and pushed aside the dupatta.

'Don't be shy,' the woman said. Tehzeeb looked at her and smiled slightly. To her amusement, some young girls and women edged Ayub out completely until they had surrounded her. They were asking her questions about herself, trying to introduce each other to her. She answered softly, but all the while, she was wondering where Ayub had disappeared.

A middle-aged woman in a slightly faded salwar kameez stood at the threshold and announced that dinner was ready. Everyone left in a rush and she wondered what she should do. The living room had suddenly emptied and she looked around properly. This was a beautiful room, she thought. One of the walls was covered with shelves and it had plenty of books. There was a large flat-screen television mounted on the wall. The room's décor was classic but slightly cluttered with a number of different artefacts. The sofas were plush and deep and the muted golden carpet under her feet was soft and squishy. She couldn't believe *this* was her home now.

'Come,' she heard a voice and looked up. It was Aafreen. She had a slight smile on her face. Tehzeeb got up, her bangles clinking, the ghagra rustling against her legs. She smiled back at her mother-in-law and walked up to her.

'Come and sit in my room for a bit. I'll get someone to send a tray for you there,' she said. Tehzeeb followed her quietly. Outside the living room, there was a huge staircase and Aafreen led her upstairs. She could hear everyone else chatting and laughing, the sounds coming from downstairs, from a room beyond. Probably the dining room where everyone was eating. Was Ayub also eating with them, she wondered.

Upstairs, it was even more opulent, if that was possible. The gold carpet that covered the floor here was lush and the wooden furniture gleamed. There were four rooms, two on each side of the landing and both had a hall sort of space outside the rooms with sofas and coffee tables. Aafreen indicated a room on the left side. 'That one's yours and

Ayub's. They're getting it ready. This is my room. Come and sit here,' she said and took her to a large room on the right.

Tehzeeb tried not to be awed by all of this. Aafreen entered her room and switched on the light. The room was airy, and as big as the living room of her house. There was a large bed covered immaculately in a light blue bedspread and there was a sofa on one side with a coffee table before it.

'Sit down anywhere you like,' Aafreen said, walking towards another door within the room. Tehzeeb thought it was the bathroom at first but Aafreen kept speaking from there and she realised it was a walk-in closet.

'You can lie down if you're tired,' she told her, emerging from there, after changing out of her lavish saree into a comfortable cotton kurta and loose palazzo pants. Tehzeeb envied her briefly. She felt like she was shackled by the clothes and jewellery and she wanted to take it all off more than ever.

'I'm fine,' she said softly. Aafreen was busy walking around, opening a chest of drawers on one side, checking for something and then pushing it back inside when she couldn't find it. She sighed.

'I'll send someone over with dinner for you,' she said and walked out of the room. The feeling of being alone in the house that was full of people came upon her suddenly. She missed her tiny house, her unkempt and haphazard Jasmine Villa where the concept of privacy was unknown and one couldn't walk into a room without banging into either furniture or walls or people.

She heard a throat being cleared and she looked up. It was Ayub and he was holding a tray.

She stood up, suddenly shy and embarrassed. What was he doing here?

'Sit, sit,' he said amicably as he came inside and sat down on the sofa beside her and placed the tray on the coffee table. 'I thought we could have dinner together.'

'I'm not hungry,' she said quickly. He looked at her and raised an eyebrow. He had changed out of his formal clothes too. Everyone except her had changed into comfortable clothes. Why was she the only one being tortured?

'I want to change out of my clothes,' she said softly.

'You'll have to ask Ammi about that,' he said as he placed a paratha on a plate along with some chicken curry.

'What?' Tehzeeb asked, outraged. He expected her to take his mother's permission to change her clothes? 'I need permission from your mother?'

He looked startled. 'No, I meant she would know where your clothes have been kept,' he said.

'Oh. Right,' she said softly.

'Here,' he said and handed the plate to her. She took it from him shyly, their fingers touching. He looked up at her then and took a deep breath. He looked like he wanted to say something but seemed to think better of it and filled up another plate with food for himself.

They ate quietly. This morning when she had woken up, Tehzeeb had been anticipating and dreading the day in equal measure. But she had never surmised that she would be sitting in her mother-in-law's room, eating dinner with her husband in silence.

TWENTY-FOUR

She looked tired. Ayub had been watching her interact with his family and had finally felt the unease of the past few months melt away. She had her reasons for keeping away from him and maybe she had been right in her own way but an explanation would have certainly helped. He had drifted away to the dining room when dinner had been announced.

His relatives would soon be leaving and it would be just them in the house – his parents, Maira, and now, his wife. There was plenty of teasing going around and lots of good-natured laughter as people sat down to have dinner.

He was tired too, he thought, rubbing his eyes. He had been awake since the crack of dawn and it had been a long and arduous day. He could only imagine how it must have been for her, dressed in that ghagra and the jewellery.

His mother came down then and pulled him to one side. Despite her initial reluctance about Tehzeeb and her family, his mother had come around. But he knew she was not fully won over. That would take time.

'What is it, Ammi?' he asked her. She looked much younger now as she stood before him, fresh-faced and dressed in her usual cotton clothes.

'Take some dinner on a tray and go upstairs to my room. Don't let her eat alone,' she said. Ayub smiled and nodded, thankful that his mother was being thoughtful and didn't care much for the other sort of decorum, where he was expected to see her only in their room, later tonight.

He was going to be aloof for a while, make her suffer a little, and his resolution only strengthened when he saw her sitting elegantly in his mother's room on the sofa. She looked startled upon seeing him but he could sense that she was also pleased. Dinner was excruciating for him, as he tried to maintain a distance from her. He took the tray and stood up when they were done and she stood up along with him.

'Wait here. I'll …' he lost track when she placed her hand on his wrist and took a deep breath. He didn't want to listen to any explanation now. Maybe later, in his room, he thought.

'I'll ask Ammi about your clothes,' he said and walked away. Her hand slipped from his wrist and he continued walking outside without looking back. He felt he had been petty though, so at the doorway, he stopped and turned. She continued looking at him, expressionless, and he nodded and left.

But instead of going downstairs, he kept the tray on a coffee table in the hall that opened up after the staircase and entered his room. Just what was taking so long to get his room ready?

Two young men were stringing jasmine strands all over the room and the fragrance was so intense that it was a wonder they hadn't been knocked out yet. There was a pile of rose petals lying in a corner of the bed and he rolled his eyes.

'Guys, this is enough,' he said to them. The fragrance already invoked the image of his wife and that was sufficient.

'But we still have to decorate the bed,' one of the men said. They had been hired by his mother, he assumed.

'Let the bed be as it is. Please don't make a heart out of rose petals,' he said, shaking his head. What a cliché. He didn't want to begin his marriage with one.

The men looked surprised.

'Ayub!' he turned around. His mother stood at the doorway, staring at him disapprovingly.

'What are you doing here?' she asked him.

'Why?' he asked.

'Let them do their job. Go downstairs now,' she admonished him.

'But Ammi,' he protested. She shook her head and turned around and walked towards her room. Grumbling, he headed downstairs. He had hardly reached when several cousins tackled him and he went along with them because there was nothing else he could do. His father was sitting in the living room watching television and he shook his head and smiled knowingly.

Now he wished he had spoken some more to Tehzeeb. He had left things awkward between them and it was going to be weird getting things back on track.

People started leaving and some of them had advice to give him. One burly uncle had pulled him aside and said, 'Show her who's the boss or she's going to rule you all your life,' he said gruffly. His wife gave him a withering stare.

'Speaking from experience, I presume?' she asked him. He hadn't realised she was there and his face turned red as he blustered and walked away. Ayub grinned. Maira walked up to him and placed her hand on his arm.

'Hey, what's up, kiddo?' he asked her.

'Nothing,' she said. He knew why she had the long face. She had been disappointed when she had heard that Luqman wasn't going to be at his wedding.

Ayub knew it wasn't his place to give any advice but felt compelled. This was his baby sister after all. 'Listen, Luqman isn't the guy for you,' he said in a hesitant tone. She flashed an angry look at him.

'Why? Why not?' she asked.

'He doesn't feel that way for you. He's made it clear already and you still chase him. Come on, Maira. This isn't like you!' he said.

Tears filled in her eyes rapidly. 'But this isn't just some crush you know. I've been in love with him for years now,' she said.

Oh dear. 'What's the point of loving someone who can't love you back?' he asked, not sure if it was the right thing to ask her.

'Why can't he love me back? What's wrong with me?' she asked. Then she frowned. 'No, what's wrong with *him*?'

Ayub shrugged, wishing he hadn't brought this up. All he wanted to do was go upstairs to his room but now he was stuck trying to counsel his sister.

'Nothing is wrong with either of you. He's always seen you as a little sister. He can't change the way he feels about you,' Ayub said. He was tempted to tell her that Luqman was in love with someone but that was not a mess he was going to make. Not now. Not tonight.

Maira shrugged. 'We'll see,' she said.

Thankfully, his mother saved him just then by calling out to him. Maira's expression changed then.

'Go. It's your big night,' she said with a sly grin. 'Go on. Make the best of it.'

'Shut up,' he muttered as he walked towards the staircase. He had to remind himself not to run or look too eager.

TWENTY-FIVE

Where was her phone? Why hadn't she thought of making sure she had it with her? She would have called and spoken to her family. She would have spoken to her sisters. Ayub's behaviour was unsettling her and she knew he was punishing her for ignoring him all these days.

She looked around his room. *Their* room. It was like Aafreen's, except there was a balcony that overlooked the lawn and the driveway below. It was a huge room, and there was a sofa here too. These people sure loved their sofas, Tehzeeb thought.

Aafreen had taken her to the room and told her to sit on the bed. Tehzeeb hadn't complied but had walked inside, a little dazed by the jasmine strands that had been made into an arching canopy above the bed. And despite jasmine being a favourite fragrance, it was quite overpowering.

Rose petals were arranged in small hearts all over the bed and she blushed. It was all getting a little too much for her.

'I told you to sit on the bed,' Aafreen repeated. She was still here? Mortified, Tehzeeb sat at the corner. Shaking her head, Aafreen stepped forward and helped her get more comfortable.

'Okay, look here and smile,' Aafreen said. What? Tehzeeb lifted her head and realised that Aafreen was taking a photo of her.

Whatever for, she thought, shocked. 'I asked you to smile,' Aafreen reminded her as she clicked some more photos on her iPhone. She didn't have time to object as Aafreen explained that this was for Maira.

'What? Is she going to put that on Instagram?' Tehzeeb blurted out. Aafreen shook her head.

'No, no, this is for a bridal look makeup that she's practising,' she explained and left.

Her breathing accelerated when she realised that Ayub was going to come inside any minute now. She had to relax. He wasn't a complete stranger to her. They knew each other. A little. She knew that there was a lot of attraction between them. Maybe even something more. She tried to control her breathing when she heard the door open and then shut. Then there was a click.

Locked together.

She wasn't going to sit here like some doll, she thought, and she got down from the bed and stepped away from the jasmine canopy.

He looked surprised. He hadn't expected her to do that. She lifted her head and straightened her back as she stared back at him. The surprise soon gave way to another expression that was hard to decipher. She swallowed and stood straighter, startled when she realised a bead of sweat was trickling down her back. The AC was switched on in the room and it was pleasantly cold. So why was she sweating suddenly?

He stepped forward. She took another step forward too. Her ghagra rustled and her jewellery clinked. He sidestepped her however, and walked towards the wardrobe that was embedded in one of the walls and opened it. What was he doing, she wondered.

'I asked Ammi. She said your clothes are here,' he said, indicating the neat rows of her clothes that had been arranged inside. She turned to the wardrobe and stepped closer but he moved away from there.

'You can change in the bathroom,' he said curtly.

'Ayub!' she said finally. He didn't look at her as he rounded the bed and sat on the other side. She shut the wardrobe door firmly and walked towards him.

'Ayub,' she repeated. He looked up at her and sighed.

'What is it, Tehzeeb? I'm tired,' he said, lying down on the bed, his forearm covering his eyes.

Stung, she stepped back. She hadn't expected this behaviour from him.

Her lips parted. This was the same man who hadn't been able to keep his hands off her during their engagement. The same man who had kissed her senseless in his car. And now that they were together, he was punishing her.

Biting her lower lip, she looked away. She was missing her family and she had hoped that Ayub would offer some comfort but he was being aloof and cold. She walked back to the wardrobe, opened it and pulled out the first thing that she saw. It was a sheer black nightie, one that had been a gift from an aunt who lived abroad.

She and her sisters had been shocked when they had opened it at home. It was nearly transparent and thin with near-invisible straps and it was the most risqué thing that they had ever seen. She didn't know how it had made its way here but she was too upset to think about anything as she took it in her hand. She realised she had to remove her jewellery first and only then she could change out of the ghagra.

She approached the bed warily and sat down on her side. Then, she removed everything – bangles, necklaces, earrings, rings. She left her nose stud because she never removed that. She was aware of Ayub sleeping so close, and glanced at him once. His forearm was still in place.

She kept all the jewellery on the bedside table and then got up slowly to go to the bathroom.

'Switch off the light when you're done please,' he said. So this was how it was going to be, she thought, her heart suddenly aching. She missed his playful banter, the flirting they had indulged in during that one week before the engagement and she missed his intense focus. Well, it is what it is, she thought as she unpinned the dupatta and walked inside the bathroom.

The bathroom was huge and spacious and with its light blue tiles and mirrors. It was simply lovely, she thought. She methodically removed the ghagra and heaved a sigh of relief when the heavy thing was finally off her. The blouse went next. Clad only in the nude bra and underwear, she shivered a little. She looked a little ridiculous now with the makeup on her face.

It took another ten minutes to wash it all off. Then she untied her hair and combed it out with her fingers. It felt good to leave it open, so she let it be. Then she wore the black nightie and gasped when she saw how transparent it was. It merely reached her knees. Swallowing again, she picked up the ghagra and blouse and stepped outside. Feeling extremely self-conscious, she dropped the clothes on the sofa, thinking of folding them in the morning. Then she looked for the lights and found the panel of switches on the wall near the door. She hit the switch and the room became dark.

She wanted to cry. This was not how she had expected her first night with Ayub to be. But keeping her back straight, she walked up to her side of the bed and dusted off the stupid rose petals from the pillow and the bedspread and lay down.

Above, the canopy of jasmine flowers mocked her. The strings spread from the centre in a symmetrical arrangement, and every breath she took reminded her of how it had felt to be in Ayub's arms.

Was she really going to lie here quietly because Ayub said he was tired? She was tired too. She still wanted him. She wanted to talk too, to explain why she had stayed away. She turned to him and tentatively touched his shoulder. No response. She edged closer to him and now that her eyes had adjusted to the darkness, she could see his chest rising up and down rather rapidly.

She knew then that he wasn't asleep. Feeling bolder, she edged closer until she was lying flush next to him.

'What are you doing?' he asked finally, in a strangled voice, as he lowered his arm and turned to her.

Smiling, she rose and before she could talk herself out of it, before reason could stop her, she straddled him quickly.

'You're my husband. What do you think I'm doing?' she asked him softly. He was wide awake now and he stared back at her. In the dark, she knew he was looking at her but she couldn't ascertain his expression.

He rested his hands on her thighs and she gasped as he pushed the flimsy material of the nightie higher.

Instinctively, she lowered her head to kiss him. He kissed

her back, his hands roaming over her bare back and one hand tugging the strap of the nightie down her shoulder. Excitement raced inside her.

He broke away from the kiss and before she could formulate a thought, he had rolled them over until he was above her. She pressed her head back into the pillow, a little shocked at how quickly everything was happening.

He looked down at her and then, to her dismay, he got up and walked away. She sat up, her hair dishevelled and her nightie half undone. He switched on a light and it bathed the room in soft colours. He walked back to her and she saw him pull off his shirt as he neared the bed. She could see his eyes glitter as he bent close.

'You don't make it easy to stay mad at you,' he said finally as he pushed her back on the bed.

'Why were you mad at me?' she asked him, her voice husky. She was busy appreciating her husband's body.

'You don't know why?' he asked, lying down beside her. She turned her face to see him.

'Because I wouldn't talk to you,' she replied. He stared back at her intensely. Words seemed to be too much effort now. She flinched a little when his palm grazed her thigh, bunching up the flimsy nightie, pulling it higher.

'Why?' he asked, letting go of the nightie and trailing a finger down her face. The finger travelled down her neck and reached the curve of her breast.

She inhaled sharply as the finger drew circles around her nipple over the nightie.

'Do we have to discuss it now?' she asked hoarsely as he lowered his mouth to her breast. She arched, hissing as pleasure bloomed from inside her, a slow rush that spread through her limbs.

He lifted his mouth and the air made her nipple pucker almost painfully. She swallowed, the pleasure of having him touch her overruling everything else.

He looked at her, breathing heavily, his eyes not moving from her face. She sat up and threw her arms around him, pressing herself close to him.

'No, we don't have to discuss it. Not this minute,' he said finally. She looked at him and without blinking, pushed off the straps of her nightie from both shoulders. She wiggled until her arms came free and removed her bra as well. She felt reckless, dangerous, powerful as she saw the different expressions flit across his face. Desire and lust was a strong combination, she realised.

'Then stop talking,' she whispered and lifted her arms. He went into her embrace and sighed as he pulled her closer.

TWENTY-SIX

'I knew I wouldn't be able to resist you. That was why I didn't answer your calls or … text you either,' Tehzeeb spoke softly in the darkness, an hour later. She was resting her head on his chest, listening to the reassuring beat of his heart. She toyed with the hair on his chest and turned her face upwards to look at him.

He was stroking her back gently, looking up at the canopy of jasmine above them. He looked back down at her, and in the faint light, she could see him smile. She traced the curve of his smile with her fingertips lightly but he still didn't say anything.

'Ayub?' she spoke softly.

'Hmm?'

'Would you have really gone to sleep if …' she trailed away.

'If you hadn't seduced me, you mean?' he asked.

'Whatever,' she mumbled into his chest and she felt his chest rumble as he laughed softly. 'Answer me. Would you have gone to sleep?'

'No. I wasn't planning on sleeping tonight. But I wanted to make you suffer a little,' he admitted.

'But why? That's mean,' she said.

'And so were you. Left me without a word about why you weren't going to even text me,' he said. He straightened up a little to sit and she had to follow suit. She faced him shyly, not sure where the bedspread was. Or her nightie.

He beckoned her closer with one finger and that move was arrogant, yet it turned her on insanely. She stayed where she was, lifting her head defiantly.

'One text to explain things would have helped,' he continued.

'You wouldn't have left it at that. You'd have convinced me to meet you and then ...'

'And then?' he asked, raising one eyebrow. She looked at him, sitting there almost majestically with his back to the black upholstered headboard, his arms crossed over his chest, staring at her intently. She shrugged.

'I don't know. I didn't want to take the chance. Now that it's over, can we please move on from it?' she asked him.

To her surprise, he leaned forward, picked up her wrist and tugged her forward until she was sprawled over him.

'Not so soon,' he said, shaking his head. He pulled her up and she was sitting astride him. But this time, they were both naked. She blushed furiously and lowered her gaze. She could feel the evidence of his desire pushing against her bottom. Her skin heated, her lips parted and she knew she wanted him again.

She had expected the first time to be awkward and fumbling but surprisingly, it wasn't. He had taken over completely, touching her, kissing her, licking her, making her shiver until she felt like she was shattering. It had hurt the slightest bit when he entered her, but looking into his eyes as he was poised above her, the physical hurt had disappeared and was replaced with something more intense.

Now, the look in his eyes was wicked as his arms wrapped around her waist, pushing her breasts up. He nuzzled them and took one into his mouth. She gasped but held his head close and shut her eyes. A strange sort of bittersweet longing awakened inside her and she realised she didn't want him to stop.

'We are so not done yet,' he said, as he lifted his mouth from her breasts and pulled her head down to kiss her.

It was just like before, but even better. She had always scoffed at sex scenes when they appeared in books, rolling her eyes at the descriptions, but Ayub made it real. Oh, he made it very real. And smooth too. The first time he had reached out for the condom, she had been surprised that it was within reach and he didn't have to leave her to go looking for it. She realised then that his intention had never been to sleep, but her thoughts were all scattered by then.

Now, their coupling was a little more frantic – they both knew what the pleasure was like and how it had ripped apart their nerve endings and they wanted to experience it again. He flipped her over and she was on her back once more. He bent her knees and pushed inside, groaning when he felt her wetness around him. She hissed with pleasure and moaned when he started moving.

He bent closer and they kissed and she threw her arms around his neck as the sensations flooded her. It was so intense and acute and heat spiralled low in her belly as he pumped into her. She was feeling everything, all at the same time and it was getting too much.

She felt like something was just within reach, that same burst of pleasure that had fired her nerve endings, but it was being elusive and she didn't know how to reach for it. Ayub bent low once more and nuzzled her neck as his hand travelled between their legs where they were joined. He did something there, she didn't know what, but suddenly she was melting and coming together once more. She shuddered in his arms, the feeling of pleasure so intense that she couldn't keep her eyes open.

She felt the soft petals of flowers kiss her body and she opened her eyes to see the jasmine strands fall on them both. She would never be able to inhale the scent of jasmine and not think about Ayub, the way he looked, how his face strained as he pushed inside her deeper.

He collapsed over her then and they both lay still, breathing heavily. She played with his hair, even as she got her breathing under control. He lifted his head to look at her and smiled. She smiled back.

'I didn't know this was my punishment,' she said. He smirked and then pulling himself out, he took care of the condom and came back to the bed. She felt limp and replete and strangely, even more desirable.

She opened her arms and he came and settled into the circle of her arms, willingly.

'This wasn't punishment, by the way,' he said. 'This was amazing.'

Tehzeeb smiled. 'I know,' she replied. She drifted off to sleep, holding him, feeling the slightest bit sore. He threw a leg over hers, pulling her closer. She had never thought she could possibly sleep like this, tangled with someone else. But sleep hit her hard and fast, ensconced as she was in his delicious warmth.

When she heard the knock later, she could barely open her eyes. Ayub mumbled something, pulling her close to his body and tightening his arm around her. The knock came again and it was louder. Her eyes flew open. She struggled to get away from Ayub but his face was buried in her neck and he kept an iron hold on her.

'Ayub. Someone's at the door,' she whispered. The dark curtains at the windows hadn't let any sunshine in but she could see a slice of light from outside the balcony door. It was morning already. Her eyes felt gritty and she rubbed them slightly.

'Ayub?'

Shit. It was Aafreen. Why was she at their door? Had something happened?

'Ayub,' she said, nudging him, pushing at his shoulders. In response, he just pulled her even closer and to her frantic horror, she realised he was hard. Even in sleep, he started kissing her neck.

'Mmm, you're so soft and sexy,' he murmured as he rolled on top of her, eyes still half-closed.

'Shut up!' she whispered, trying to push him off her but he was too strong. She pinched his thigh.

'Ouch,' he said loudly, opening his eyes wide. He looked down at her and frowned, rubbing at his thigh.

'Your *mother* is at the door,' Tehzeeb whispered furiously. 'Go see what she wants.'

'Fine,' he grumbled and rolled off her.

'Shit. Wear your clothes!' she said, looking around for his shirt. She found it under the bed, dusted it and handed it to him. He gave her a cheeky grin as he slipped on his clothes.

'You're going to stay there in bed like that? Naked?' he asked.

Shaking her head frantically, she grabbed her nightie and ran to the bathroom just as he opened the door.

TWENTY-SEVEN

Ayub rubbed his eyes and then opened the door the slightest bit. He was annoyed at being woken so early. He wanted to stay in bed and make love to his wife once more. But … never mind … he would continue after his mother left.

'What is it, Ammi?' he asked, frowning.

'Guests are coming for breakfast and Tehzeeb needs to be ready. Let me in. I need to show her which dress to wear,' his mother said, pushing insistently against the door.

'Ammi, wait. She's, um, in the bathroom. Just tell me which dress she has to wear and I'll tell her,' he said, horrified at the thought of his mother coming inside his room. Certainly not after last night.

She looked at him, exasperated. 'As though you will know which is which. Let me in,' she said.

'Ammi, no. Wait. Tehzeeb will come out and talk to you,' he said, and pushed the door shut on his mother's incredulous face and locked it.

He looked around at the bed. Shit. The jasmine canopy had fallen over them and they hadn't even noticed. The bed covers were tangled beyond recognition. He tried straightening up as much as he could, and despite the horrifying thought of his mother outside, he couldn't stop grinning.

He turned around when Tehzeeb opened the bathroom door and peered outside. 'Is she gone?' she asked, wide eyed.

He shook his head, still grinning, holding on to her bra that he had found somewhere on the bed. 'On the contrary, she's waiting to come inside. She wants to talk to you about what to wear,' he explained, jiggling her bra in his fingers.

Her mouth dropped open. 'What? I … no … I …' she stammered. Her face had turned pink. She was holding on to the edge of the bathroom door tightly, the henna designs on her hands, a deep crimson. She shook her head.

'No, no. Please don't let her inside. I need to … I need to shower and I need to change and …' she looked lost.

'Hey, relax,' he said softly. 'I'm not letting her inside until you're ready.' He jumped when his mother knocked on the door once more, and Tehzeeb rolled her eyes. Didn't his mother have any boundaries?

'This will take just a minute, Ayub,' Ammi said from outside.

'Or you could stay inside and I'll let her in and she could keep out the clothes that you're supposed to wear. Hmm?' he asked and before she could say anything, he was walking towards the door, still holding her bra in his hand.

'Ayub!' she squeaked. 'Stop! Look at the mess … at the mess we've made!'

He realised he appreciated the nightie in the day far more than he had in the night. Last night, he'd been too frustrated and aroused to notice much except how soft she had been when she'd rolled over to his side.

She walked up to him and snatched away her bra from his hand unaware of the direction his thoughts were taking. Outside, his mother was getting impatient.

'Ammi, wait!' he called out, while Tehzeeb tidied up the room as much as possible. The jasmine had started to become a little stale now and she bunched most of it and placed them in a heap in one corner.

'You don't have to do that,' he said.

She turned around, surprised. Uncertainly, she walked over to the wardrobe where her clothes were kept and opened it quickly. She pulled out a couple of things hastily was walking past him to go to the bathroom when he caught her elbow and whirled her around in the centre of the room.

'Ayub! Let me go!' she whispered loudly.

He pulled her flush against him and kissed her. She kissed him back almost perfunctorily and he laughed.

'This won't do,' he said.

Groaning and hitting her forehead lightly with the tips of her fingers, she shook her head. 'Later, you idiot,' she said and ran into the bathroom.

'Whatever is taking so long, Ayub?' Ammi asked from outside. Was she seriously asking her newly-married son that question?

He looked around the room once and well, at least the incriminating evidence was out of sight. Sighing, he opened the door.

His mother walked inside, shaking her head. 'I don't have time for this. I just needed a moment to discuss Tehzeeb's wardrobe for today,' she said. On cue, the shower started in the bathroom.

'Just put something out for her to wear. She'll be fine with whatever you decide,' Ayub said. But an uneasy part of him remembered that Tehzeeb wouldn't take too kindly to others deciding anything for her.

Ammi looked around the room, taking in the mess, and sighed. 'You were always such a jungli,' she said, shaking her head and he blushed. She walked up to the wardrobe where Tehzeeb's clothes were kept. Since she had been the one to arrange them, she obviously knew where to look. She saw the jewellery kept on the bedside table and frowned.

'Please tell her to take better care of the jewellery,' she said as she opened the wardrobe and then stood back and perused. Finally, she pulled out something and kept it on the bed. She looked at the jewellery and selected a couple of things from there and kept those on the bed too.

'Tell her to wear these with this outfit,' she said and walked away. Turning around, she spoke again, 'Raheema Auntie and her daughter-in-law are coming along with Shireen Auntie and Nadia. They're all going to be here for breakfast by 11 a.m. Please tell Tehzeeb to be ready by then. Maira can help with the makeup,' she said.

Ayub nodded, wishing it could have been just the family for Tehzeeb's first breakfast in the house. And hadn't Ammi been trying to get him interested in this Nadia? Why had she invited her for breakfast then?

'Why are they coming?' he asked.

Ammi frowned as though it was obvious. 'We have to plan our next party. And I have to show Tehzeeb off to my friends *before* the valima tomorrow,' she said.

She left and the shower in the bathroom stopped. Some moments later, Tehzeeb opened the door slightly.

'She's gone?' she asked. A towel was tied on her head Turkish style and she clutched another towel to her front.

'Come and see for yourself!' he said, waving his arm about expansively.

She stepped out, looking around. He was never going

to leave this room if she looked like this, he thought as he walked up to her. She was glowing, rosy and extremely fuckable. At his approach, she backed up a little.

'W-what did she want?' she asked, apparently trying to pretend that he wasn't ogling her.

'Maybe you should start by asking what I want,' he said, bending down and licking a droplet of water from her round, creamy shoulder.

'Ayub,' she whispered. 'Stop it. I have to get ready. What did your mother want?'

He explained that some people were coming for breakfast, and she frowned. 'I have to dress up and wear jewellery again?' she asked.

He smoothed the frown on her forehead with his index finger. 'Yup,' he said, not really thinking of the breakfast ahead of them. He was wondering what it would take to convince her for a quickie. She tried to sidestep him but he trapped her against the wall.

'Your mother is waiting,' she reminded him, but he could see the flush rising up her neck. He wedged his knee between her legs and the knot on her towel slipped open. She gasped.

'You are unbelievably beautiful,' he said, kissing her. She kissed him back but then pushed him away slightly.

'Can we do this later? Please?' she asked.

Regretfully, he brought the panels of her towel back together, hiding those luscious breasts from view.

'Fine. But I'm holding you to it,' he said, handing the edges of the towel to her and pressing a quick kiss to her nose.

'I'm hoping you will,' she said as she walked past him to the bed where her mother had placed the outfit. Grinning, he went on to the bathroom to shower and when he emerged ten minutes later, towel wrapped around his hips, she was wearing an ivory ghagra and sitting at the dressing table, her hair flowing behind her, the back of her blouse open.

She looked at him in the mirror and he realised she was eyeing him rather appreciatively. He felt like preening, glad he had been going to the gym for the past five years and happy his wife liked what she saw.

She licked her lips. 'I need help with these buttons,' she said. Nodding, he walked up to her and buttoned up the blouse, hiding her lush skin when he wanted to do nothing but the opposite. The ivory material ended at her nape and he kissed her there lightly. She turned a delectable pink and cleared her throat.

'Isn't this too grand to wear at home for breakfast?' she asked. She picked up the gold necklace his mother had kept out for her and handed it to him. He helped her wear it and she stood up, turning around to face him.

'Do I look all right?' she asked.

He picked up her hand and kissed the centre of her mehendi-covered palm, all the while looking into her eyes. 'Stunning,' he said, and she blushed, pushing his chest lightly with her other hand.

Then he remembered what Ammi had said about Maira helping with makeup.

'Makeup? I need to wear makeup in your house?' she asked.

'It's your house too,' he said. She walked away from there and sat down on the sofa.

'What are you doing?' he asked.

She shrugged. 'I don't know. I can't just go downstairs myself. I thought your mother had some protocol for everything,' she said.

He didn't reply as he walked over to his wardrobe and pulled out something to wear. She raised an eyebrow when she saw that he was holding a shirt and jeans.

'You get to wear this and I have to wear ...' she said pointing at her clothes.

He didn't say anything but merely grinned.

TWENTY-EIGHT

'I almost didn't recognise you,' Ana said, sitting next to Tehzeeb the following night at the Valima, the reception that Ayub's parents were hosting for friends and relatives and everyone else. It was not at a wedding hall but at a hotel, just like their engagement. Tehzeeb was sitting on a small raised stage, dressed in a dark green ghagra, richly embellished with gold zari work.

She turned to her sister and hugged her. 'Where were you guys? What took you so long?' she whispered.

'You know how slowly everyone gets ready and Abbu wanted everyone to come home and leave like he did at the engagement,' Ana explained. Tehzeeb looked at her sister's face, and smiled tremulously.

'I missed you,' she said. 'Where's Athiya?'

'There she is, coming towards us. What's up? You all right?' Ana asked.

Tehzeeb nodded. 'Where's my phone? I've been looking for it for the past two days. I wanted to talk to you guys but ...'

'But got too busy with your husband. I can see that,' Ana said teasingly. To her horror, tears filled up in Tehzeeb's eyes.

'Hey! What happened? You okay?' she asked. Tehzeeb picked up her clutch purse and pulled out a monogrammed handkerchief and carefully dabbed at her eyes. Ana stared at her sister, and at the handkerchief in her hands.

'Maira will kill me if I cry now. She's spent two hours doing my makeup,' Tehzeeb explained.

'What? No wonder you look like this. Why didn't you say no?' Ana asked.

Tehzeeb took a deep breath. 'Their house ... the people, they're very different from us. They're all so put together, even at home,' she said, sniffling the slightest bit.

Ana listened in silence and just then Athiya joined them. 'Whoa,' she said, inspecting her sister's face.

'Have you been crying?' she asked, frowning.

'No, I just got a little emotional thinking about ...' Tehzeeb trailed off. She didn't think she could explain anything to her sisters at the moment. This wasn't the time.

'What's wrong?' Athiya asked.

'Nothing is wrong. Everything is good,' Tehzeeb said, but she knew she wasn't convincing her sisters.

'When are you coming home?' Athiya asked. 'Then we can bitch about your horrid in-laws in peace.'

'Athiya!' Ana reprimanded her, frowning.

Tehzeeb grinned. 'Hey, they're not horrid, okay? They're ... just very different.' She was bursting to tell her sisters everything about them.

Athiya lifted an eyebrow. 'Different is the polite word for ugly, mean, horrid, stinky-ass ...' and at this, Tehzeeb burst out laughing.

'Hey, I'm fine. Really,' she said, holding both their hands in each of hers. 'Really.'

'I'm sure a lot of that has to do with your very dishy husband,' Athiya said.

'Shush!' Ana said, leaning across Tehzeeb and smacking Athiya's hand. 'You can't talk about your brother-in-law that way.'

Athiya made a face.

'You guys, I actually missed your bickering,' Tehzeeb said, squeezing their hands tightly. 'But first, where's my phone?'

'I have it with me,' Athiya said, pulling it out from her purse.

'Oh, thank goodness,' Tehzeeb said, taking it from her. 'I felt so handicapped without it.'

'I thought you wouldn't need it and that your rich in-laws would have bought you the latest iPhone already,' Athiya said.

Tehzeeb rolled her eyes but she knew what Athiya was saying was right. She had observed the people in Ayub's house since yesterday morning and didn't quite know what to make of them.

Maira had sat down and done her makeup extensively, talking all the while to her about how she loved doing makeup videos for Instagram and how she was always on the lookout for the best products on her trips abroad. Then, those relatives had shown up and all four women sat down with her in the living room and talked amongst themselves, while she listened to them quietly.

The four women who had arrived for breakfast had each brought over a dish that they placed on the dining table. They then discussed how they had ensured their maids had cooked it properly.

'I mean, she doesn't know what fajitas are and I had to explain to her ten times not to put garam masala in it, but she works hard, you know,' one of the women whose name was Shireen said. The other women tittered. Tehzeeb smiled slightly, thinking they were expecting at least that much from her but apart from looking at her cursorily when they entered, the women had ignored her.

She took in their appearance – they were dressed elegantly, each one of them. Tehzeeb thought of her own aunts. First of all, no one would leave their house and come to someone else's for breakfast. They had too much work to do in their own houses. And all these women looked like they had spent at least an hour getting ready. There was a clash of so many different perfumes here.

The living room looked different in the light of the day. Aafreen had pushed open the heavy curtains and Tehzeeb could see everything much more clearly now. It was packed with knickknacks and elegant showpieces but it was all a little too much. The room wasn't breathing easily and neither was she.

The two older ladies then started discussing something with Aafreen, planning a party for the following week, and the younger women sat down closer to her. Tehzeeb expected them to talk to her but apart from smiling at her, they spoke amongst themselves.

Tehzeeb didn't have to strain too much to overhear them. Someone they knew had made it to third page of *Bangalore Times* and they were annoyed about that.

Thankfully, she didn't have to endure this vapid nonsense for too long because Maira came flouncing inside the living room and greeted everyone but made a beeline for her and sat down, holding her hand.

Tehzeeb smiled at her. Maira was um … to put it mildly … an airhead. But she was sweet. She turned to the other girls and included them in the conversation, making sure that Tehzeeb was also a part of it. Later, when they rose for breakfast, she had whispered to her that the girl in the white outfit with the multihued dupatta was Nadia and her mother had been trying to get her married to Ayub. Not helpful, Maira, Tehzeeb wanted to tell her. Not helpful.

Nadia was gorgeous – her hair cut in waves with blonde streaks running through, eyes done up perfectly and her lipstick made her lips look lush and inviting. She was almost glad Maira had done her makeup that morning or she would have looked washed out in comparison despite wearing the ivory ghagra with the minute thread and zari work on it.

Maira was dressed grandly too, in a light pink anarkali suit. This, on a Monday morning for a breakfast at home. Aafreen was wearing silk palazzo pants with a silvery grey tunic that was stylish and classy and like nothing she had seen women in her family wear. Her hair was open and she was wearing an exquisite silver necklace that was shaped like petals falling off a flower. She noticed that it was studded with sparkling stones and belatedly realised that it was probably a platinum piece with diamonds.

'We need to do something about your hair,' Maira said, lifting a strand and inspecting it. Tehzeeb hadn't known what to do with it and had left it open, thinking that her dupatta would anyway cover her head.

'Do what?' she asked, surprised. She had always loved the rich, natural brown colour of her hair.

'Get you some highlights, Bhabhi,' she said. 'Okay, come on, girls. I need a selfie for my Insta!'

The three of them clustered close to her and posed for the camera, tilting their faces to get their good sides.

'Bhabhi, smile,' Maira said, and Tehzeeb smiled automatically. Maira posted the photo and they returned to discussing something in low tones. Tehzeeb missed her sisters and their camaraderie and she had understood that her life was not going to be the same any longer.

She looked at them now, sitting beside her and smiled. My sweet little fools, she thought fondly.

'Enough of that dreamy smile,' Athiya said. 'You're looking like a lovesick fool.'

'Idiots. I was thinking of how much I miss the two of you,' Tehzeeb said.

'I don't. I like having more space on the bed to sleep,' Athiya said, sticking out her tongue.

Ana rolled her eyes. 'Yeah, that's why she's been crying into the pillow the past two nights,' she said. Athiya looked horrified.

'You saw?' she asked in a whisper. Ana gave her a look.

'Nothing escapes my eyes,' Ana said loftily.

'Why were you crying?' Tehzeeb asked Athiya.

'Too much kachra in my eyes,' Athiya explained.

'Because she's missing you. Why else?' Ana said.

They fell silent because someone came up on stage to see Tehzeeb and handed her a gift-wrapped box. She took it silently and smiled at the woman. She didn't know many of these people. The woman lifted her chin, inspected her face with a faint smile and then nodded approvingly.

'God. How do you bear it?' Ana asked, bristling as the woman left the stage.

'Bear what?' Tehzeeb asked, surprised.

'All these people groping your face, looking at you all the time. Don't you feel like ... snapping at them? Or running away?' she asked.

Before Tehzeeb could reply, Athiya bumped her shoulder. 'Speaking of running away, where's the honeymoon?

'I don't know,' Tehzeeb replied softly. She hadn't seen Ayub after breakfast yesterday. She didn't know where he was and she couldn't just ask for him outright. He had come home for lunch and only then had she realised that he had been out.

When was *she* going to go out? She felt suffocated, sitting in the living room, dressed up like a doll. Thankfully, the ladies had left before lunch and Tehzeeb wanted to change out of the ghagra into something comfortable. But Aafreen informed her that more people were coming later in the evening and if she wanted to change, she would come upstairs and help her pick out another ghagra.

She wanted to groan but she kept quiet. She caught Ayub's eye but he didn't bat an eyelid. He had loudly proclaimed that he was sleepy and wanted to take an afternoon nap. Tehzeeb looked down at her plate, hoping he wouldn't make it obvious that he wanted her to join him. It would be so embarrassing.

But oh, what she would do for a nap, she thought wistfully as she watched him leave. He turned to look at her and indicated with his head that she should follow him. She had looked at Aafreen who seemed to be oblivious and was talking to her about the plans they were making for a party next week with the ladies who had visited them in the morning, and she knew she couldn't just get up and go from the table right then.

Ana cleared her throat then, bringing her out of her reverie which was a good thing because Ayub was being led to the stage where he would be joining her. She didn't need to think of how the previous night had been with him. She blushed when she remembered how he had picked her up in his arms the moment she entered the bedroom and kissed her senseless. And then proceeded to show her how he completely owned her body.

He looked different today—no more sherwanis—he was wearing a charcoal black suit paired with a light blue shirt and a dark blue tie. She had watched him get dressed earlier in the evening and he'd caught her looking at him in the mirror. Her belly dropped every time he gazed at her in that particular way and she knew what was on his mind. But he merely shook his head and smiled as he fixed his cufflinks.

Her sisters got up and vacated the seat next to her and he joined her filling up the space, not letting her breathe. She nudged him with her elbow. He turned the slightest bit towards her and raised an eyebrow.

'I can't breathe,' she whispered. He frowned.

'What happened? You're not well?' he asked, concerned. He didn't seem to care for the people looking at them as he picked up her hand and touched her wrist. She shook her head and pulled her hand back.

'You're taking up all the oxygen,' she said.

'What … I …' he looked confused.

'Maybe bring down the sexy a little bit,' she added. He stared at her and threw back his head and laughed. To her mortification, he lifted her hand and kissed it in front of all their relatives.

Several throats were cleared but Tehzeeb continued to look down demurely.

TWENTY-NINE

A week after their wedding, they had gone to Mauritius for their honeymoon. Maira had packed some really strong sunscreen for her, saying that it would be disastrous if she came back with her clear, pale skin ruined. Aafreen had merely nodded. Tehzeeb had been excited at the prospect of spending proper alone time with Ayub without having to see him off in the morning or wait for him to come home in the evening.

She must have applied the sunscreen just once or twice when they used the private swimming pool that came with the villa where the two of them were staying. In the evenings, they walked down to the beach to watch the sunset, hand in hand, feet sinking into the soft, warm sand. The rest of the time, she and Ayub stayed holed up in the room, watching TV, talking, getting to know each other and making love.

Ayub couldn't keep his hands off her and she felt the same way. When they tired themselves out, they lay back, replete, hands still touching the other, maintaining some form of contact as they talked. At one such time, Tehzeeb told Ayub that she would like to get a job.

He smiled and nodded. 'I was wondering when you would bring it up,' he said, sitting up straight. She was lying in the opposite direction, her head resting on her elbow, her body lightly covered with a sheet and she frowned even though the sight of his bare chest was distracting her.

'What do you mean?' she asked.

'Abba had told me that you were working for an NGO when he set me up on that fake interview with you,' he said with a teasing smile, his toe rubbing circles on her leg. She retracted her leg and shot him a look.

'Yes, the time I asked if you were gay,' she reminded him archly. His eyes darkened and he raised an eyebrow.

'I'm going to pretend you didn't just say that,' he said crossly.

She sat up, pulling the sheet with her and covered her mouth as she giggled, shaking her head. 'The look on your face when I said that. I'll never forget it.'

He went still and then before she could realise it, he was on her, pulling her down while he straddled her.

'How about the look on my face now?' he asked, pushing aside the sheet roughly, his hands kneading her breasts, playing with her nipples. She gasped and arched as he bent his head to suckle them one by one.

'So, Ayub, about the job?' she asked him breathlessly and he looked up at her for a second, surprised she was still talking about it but he went with the flow immediately.

'Would you like to be my assistant?' he asked, bending his head close to hers, until their lips were almost touching.

Her tongue shot out and licked his upper lip. His eyes widened. She sensed him getting hard but she continued with the questions. It was seriously hot pretending to talk while … while … his hands had just reached between her thighs.

Gasping, she shook her head. 'No, I don't think I'd be

very good at that job,' she said as his fingers teased her.

Ayub continued to stare at her even as he reached behind him blindly for the rapidly diminishing pack of condoms that had been there on the bedside table since the time they had come here.

'Why not?' he asked, watching her face closely as his fingers continued to do their magic. She knew her face had turned pink and she arched her neck. He bent down and licked the spot below her ear.

'I'm not good at listening to instructions,' she gasped as he pushed into her and started moving.

Without breaking his tempo, he reached out for both her hands and pulled them above her head, so her breasts jutted out.

'What sort of job do you want then?' he asked.

'I like helping people,' she said, her voice faint.

'I'll see what I can do. Some of Ammi's friends run charities,' he said, without breaking stride.

'Can we not talk about your mother now?' she breathed out, as he nuzzled her breasts and continued riding her.

'Sure. What do you want to talk about? You want to join a CSR team somewhere?' he asked, playing with her nipple and she twisted under him.

'What's CSR?' she asked, shuddering as she came.

'Corporate Social Responsibility,' he gasped, as he collapsed on top of her.

They were both breathing heavily, sweating profusely but she touched his face and he looked at her, shaking his head.

'I'm never going to be able to talk about CSR without thinking of what we just did,' he said softly, playing with a strand of her hair.

She smiled. 'Neither am I. But … seriously, I want to get a job,' she said.

He watched her face and bent down to give a quick kiss on her lips before pulling out. 'Fine. Let's take a look at your resumé then.'

'Okay. But I think we'll have to update it,' she said, stretching her arms lazily and watching him through lowered eyes.

'With what?' he asked, lying back next to her.

'Expert at CSR,' she said with a straight face.

'Oh yeah? Expert, is it?' he pulled her close to him.

They fell asleep that way, tangled in each other and Tehzeeb felt her heart open up to him. What had started as attraction and lust had turned quickly into something stronger, something she was no longer hesitant to define as love.

She just couldn't bring herself to tell him yet. And maybe she was waiting for him to feel the same way too.

THIRTY

One month later

Tehzeeb was still getting used to life in Ayub's house. She couldn't think of it as her home yet. It was too big, too opulent and too much of everything. She also had trouble getting used to the concept of servants, people who cooked and cleaned and did everything that she and her sisters did at home whenever they tried to make their humble Jasmine Villa presentable.

She missed her family and her work. She was waiting for Ayub to begin the job discussion at home with his parents and he had promised her he would do it soon. Sometimes she wished she hadn't quit her job, because now her days seemed endlessly filled with nothing to do but looking pretty and waiting for Ayub and she wasn't on board with that. She wanted to be useful in a way that made her feel accomplished too. She often looked at Aafreen who seemed so put together at any time of the day and she wondered if her mother-in-law expected that sort of tedious perfection from her as well.

Tehzeeb couldn't get a read on her mother-in-law yet. She was elusive, quiet and elegant when she was with her.

She became animated only in the presence of Ayub, Maira or Abba. But Abba was a different matter altogether. She had connected with him instantly, finding it easy to talk to him and call him Abba just like Ayub did. He always seemed happy whenever he saw her. He would pat her head and smile widely and she would miss her father just the slightest bit less in his presence.

In the one month since they had been married, Tehzeeb had gone to three ladies-only parties with her mother-in-law and Maira. Two of the parties had been hosted by other ladies, friends of Aafreen, with houses just as perfect and spotless. One had been in a restaurant. Tehzeeb sat back and watched these interactions, amused, because she didn't know how to participate in these conversations.

They never discussed anything other than the latest salon treatments, the newest clothes that had arrived at someone's boutique (of course some of these people had boutiques), whether anyone was planning to go for the Dubai Shopping Festival this year and if they did, the best places to go shopping there.

Maira had her own set of friends at these events, some of the younger women who were either daughters or daughters-in-law of the older women. To her credit, Maira did try to include Tehzeeb in the conversation but there wasn't anything to say so she often just nodded along, pretending to be interested.

At one of these lunches, Maira started an Instagram live and turned the camera to each of her friends who waved and made some sort of outrageous pouty face. When it came to her, Tehzeeb just smiled and wished she'd move on from there. Maira, on the other hand, was giving a commentary about where they were, what they'd just eaten and what they were going to do after this.

When she ended the Instagram live, she sat down next to Tehzeeb and took the compliments that came her way graciously. Her friends thought she was doing a great job.

'I've been telling you for ages to come to my boutique. You should do one of these things there,' one of the young women said. She was wearing a red flowy silk top paired with a cream churidar. Her face was a fraction less white than a geisha's and she wore dark red lipstick. Maira looked pleased and nodded.

However, she said, 'I have to see how my schedule is. I'm quite busy with different collabs these days you know.' Tehzeeb stared at her but kept her face impassive.

Maira was the same age as Athiya and she had never seen *her* sister get up at 11 in the morning every single day. And what collabs? But she figured that Maira was trying to play hard to get. Good for her, Tehzeeb thought.

She glanced at her mother-in-law who had heard the conversation too and was smiling at her daughter proudly. The next such event was to be at their house and it was a potluck lunch. All the ladies started discussing what each one would bring and Aafreen looked over at Maira.

'Set up the Whatsapp group, dear,' she told her daughter. Maira nodded importantly.

'Bhabhi, you should invite your sisters too,' she said suddenly. The talk at the table died down and Tehzeeb felt every eye turn to them.

After a prolonged pause, Aafreen smiled at Tehzeeb but it didn't reach her eyes. 'Wonderful idea, Maira. Yes, please do invite them, dear,' she said.

Tehzeeb smiled and shook her head. 'It's all right. They can't come. This is on a Thursday and they both have college then.'

'How come your sisters are still studying?' a woman seated near her mother-in-law asked. Tehzeeb remembered her from the day after her wedding as the woman who had come home for breakfast. Raheema Auntie.

'Ana is doing her master's in psychology. This is her final year. And my younger sister just started her master's this year in economics,' she explained.

Nadia shuddered. 'Psychology and economics?' she repeated. 'Just thinking about those subjects is making me sweat.'

'What about you? Do you also hold a master's degree?' the woman in the red flowy outfit, the one with the boutique, asked her curiously.

Tehzeeb nodded. 'I did mine in accountancy,' she said, feeling the stares upon her. Aafreen cleared her throat, in an attempt to bring back the topic to what she felt was more important.

'Let's try and make healthy food this time. I don't want any oily samosas and spring rolls, okay?' she said.

The others nodded solemnly.

'Also, do you ladies think we should try a vegan theme this time?' Aafreen suggested. There were loud protests from every side. 'Okay, okay, no to the vegan theme,' Aafreen amended quickly, shaking her head. They did love their kababs and their custard after all.

Tehzeeb was itching to tell her sisters about all of this. So far, she hadn't told them about these events because she knew it would just highlight how different her life had become. Maybe once they hosted one such event in the house, she'd have more fodder for them.

The prospect of relating all this to her sisters, thinking of their reactions and how she would relate it to them suddenly made her feel better than she had in a long time.

THIRTY-ONE

Ayub grinned when he opened the email from Tehzeeb. She had sent him her resumé with the subject line 'CSR' and he drew in a breath, remembering how they had made it code for sex. Earth-shattering sex, actually. He looked at her photo on his desk and he sobered a little. It was a photo from the Valima, where she was dressed in that dark forest green ghagra and she was looking straight at the camera with such self-assurance while he was gazing at her. Like a lovesick fool. He had snuck away this photo for himself, hoping no one would notice because he wanted to look at her all day even when he was at work.

But what irked him was that she seemed to be in complete control of her emotions when it came to him. He wanted her to be as helpless as he was, to feel like she couldn't wait another moment to see him. Because that's how he felt all the time. He dragged himself to work every morning, wishing he could stay snuggled against her warm body for a little while longer.

His cynical mind had bent over backwards when he had seen her in the café for the first time four months ago, and he knew that he had fallen in love with her instantly. It had taken him some time to accept that fact though. Every time he looked at her, his heartbeat became a little faster. When she smiled at him, he knew he would do anything she asked. When she walked towards him, his gaze could never waver from hers. He had thought this was infatuation and lust at first. But he knew better now.

He thought of this morning, when she had sleepily woken him up so he wouldn't be late for work. She fell asleep again as he readied himself but when he went down for breakfast, she came down too and sat opposite him, her hair wet from a shower, her skin sparkling with stray droplets of water. She looked surreal to him.

When he looked at her surprised, she shook her head. 'I just wanted to have breakfast with you,' she explained as Haleema Auntie served them. She even got up and helped Haleema Auntie in making some of the parathas, much to the older lady's mortification. It made him happy to see Tehzeeb up early so she could spend time with him.

They spoke quietly over the food as Haleema Auntie finished making their tea and shuffled off to the backyard where she always had some work to do. Ayub realised how rare it was that they could spend time with each other outside the bedroom without anyone breathing down on them. Maybe Tehzeeb too had the same idea. Anyhow, he enjoyed her company, loved making her laugh, especially when she threw her head back and laughed guilelessly. He couldn't help but be fascinated.

Clearing his mind from these thoughts, he went back to her email and opened the resumé and perused it. She had listed her achievements in college and the work she had done in the NGO as experience and he mulled over what he could do for her. He realised then that he had to inform the family about her decision too.

He knew that for some reason Ammi hadn't taken a liking to Tehzeeb right away. Well, the obvious reason was her background, that she didn't come from money and her family didn't share the same social circles as his but he liked to believe his mother wasn't that shallow. But then what else could it be? That she had no hand in choosing her? That Abba had been the one to set the wheels in motion and Ayub had happily complied? Why was she taking it out on Tehzeeb?

On the outside, there was no animosity from her. But Ayub knew that the excessive politeness was also not the mark of his mother's genuine warmth. Take Maira, on the other hand. His foolish, guileless, selfie-obsessed sister seemed to really love Tehzeeb like a sister and he hadn't honestly expected that from her. But she and Tehzeeb got along well and he realised that maybe Maira had missed having a sister of her own, someone to share common female experiences.

Thinking of Maira made him think of Luqman. He shook his head. That way lay disaster. Luqman had made it clear to him that he could never think of Maira as anything but a little sister and her constant attempts to get his attention were only embarrassing him and his family.

Luqman's father had a real estate company where his two older brothers worked. He wondered if he could get a job for Tehzeeb there. But would that be a good idea? He realised that the best thing would be to apply for a job neutrally through some portal and he picked up his phone and texted her.

She replied back saying that was fine too and she had sent him her resumé just as a reminder.

'Of what? CSR?' he typed back with a grin on his face.

'No, to talk to your parents about this,' she replied. He went back to work with a smile on his face.

*

Later that evening, as the four of them sat down for dinner—Maira had gone out somewhere with her friends and would be coming in later—Ayub brought up the topic. Abba smiled and nodded but Ammi frowned just the slightest bit before her brow cleared up again. Keeping her face impassive, she cleared her throat.

'But why does she want to work?' she addressed Ayub even though Tehzeeb was sitting right in front of her. He sensed her stiffen beside him and he reached out below the table, held her hand and gave it a slight squeeze. She took a deep breath.

'Because I want to, Auntie,' she said. Ayub kept his face expressionless. He wondered why Tehzeeb didn't call her Ammi like he did but had readily adopted 'Abba' for his father.

Ammi still didn't look at her but instead focused on what was on her plate. Abba cleared his throat.

'That's great, Tehzeeb. Do you have any idea of what sort of work you want to do?' he asked her. Tehzeeb smiled at him gratefully and launched into an explanation of why she wanted to work and especially somewhere where she could make an actual difference.

Ammi remained quiet as Tehzeeb spoke animatedly with Abba. Ayub kept looking at her, wishing she would look up so he could communicate to her, tell her how this meant a lot to Tehzeeb and he just wanted her to be happy.

'And what about when you have children?' Ammi said suddenly.

Tehzeeb's face flushed red and she opened her mouth to say something but shut it. Abba looked embarrassed for her.

'We got married just a month ago, Ammi,' Ayub said, laughing uneasily, trying to reduce the tension in the room.

Ammi shot him a look.

'For now, I'd like to work and make myself useful, Auntie,' Tehzeeb said, meeting his mother's gaze.

The tip of Ammi's nose had turned red, a sure indicator that she was about to lose her temper. Ammi rarely got angry, but when she did, it was spectacularly scary. Ayub didn't want Tehzeeb to be subject to it for no reason at all.

'Are you done? I thought we could go see your family for a bit,' he said to Tehzeeb. She turned to him, almost incredulous.

'Now?' she asked. He shrugged.

'Why not? I never get to come with you,' he said.

A look passed over her face, something that he couldn't decipher. Abba cleared his throat.

'Great idea, Ayub. It's not too late yet. Give my salaams to your father,' he said, pushing his chair back and getting up from the table.

Ammi continued to sit there rigidly as they all got up. Why was she being so bullheaded about this, he wondered. He hadn't thought that there would be any problem whatsoever. But as they left, he overheard her telling Abba, 'Does she mean to imply that we are not useful in some way?'

Thankfully, Tehzeeb had gone ahead of him and didn't hear anything as Abba tried to mollify Ammi and convince her that Tehzeeb meant no disrespect.

THIRTY-TWO

Tehzeeb sat in her old room with her sisters and they kept talking over each other. But every few seconds, she would tune out and try to overhear the discussion between Abba and Ayub.

Ayub had visited her home just once before, a few days after their wedding. At least then the house had been a little spruced up for the wedding and she hadn't minded that it was so small. But now her house had reverted to its earlier shabbiness and she was embarrassed to take him there. She had texted her sisters to tell them that they were coming and she hoped they had the sense to clear out some of the clutter at least.

He didn't say anything as they parked the car outside her house. She looked over at the faded sign on the wall near the pink gate that read 'Jasmine Villa' and she felt an overwhelming sort of love for her house despite everything. Ayub's house was an actual villa but she had never felt at home there, at least not yet.

If her house was a person, she would have hugged it, she thought as she pushed open the creaky gate and walked inside.

'This whole garden smells like you,' Ayub said softly,

reaching out and holding her hand. She squeezed his fingers lightly and smiled. The porch light was weak and it flickered, throwing shadows over them. Abbu would have heard the gate open and would open the door any moment now.

'My mother brought this jasmine plant from Vellore when she got married and moved to live here with Abbu,' she explained, showing the malligai poo plant that had remained here all these years. Ayub walked over to it and sniffed and closed his eyes.

'I remember this fragrance from the moment I first met you,' he said, turning to her and tugging her close.

'Ayub,' she whispered, shaking her head. Just then, the door had opened, and Abbu stood there, a surprised smile on his face. Both embraced like they were old friends and they all walked inside. Ayub sat down in the living room which was thankfully a little cleaner than it normally was. Ana and Athiya emerged from their rooms, happy to see her and they hugged.

They lingered in the living room for a while until Tehzeeb realised that it was very crowded with all of them there. So she dragged her sisters to their room, her old room, where she plonked down on the bed and they started talking.

'How come you two came now?' Ana asked. 'I mean it's a lovely surprise but ...'

Tehzeeb shrugged and then went on to explain the situation at dinner. 'I think he wanted his parents to discuss my job without us around so he suggested this. What I don't understand is why his mother would have a problem,' she said.

Athiya looked at her impatiently. 'Rich people problems,'

she said, dismissing it. 'Tell us other stuff. How's married life?'

Tehzeeb related to them about the many lunches she had gone to with Maira and Aafreen and how they bored her. She lowered her voice because she didn't want it to carry outside.

'It's all they do. Meet for lunch, size up each other's outfits and jewellery, talk about their latest shopping secrets and then make plans for the next lunch. There's one being planned for next week and it's going to be in Ayub's house,' Tehzeeb said.

Ana and Athiya were listening to her with a great deal of interest. 'And what do you do at these lunches?' Ana asked.

'Wear one of the silk suits dear, and pleeeeeease wear some makeup. Mascara and lipstick at least. Barefaced won't do. And none of the chunky gold jewellery. I'd prefer it if you wore something restrained, like that pearl necklace I got for you last week,' Tehzeeb said, imitating Aafreen's breathy voice, her accent and her expressions. Her sisters stared at her, mouths open in shock and then all three burst out laughing.

Ana was wiping the tears from her eyes and she shook her head as she shushed them. 'Ayub Bhai will hear us!' she said, hiccupping as she laughed.

'Let him!' Athiya said, making a face. Tehzeeb shook her head.

'No, no. I don't want him to hear this,' she said. But she lowered her voice and then imitated Maira, picking up her phone and taking a selfie, pouting. She took on Maira's slightly nasal tone as she talked about 'collabs' and how important it was to be a social media influencer.

Athiya and Ana couldn't stop laughing. 'Do more!' Athiya said.

'Later. When I have more fodder for you guys,' Tehzeeb said, grinning. She felt a little bad about poking fun at Maira who had always been nice to her. But she was frustrated over Aafreen's behaviour at the dining table tonight and her strange reluctance to address Tehzeeb directly.

The three of them drifted to talking about a number of different things until Abbu called out to Ana to make tea.

'Shit, I forgot completely,' she said. But turning to Athiya, she pleaded, 'You make, no? Please.'

Making a face, Athiya got up from there and went to the kitchen. 'One for me also,' Tehzeeb called out. Ana turned to Tehzeeb then and spoke softly.

'So? Are you happy? With him?' she asked.

Tehzeeb smiled and nodded. 'Yes, I am. We get along so well together, Ana. I feel so happy when I'm with him. It's just so surprising when you think that last year, I didn't even know he existed. And now … now I can't imagine spending even a day without him,' she said.

'Wow. You've been married for just a month now,' Ana said, shaking her head.

Tehzeeb shrugged. 'I can't deny what I feel. It's very real,' she said.

'Do you love him?' Ana asked, eyes wide.

'I think I do,' Tehzeeb said softly, lowering her eyes. 'It's stupid. But I've never felt this way before and I've always been slightly cynical about love but …'

'Are you sure it's love and not just sex?' Ana asked bluntly.

'Ana!' Tehzeeb admonished her. Ana shrugged.

'It could be true. Love needs to grow and that takes time. You don't get smacked in your face with it in just a month of marriage,' Ana said.

'And you would know this how?' Tehzeeb asked her, annoyed.

'Common sense,' Ana said, shaking her head.

Tehzeeb didn't reply but Athiya had made tea and she called out to them to come outside and have it. She and Ana got up from the room and walked outside, where Ayub was deep in discussion with Abbu. She wondered what they were talking about but he looked at her and gave her one of his heart-stopping smiles and her steps faltered.

'Come, sit,' Abbu said to her and she sat down beside him on the sofa. Abbu put an arm around her shoulders and drew her closer. She shut her eyes and felt at home. When she opened her eyes, she saw that Ayub was looking at her with an unreadable expression on his face. She raised her eyebrows in a questioning manner but he shook his head the slightest bit.

She straightened up when Athiya handed them the teacups and she took a sip of her sister's famed ginger tea. Ayub took a sip as well and his eyes widened in appreciation.

'I married the wrong sister,' he whispered.

Athiya gasped and sat down next to Tehzeeb. '*Such* a charmer! No wonder you like him so much,' she said and nudged Tehzeeb. Ayub looked at her then, and raised an eyebrow just as she had done a while back.

Abbu laughed and Tehzeeb looked at him. Her father looked truly happy.

THIRTY-THREE

Ayub didn't return home right away. Since they had come back from the honeymoon, the only time they spent alone together was in the bedroom. It was nice to be outside for a change, looking at his beautiful wife sitting in the car with him.

Sometimes he would wake up from sleep, unaccustomed to having another person share his bed, and he would turn and look at her, sleeping on her stomach, her hair sprawled behind her. He would thank his lucky stars his father had taken this gamble and brought them together. But every time he thought of his father, something would clutch at his heart too. He knew Tehzeeb wouldn't take it kindly if she ever found out about his father's machinations. Neither would Yusuf uncle.

As they drove away from there, he glanced at her once or twice as she looked solemn.

'What's the matter?' he asked her. She turned to him and shook her head. Her earrings clinked and she smiled slightly.

'Nothing. It just feels weird that I'm not there with them and I'm a visitor now,' she said.

'Did you want to stay a while longer?' he asked as they stopped at a signal.

'No. It's okay. I'd have to leave eventually. I would like to come and spend a couple of days here though, with them,' she said softly, looking down.

'Yeah, so why haven't you?' he asked. She looked at him sideways.

'Because I didn't want to leave you,' she said.

Her words hit him directly, and happiness bloomed in his chest.

'And now you want to go because?' he asked, unable to stop himself.

'I miss them. I miss the chaos and the ...' she stopped herself, took a deep breath and then continued. 'My house is nothing like yours. It's crumbling down around us and it's small and we have forever been lamenting about something or the other that's not working. Abbu tries his best but after Ammi died, he just kind of gave up, you know. But with all its faults, it's where I grew up. It's home for me.'

He listened to her in silence. The signal changed and they were moving once more. He had no clear idea of where they were going but he turned to look at her once. She looked at him too.

'My home is you,' he said quietly.

When he looked at her again, her eyes were shining and she reached out to hold his hand. 'Athiya was right. You *are* a charmer,' she said.

He didn't know why he had said those words. But now that he had, he expected her to say something, anything, to show that she felt the same too. But she didn't. It irked him but he smiled.

'I know that. But I didn't say it to be charming,' he replied, letting go of her hand to shift gears.

There was silence in the car and he glanced at her. She was looking straight ahead.

'I said it because I meant it,' he spoke in the tense silence in the car. 'I'm in love with you.'

She stiffened and then looked at him. She spoke after a pause. 'I ... I've never been in love before so I don't know if what I feel is love. And I don't want to say it just because you said it. But I have never felt this way about anyone else in my life.'

Ayub hid his disappointment. She would say it eventually, he knew, and for now he would have to be satisfied with that.

'Tell me more about the NGO you worked at. What were your duties there and what you enjoyed doing. And we'll figure out a job situation for you soon enough,' he said. She looked at him, surprised at the change in subject but she accepted the lead.

She told him about how she managed the accounts at the NGO, taking care of the contributions and she also did a bit of admin work. But what she loved was talking to the women, assuring them, offering them hope.

'I'm quite sure I don't want to work in a corporate set up,' she said. Ayub nodded. He thought of his mother suddenly, wondering how she would take this. He knew things weren't smooth between Tehzeeb and her and he wondered why. Surely his mother wasn't still holding out a grudge against Tehzeeb because Abba had intervened and sent out the proposal?

He thought back to the scene earlier tonight at dinner when Ammi was behaving strangely. Why had Tehzeeb's words made her so angry? He hoped Abba would have smoothed things out so that when they returned, they could pick up like before.

'Ayub, let's go back,' Tehzeeb said.

'Why?'

'We're just driving aimlessly. I'm tired. I want to sleep,' she said, yawning.

'Sleep?' he asked, feigning disbelief.

'Why not?' she asked, turning to look at him, eyes wide in fake innocence.

There were times like these when he just wanted to grab her and kiss her senseless. But he restrained himself and started the journey towards home.

'But I was also hoping we would discuss a little CSR,' she added softly.

'Come here,' he said, pulling the car over to a stop at the side of the road. Cars whizzed past them and she looked at him, surprised.

'What? Why?' she asked, not unbuckling her seatbelt. 'Why did you stop?'

'Let's discuss it now. Right here,' he said. Her eyes widened as he unclasped his seatbelt and moved to undo hers.

'Ayub, no! I ... not here, please,' she said, looking panicked.

'Why not?' he asked, running his hand up her arm. She shivered the slightest bit.

'Because ... because we'll get caught and ...' her face turned red and she shook her head.

'Let me get this straight. We'll get caught because we're discussing CSR?' he asked, looking genuinely confused. She glared at him then, understanding what he was doing.

'You ass,' she muttered under her breath.

'I do have a fine ass, thank you,' he said, still making no move to buckle up and drive.

'I'm *really* going to sleep when we get back home,' she said, sniffling.

'We'll see about that,' he said, leaning over and turning her face to him. He kissed her lightly and was about to turn away when she held the back of his head and deepened the kiss. He held her arms, wondering how it could feel like this was their first kiss. When he set her back, her face was flushed, her lips swollen and her eyes were wide with desire. She sighed.

'What happened to worrying about getting caught?' he asked, tipping her face up.

'It was just a kiss and I'm allowed to kiss my husband in the privacy of his car,' she replied. 'Now hurry up and head home please.'

'So you can sleep?' he asked, vaguely pleased by her reply.

She shook her head. 'So you can finish what you started,' she replied tartly.

He didn't need to be told twice.

THIRTY-FOUR

Things were awkward at home after that dinner. Aafreen continued to maintain her polite distance, deepening it even, and hardly spoke to her. Tehzeeb felt isolated and if it weren't for the many maids who worked at home, or Haleema Auntie with whom she could always chat about something, or Maira, she would have been very unhappy.

Plans were underway for the party that was going to be held at home. What was the point of this party, she wondered as she saw the maids clean up the living room and start working in the kitchen on the day of the party. Aafreen supervised them and Tehzeeb wished there was something she could do to help but she knew she wasn't required in any capacity.

At the same time, she didn't want to retire to her room, so she lingered in the living room, perusing magazines and books, waiting for Maira to join her. She thought back to the job applications she had sent out and the responses she had received. She was overqualified for most of the jobs, just as she had been for the NGO. But she didn't mind.

The job was to give her a sense of independence in this house where her wardrobe was still being controlled by her mother-in-law. She had grown tired of wearing the flowy ghagras and anarkali suits and she was waiting to get a job so she could ditch them altogether. She had considered discussing it with Ayub but he seemed oblivious to this tussle between his mother and her and she didn't want to add to the tension at home.

She did wonder why she wasn't being defiant enough to just wear what she wanted. Why did she have to listen to Aafreen at all? The very idea that Aafreen thought she could dictate what clothes she could wear made her very angry, but to maintain a form of peace in the house, she had gone along. But she knew it was a temporary sort of peace. She was going to pull out all the stops once she landed a job.

'Bhabhi!' Maira said, coming inside. She was wearing jeans and a pink top with dangling bell sleeves. 'Guess what?'

'What?' Tehzeeb asked her with a smile. She could always count on Maira to cheer her up.

'My evening glam makeup tutorial video got 800 views on Instagram!' she said, jumping up and down as she sat on the sofa next to her.

'That's great!' Tehzeeb said, genuinely happy for her.

'But you know what will help?' Maira asked, reaching out and holding her hand.

'What?'

'I'm sure I'll get way more likes and views if I post a video of me doing makeup for you!' she said, smiling brightly.

'Err … but …' Tehzeeb didn't know what to say.

'Please, Bhabhi! You're so beautiful and you have such clear skin and I am positive I'll get more than a thousand likes and even new followers if you do this for me!' she said.

'Okay. Sure,' Tehzeeb replied, smiling at her.

'Do you need to ask Bhai about this?' Maira asked suddenly. Tehzeeb frowned and shook her head.

'No. I don't need to take anyone's permission,' she said. She did wonder what Aafreen would say to this but that only strengthened her conviction. She was going to wrest control back over her body and her clothing and this was the first step.

'Okay, great. So, Ammi has asked me to set up a game after lunch today. And we'll have prize winners and everything and ...'

'Oh, how fun!' Tehzeeb said. 'Do you need my help?'

'Yes, can you help me in wrapping the prizes please?' Maira said.

'Sure,' Tehzeeb said and the two of them got up and went to Maira's room. Maira's room was not like hers or Aafreen's. Tehzeeb had been here a few times before. It was large like the other rooms but the bed had been pushed to one side to create more space in the room. One of the walls was painted a deep textured pink and it had a border of flowers, done in a light cream colour. This was the backdrop that Maira often used for her videos as a frame. Another wall had a collage of frames – photos of Maira from the time she was a cherubic baby to when she was a graceful teenager and then, graduation and of course, photos of her now being celeb-like.

Tehzeeb tried hard not to be judgemental. She tried hard not to think of her cramped bedroom in her house with her sisters sharing every breathing space. How much they had irked her but how at the same time, she had never wanted that equation to change. How foolish she had been to think that it wouldn't change. She snapped out of her melancholy mood and got down to work.

The prizes were on Maira's bed. Tehzeeb picked them up and inspected them. There were three matte cream lipsticks and each of them was just a little short of Rs 2000.

Her mouth dropped open but she quickly pretended like seeing the prices hadn't jolted her.

It was getting really hard now to not think of her sisters and herself, of how they did part-time jobs and how even when they got some extra money, they often used it for the house and never really considered splurging on cosmetics. Sighing, she wished she had invited Ana and Athiya over for the lunch. She was sure they would have won whatever game Maira had planned and they would have at least gotten these fancy prizes, she thought as she reached out for wrapping paper and cello tape.

*

Four hours later, Tehzeeb was really beginning to wish she had invited her sisters. This was worth missing college for. She sat through the game, a quiz, with a straight face.

Everyone had just finished lunch. Each guest had brought over something from their homes, so there was a lot of food that had been kept on the dining table. There was a pasta salad with cherry tomatoes, chicken mince crepes, kebabs, cheese rolls, caramel pudding and a number of other things while Aafreen had instructed Haleema Auntie to make mutton biryani.

The ladies, most of whom were familiar faces now, sat daintily, cross-legged with hands over knees. Some of them made sure their Fitbits were visible. The questions were something children in seventh grade would know answers to, but which had most of the women scratching their heads over.

Maybe they're faking it, Tehzeeb thought when Maira asked for the full form of WHO and no one knew. How could anyone not know that?

She had refused to participate because they were hosting lunch, and for the first time, Aafreen looked at her with some sort of approval. Great. Pretend to be dumb and you score points, Tehzeeb thought to herself a little while later as they tried hard to guess the name of Harry Potter's best friend who is a girl.

It was indeed getting too much for her, she thought, as she watched the expressions flit over their faces. How did she end up here?

She thought of the evenings her father spent reading poetry out to them, especially when he missed their mother acutely. She thought of his cadenced voice, the lilting rhythms and the way he would look upwards sometimes, as though Ammi was watching from above.

She was brought back to the present when someone clapped loudly. Raheema Auntie looked positively thrilled. Her daughter-in-law Ayra had guessed something correctly. Some of the ladies looked bored, inspecting their fingernails, and she realised the quiz had ended.

Her phone pinged with an email. It was from one of the applications she had sent out. They wanted her to attend an interview the very next day. Happy, she looked up and met the unwavering gaze of her mother-in-law who was looking at her speculatively, eyes narrowed. Aafreen then turned to Maira and nodded proudly.

Who cares, Tehzeeb thought, tucking the hurt away somewhere. Aafreen was not her mother and that was why she would never call her Ammi. Talk erupted about whether anyone had seen the latest Sabyasachi designs and who had the address of the girl who sold those designer Pakistani suits.

She was going to get a job!

THIRTY-FIVE

One month later

Tehzeeb and Ayub sat at the breakfast table early one morning, eating quietly. Ayub read the news on his phone and he looked up at Tehzeeb. She had started her job two weeks ago and she seemed to love it. He was really happy for her. She was reading something on her phone too but she seemed to have felt his gaze on her and she looked up and smiled brightly.

Would his heart always jump like that when she directed her smile at him, he wondered. He hoped so. He loved this feeling of being alive. He loved the buzz he got from just being near her, inhaling her special jasmine fragrance. She insisted she used no perfume whatsoever and that just intrigued him even more. Every night, when they snuggled together after making love, he would press a kiss to the back of her neck and go to sleep, her fragrance within reach, reminding him of something elusive, something happy, something sad.

He cleared his throat as she sipped tea. She seemed happier at this time when everyone else was asleep. Normally, he would be sleeping in too but since she got the job, they both woke up early and had breakfast together and he would drop her off at her office, insisting that he didn't mind the extra time it took for him to get to work. He loved leaving for work with her, watching her get into her professional mode and he loved how serious she was about everything.

He noticed that she had changed her attire from the flowing ghagras and suits since they got married. She had switched to cotton suits, simple outfits like the one she had been wearing when they met for the first time. She had gone shopping with Maira one weekend and came back with some classy cotton outfits that excited her. She wore no jewellery except for a single bangle on her left wrist and diamond studs in her ears.

He knew there was some sort of tension between Ammi and her – over the clothes, the lack of jewellery and even the job. At dinner one night last week, Ammi had informed her and Maira that they were going for lunch at Shireen Auntie's home and they had to figure out the potluck dish to take so that she could inform Haleema Auntie to cook it.

Tehzeeb had looked at Ammi and asked if the lunch was being held on a weekend.

'Oh goodness, no. You know these are ladies-only events. And we don't want bratty kids running around or husbands dropping by asking us what we're doing. That's why we hold them during the weekdays,' Ammi had said, as though it was obvious.

Tehzeeb lowered her gaze and then shook her head. 'I'm afraid I can't come, Auntie,' she said softly. Ammi glared at her. 'What do you mean?'

'I have office,' Tehzeeb said, meeting Ammi's gaze. 'I can't take leave just a week after joining.'

Ammi hadn't said anything to her but she had glanced at Maira, who seemed oblivious. Tehzeeb had gotten a job managing the accounts of a small interior designing firm that was run entirely by women. She knew she was overqualified for the job but her bosses had told her that she could take over their unofficial CSR activities entirely because they didn't have the time to invest in it.

'Ready?' Ayub asked, pushing back his chair. Despite the late nights and early hours, now he anticipated the weekends more because that meant they could both stay late in bed. What he loved more was the look of contentment on her face as they drove out together, talking about various things, discussing the day ahead or making plans for the weekend.

'Yes, ready,' she said, pushing her chair back and getting up. He watched as she rinsed out the plates and kept them in their place, despite the many bemused looks Haleema Auntie was giving her, trying to take them from her hand.

'Here. I packed lunch for you,' Haleema Auntie said, handing her a dabba. Tehzeeb took it from her with delight.

'Thank you so much Haleema Auntie! I was getting tired of eating lunch outside every day,' she said, hugging the middle-aged lady impulsively. Ayub watched as Haleema Auntie blushed and patted her shoulder awkwardly.

'What about me?' Ayub asked, feigning indignation.

Haleema Auntie gave him a sharp look. 'You?' she said, sniffing. 'You used to bring back lunchboxes even from school, uneaten. And the stories I have to tell about your uniforms! All those oil stains in your pockets from hiding papads and kababs!'

'Really? You must tell me more someday,' Tehzeeb said, looking at Ayub slyly.

'He would eat only papads and kababs and not touch anything else in his tiffin,' Haleema Auntie informed her in a conspiratorial tone.

'What have I unleashed?' Ayub groaned but he winked at Haleema Auntie who smiled at him as he put an arm around Tehzeeb's shoulders and they walked outside.

She was wearing a white cotton kurta today with jeans and beaten silver earrings. Her arms were bare except for a watch and she looked fresh, young and free.

As they drove out from the house, she kept up a continuous chatter of work-related anecdotes and things that made her laugh and how wonderful it was that this new workplace already felt so right for her.

'It's amazing how much work a bunch of women can get done,' she said as he neared her office. 'I mean, there's no bullshit and honestly, men gossip way more than women during coffee breaks. We're all so supercharged that we're always raring to get back to work.'

At a signal, while they waited, she put her hand on his elbow. He turned to her and raised his eyebrows.

'Thank you,' she said.

'For what?' he asked, surprised.

She shrugged. 'I know the job decision didn't go down well with … your mother. So I just want to thank you for sticking by me,' she said.

'Always,' he said, reaching out and pushing his favourite strand of her hair behind her ear. She leaned into his touch and closed her eyes. The signal cleared and the moment evaporated. She straightened and he drove them to her office.

It was in one of the by-lanes, and the office was in a house, surrounded by other residential homes. He parked the car outside the gate. She unbuckled her belt, turned around in her seat and took the lunchbox that Haleema Auntie had given her along with her handbag and other things. He watched her movements quietly and was surprised when she leaned forward and kissed him before getting down from the car.

'Love you,' he muttered as she opened the gate and walked inside. He wondered when she would say that to him and what was stopping her.

THIRTY-SIX

Malini and Chandni, the two women who ran Niche Space, were almost always there before her because they lived nearby. There were a few other staff members, designers, interns and now, Tehzeeb, and altogether they were around ten employees, all women. It was a very small set up, but Tehzeeb loved it. She loved the family-like feeling here – everyone knew each other and there was a lot of banter and fun.

Her thoughts were still with Ayub as she pushed open the door and walked inside the reception. There was a desk and a phone but no receptionist. They didn't really need one because not many people called the front office anyway. If the phone rang, any one of them answered it and it worked well enough.

She pushed open the door that led to the inside office space and smiled when she smelled coffee. Sneha Akka, the lady who worked for them, making sure everything was clean and tidy and who did small jobs, etc., made some of the best filter coffee she'd ever had. The original kitchen of the house had been retained as a kitchen where Sneha Akka could often be found pottering around.

Tehzeeb waved generally at everyone as she settled down

before her computer. Malini walked over to her, typing something on her phone. She was in her late thirties, tall and almost statuesque-looking. She had a few greys in her shoulder-length hair that she never got around to touching up and she wore a large nose pin, often in different designs to suit her mood. She was married but had no children. Her husband Alok worked in an advertising firm. She sat down at the chair opposite her and they talked a bit about this and that.

'Chandni hasn't come yet?' Tehzeeb asked, settling back in her chair.

'She's on her way. A little late today. There she is,' she said, turning to greet Chandni who had just walked inside, looking a little harried. Chandni had just turned thirty this year and she was the mother of a four-year-old which meant that there were days when suddenly something would go wrong and she would have to take care of the situation before coming to work. Chandni was dusky and petite and almost always tied her hair in a ponytail. She reminded Tehzeeb of Rani Mukherjee on some days.

'Where's everyone else?' Tehzeeb asked, looking around.

'You know how they are. Always late,' Malini said, referring to the intern, Chaya, who had joined them a few months ago as a stopgap job after finishing her studies and figuring out what to do next.

'And Lisa?'

'Lisa has a client meeting today. She's taken the other intern with her. Let's hope she bags the deal,' Malini said, talking about the other designer on their team. Lisa was just a couple of years older than Tehzeeb but she already seemed so much more accomplished than her.

They all settled down to work peaceably and then a while later, Sneha Akka got them all coffee. Tehzeeb took her mug gratefully and took a break from work. She picked up her phone to check for texts and to browse the internet for a bit.

There was a message from Athiya asking her how she was and what the new job was like. There was one from Ayub – he must have sent it after reaching work. It was a simple text asking her if they could go for a movie that evening. Smiling, she said yes to him and then frowned when she saw a message from Maira.

'Bhbhi, need ur hlp,' it read.

'Sure. What do you need?' she typed back.

Maira called her back instead and warily, Tehzeeb answered it. Maira sounded on the verge of tears but also panicky at the same time. She walked outside the office to talk to her in privacy. It took some time to coax her into calming down.

'Can I meet you for lunch today?' she asked Tehzeeb. The beseeching tone in her voice had her worried. What was wrong? Was everything all right at home?

'What's wrong, Maira? Should I call Ayub?' Tehzeeb asked, her stomach sinking almost painfully. She had come to care for the flighty young girl in the past two months that she had been married. She was the one, apart from Ayub, who had made the house bearable for her.

'No! No, don't tell Bhai anything. This is between you and me,' Maira said quickly. Tehzeeb was worried but she agreed.

'Sure. Where do you want to meet for lunch?' she asked Maira, thinking of the lunch box Haleema Auntie had prepared for her so sweetly this morning. She'd have to give it here to someone to eat.

Maira named a restaurant in Indiranagar and Tehzeeb found herself nodding. They made plans to meet by 1.30. As Tehzeeb was about to end the phone call, Maira spoke again.

'Thank you. Thank you so much for this,' she whispered and ended the call.

Anxious and worried, Tehzeeb found she couldn't concentrate on work. When it was 1 p.m., she got up and spoke to Chandni, telling her about needing to go out for lunch. Malini had gone out for a meeting.

'Sure. No problem,' Chandni waved her away and Tehzeeb left the office, booking an auto to the restaurant where she would meet Maira. She only hoped that Maira wouldn't be too late because she didn't want to overstay her lunch hour.

THIRTY-SEVEN

When Maira walked in ten minutes after Tehzeeb reached, she forgot her irritation over the younger girl's lateness. Maira was wearing dark glasses but she had left her hair open, a little untidy, as though she couldn't be bothered to brush it out. She scanned the room and walked up to Tehzeeb when she spotted her.

She sat down opposite her, putting down her handbag beside her and carefully removing the dark glasses. Tehzeeb gasped. Her eyes were rimmed red and she saw that Maira's nose was also quite pink.

'What happened?' she asked, reaching out and holding Maira's hand.

'Bhabhi,' she started and tears started falling down her face rapidly. Tehzeeb abandoned her seat and went up to Maira's booth and sat down next to her to comfort her. Maira turned to her and hugged her, sobbing into her neck.

'Shit, I'm so sorry. I'm making a scene here,' she sniffled. Then, straightening up, she took a deep shuddering breath and tried to calm down visibly. Tehzeeb was getting really worried now.

'What is it?' she asked her, holding on to Maira's hand and squeezing lightly.

Maira nodded and then pulled out her phone from her bag and tapped it open. She opened something and handed the phone to her. Tehzeeb took it from her, wondering what it could be. It was the photo of a young man, a very good-looking man, and he was smiling straight ahead at the camera. There was something familiar about him.

'This is Luqman,' Maira said, softly. 'He ... he's Bhai's best friend.'

'Was he at our engagement?' Tehzeeb asked suddenly. Pieces fell together in place and she blushed when she remembered where she had seen him.

Maira nodded. 'That was the last I saw him. He ... he ...' Her lips quivered.

'What happened to him?' Tehzeeb asked anxiously even though she had a feeling she knew where this conversation was going.

Maira licked her dry lips. 'I've been in love with him since the time I was sixteen, Bhabhi. I ... I've ... I don't know how to explain this to you, but he's ... he's ...' Maira's pale face coloured a little and she swallowed.

'He's the love of my life,' she told Tehzeeb. Wow, Tehzeeb thought.

'And?'

Maira took another deep breath. 'I heard my parents talk about my marriage this morning. And it's obviously not with him or why would I be crying?' she asked. Her eyes filled with tears once more.

'Oh!'

'Ammi was telling Abba that she has started receiving proposals for me and ... and they should consider one of them seriously,' Maira continued.

Tehzeeb wondered how Maira expected her to help

in this case. She held no influence over her in-laws. But surely Ayub would put in a word for his sister. He loved her to bits.

'I'm sure Ayub can help,' Tehzeeb said softly. Maira shook her head.

'No, I mean your parents will listen if he speaks to them. They know he has your best interests at heart,' she said.

'No, Bhabhi. Bhai won't speak to them,' Maira said flatly.

'But why?' Tehzeeb asked, mystified.

'Bhai doesn't think Luqman is the right person for me,' she said.

'Why not? How does he even know that?' Tehzeeb asked, a little indignantly.

'He thinks Luqman considers me to be his younger sister.'

'Wait. Luqman also … feels the same way about you, right?' Tehzeeb asked, understanding dawning.

Maira took a deep breath. 'He just needs a little convincing. From you,' she said, looking at Tehzeeb suddenly.

'Me?' Tehzeeb asked, shocked.

'Yes! Please. You have to meet him and tell him about this situation at home. Tell him that my parents are getting me married. That will knock some sense into his head,' she said.

Tehzeeb was dumbfounded. She sat back and looked at Maira, thinking of how she could possibly get embroiled in this.

'Why me? How can *I* convince him that he loves you?' she asked Maira.

'He might listen if you tell him how upset I am over this! If my parents get me married somewhere else, it will ruin my life. I won't be able to ... I can't imagine ...' Maira said, bursting into tears once more.

Tehzeeb patted her shoulder awkwardly. 'But ... why would he listen to me? He doesn't even know me,' she said.

Maira shook her head. 'Bhai refuses to see my point of view. He thinks I'm a kid. But ... you're my sister now and you're like my best friend too. I think he will listen to you if you tell him how much he means to me,' she said.

Tehzeeb pondered over this in silence. This was very sticky territory. She could get into a lot of trouble with various people, especially her in-laws. But she wanted to help Maira.

'Won't it be strange if I ask to meet him? He's your brother's friend. And what's to stop him from telling Ayub everything?' she asked.

Maira looked at her thoughtfully.

'What if I can arrange a meeting accidentally?' she asked.

'What?'

'Yeah,' Maira nodded. Her eyes were still red-rimmed and she sniffled a little but she seemed more focussed now.

'Maira, whatever you're planning, please remember it would be highly inappropriate for me to meet your brother's friend alone,' Tehzeeb said.

'What if ... what if you took someone along with you?' Maira suggested.

'Who? Haleema Auntie?' Tehzeeb joked. She was already getting a bad feeling about this.

Maira shook her head. 'No. I meant, take one of your sisters with you. Then it would be fine, right?' she asked. She looked extremely thoughtful.

She seemed to have thought of everything, Tehzeeb

thought frantically. It seemed like she had been played somehow, manipulated into doing this. But she was very fond of Maira and she wanted her to be happy. What worried her was how she could possibly convince Luqman about this.

Marry her because she loves you and you'll eventually fall in love with her?

THIRTY-EIGHT

Ana was still not used to seeing this polished veneer on her sister. Tehzeeb claimed that she hadn't changed but she had. From the slim silver watch on her wrist, the quiet diamond studs in her ears, to the soft cotton outfit she was wearing, her sister's style had been streamlined, downsized and made more acceptable for her in-laws and this annoyed her the slightest bit even though it was to be expected.

'I still don't understand what we're doing here,' she said to Tehzeeb as she sat beside her in the coffee shop, fidgeting a little.

Tehzeeb was looking at something on her phone and she frowned. Even that frown didn't mar her beauty, Ana thought, pushing away her resentment and focusing on how nice it was to spend time with her for a change.

'I already explained it to you, no?' Tehzeeb said softly, looking up and around. They were sitting outside one of the coffee shops in a business park, where there were several offices and employees walking past them, busy talking, discussing and making plans.

'No, it didn't make much sense to me,' Ana said, crossing her arms.

Tehzeeb narrowed her eyes and then sat straighter.

'Okay, here he comes,' she whispered. She looked nervous and rightly so. This plan was outrageous and Ana was sure Tehzeeb was going to get into a lot of trouble with her in-laws. Even her husband.

Tehzeeb turned to Ana and started talking to her animatedly. Ana took the cue and went along with the ruse. Someone walked past them and Tehzeeb turned to look at the person and she called out, apparently surprised.

'Luqman?'

The man stopped and turned around, a frown on his face that shifted when he saw them. He was tall, attractive and fit. He had nice hair and … oh, geez, Ana realised who it was. The man who had accompanied her when she had been searching for Tehzeeb after her engagement.

He walked back to them, looking dumbfounded.

'Tehzeeb?' he said. 'Ayub's wife? What are you doing here?'

'My sister, Ana, had an interview here in one of the offices. I came with her to offer moral support,' Tehzeeb improvised smoothly. That's when he turned to look at her and did a double-take.

'You!' he said, and then seemed to steady himself.

'Hi,' Ana said, flashing a bright smile at him. He looked disconcerted and smiled back uneasily.

'Are you very busy?' Tehzeeb asked him and he shook his head.

'Just headed out for some coffee,' he explained.

'Then join us?' Tehzeeb offered. He looked uncomfortable. Ana marvelled at how well her sister seemed to be play-acting this entire thing as if it was scripted.

'Ana is just concerned about the work culture here and how convenient it would be for her, generally speaking and …' Tehzeeb trailed off and he nodded.

'Sure,' he said, looking around for a place to sit. He snagged a chair from one of the other tables and sat down, adjacent to both of them.

Ana tried hard not to stare at him. She hadn't paid him much attention the last time she'd seen him but now she was suddenly aware of him, how his knee almost brushed hers.

'What do you want to know?' he asked, turning to her with a slight smile. In such proximity to him, Ana got tongue-tied and couldn't seem to order her thoughts. Her stomach flipped and settled and then flipped again when he leaned closer. She could see his clean-shaven jaw and it was very unnerving.

She looked at Tehzeeb for help, feeling silly about not being able to hold her own in a conversation. But she hadn't expected this lurch inside on seeing him.

'I ... err ...' she said and she felt her face turn warm. What must he think of her!

'How come you didn't come for our wedding, Luqman?' Tehzeeb asked and he turned to her sister. Ana exhaled in relief.

'I had to go to the US on a project,' he explained.

'But ... you're his best friend,' Tehzeeb said, smiling a little slyly. Ana marvelled at how well her sister was doing this.

'I know. I ...' Luqman looked uncomfortable.

'Never mind. There's another wedding happening soon enough in the house. I'm sure you'll be happy to attend that,' Tehzeeb said with a smile.

He was silent for a few seconds.

'What? Really? Oh my god! Thank GOD!' he said, throwing his head back and shutting his eyes, as though relieved. Tehzeeb looked at him, alarmed. This wasn't the reaction she had been expecting. She straightened up and cleared her throat.

'You're *happy* Maira is getting married?' she asked, softly.

'Yes!' Luqman said emphatically. He turned to her suddenly and grinned so happily that she didn't quite know how to react. He shook his head and rubbed his forehead.

'I swear Tehzeeb, this is the best news you could have given me,' he said.

'Hold on,' Tehzeeb said sharply. She looked anguished. Lowering her voice, she spoke softly. 'But Maira is in love with you.'

Luqman stared at her in shock. He suddenly seemed to understand something and he pushed his chair back, still seated. The chair's legs scraped sharply on the pavement and she winced.

'Is she here somewhere?' he asked quietly. She could sense he was angry and she knew it was valid.

Tehzeeb shook her head but she leaned forward. 'Listen. She's very distraught. Her parents are fixing her marriage. They've started looking at proposals already. But she's been in love with you since she was sixteen …' Luqman was already shaking his head as he stood up.

'Luqman, please listen to me,' Tehzeeb said, spots of colour on her face.

'Did you know about this too?' he turned to her suddenly. Ana didn't quite know how to respond to that. She shrugged.

'This is ridiculous. I have made it clear to her that I don't see her that way. I never have and I never will …'

'But why not?' Tehzeeb asked. Ana frowned.

'What do you mean?' Luqman asked, still standing,

towering over both of them. She acutely sensed the vacuum of his abruptly emptied chair, almost making her wish he would sit back down.

Tehzeeb looked confused. 'I know this isn't my place and I don't want to meddle but she's such a sweet girl and she loves you so much. Why *can't* you consider her as a possibility?' she asked.

Luqman exhaled and then pushing his hands into his hair, he blew out a breath. He sat back down. Suddenly, all that space seemed constricted and Ana realised she couldn't breathe freely again.

'Look. I'm the youngest son of my family. My older brothers are still unwedded. Even if I wanted to marry her, I couldn't. My mother is seeking a bride for my oldest brother. My turn won't come for at least a few years. Maira's parents aren't going to wait that long. And my mother is very conservative. She will definitely not like any of this,' he said.

Tehzeeb looked downcast at this and Ana felt sorry for her sister-in-law. 'I'm sorry, Luqman. I really didn't want to get involved but you know how she is,' she said.

'Exactly. I ...' he looked around, suddenly seeming to realise that Ana was with them and he shook his head ruefully. 'Is she really your sister?'

'What? Of course she is!' Tehzeeb glared at him.

'And the job part?'

Tehzeeb had the grace to look a little abashed. She shook her head.

He exhaled. 'It was nice meeting you guys. And I won't bring it up with Ayub. You don't have to worry about that. BUT. It's a no from me. I was really happy that she was getting married. I actually do want to see her happy you know,' he said.

'So do I,' Tehzeeb said softly. 'I just ...'

'Please, Tehzeeb. This was never going to happen. She's outdone herself this time in getting you to plead her case. Is there even a proposal happening or was that also part of the plan?'

Tehzeeb shook her head. 'I heard them speak about it at home too. They're planning to get her married in a year. What do I tell her, Luqman? She asked me to help her and ...'

'Tell her ... tell her I've fallen in love with someone,' he said, nostrils flared.

'What?'

'Yes, tell her that I'm in love with someone who's willing to wait till my mother gets my brothers married. Ayub told me that the only way she'd stop focusing on me was if I got married or at least got a girlfriend. I should have listened to him,' he said, playing with a paper napkin on the table.

'She's going to be devastated,' Tehzeeb said, curling her fingers into her palms.

'It can't be helped. I have to be cruel to be kind,' he shrugged.

'She'll want proof,' Tehzeeb said.

'Shit. I hadn't thought of that. Why don't you ... why don't you take a photo of me with ... Ana, right?' he said.

'I'm not taking part in this!' Ana said, outraged.

'You already are. Just help a man out, please. We'll blur out your face and I'll just sit next to you and look at you like I'm madly in love with you. If you don't mind,' he said.

Tehzeeb looked at Ana helplessly. 'He's right you know. This is the only way she'll let go of him.'

'Listen, don't tell her my girlfriend is a colleague. Or she might even land up here to find out who that is. Just ...

tell her that you were coming to speak to me here and you found me, like this,' he said, turning around in his chair and shifting it close to Ana's. To her shock, Tehzeeb got up and backed away.

'Where are you going?' she called out, suddenly feeling like she'd been dropped right in the middle of an intense scene from a film.

'I have to take the photos from a distance, no? Or how will it look convincing to her?' Tehzeeb called out. It was only her and Luqman at the table now, and Luqman turned to her. It felt like they were inside a protected bubble and everything that she needed was right here. Her heart constricted and she paled. It felt like her lips had dried completely. Her tongue came out to moisten her lips and she saw him follow the movement with his eyes. Keeping still, she spoke softly. 'Fine. Just do it fast.'

'No, it has to be done properly or she won't believe it,' Luqman said, leaning close to her and picking up her hand. He looked into her eyes and leaned close to her face. Ana felt her face heat up and she heard the photos click in the background as Tehzeeb took pictures.

Luqman lifted his hand and brought some of her hair forward to cover her face partially. 'Better,' he said softly, still gazing at her.

Ana's lips parted. Her heart raced. What the hell was happening? She wanted to put a stop to this. She wanted to lean closer to him and … she wanted to kiss him. Startled at the direction her thoughts were taking, she spoke from the corner of her mouth.

'Are you done, Api?' she asked.

'Yes. I think she should be satisfied with this,' Tehzeeb said, coming back to the table. Luqman shifted the chair back and took the phone from Tehzeeb to see the photos and Ana could breathe again. She was mortified at what had just happened. At where her mind had taken her. She hoped none of it was visible on her face. She hoped she never saw him again. Well, that was a lie. But she was going to believe it for now.

THIRTY-NINE

Maira's room was dark. Tehzeeb was lying down on her bed with her, holding her as she cried, her shoulders shaking with sobs. Tehzeeb hated being the one to do this to her and she thought that Luqman had gone overboard in taking the photos. He really looked as though he was in love with the girl sitting with him. Thank god no one could see that it was Ana.

'Shh,' she soothed Maira who had begun sobbing even harder.

'Bhabhi, my heart feels like it's breaking,' she said, her voice shaky. 'Why did this happen to me?'

Tehzeeb rubbed Maira's arm briskly. 'Listen, it's for the best you know. I'm glad I saw him with this girl there. I'm glad I didn't have to talk to him, to tell him about you. Now you can just pretend that none of this happened and move on.'

'How do I move on?' Maira asked, hiccupping. 'Five years, Bhabhi! Right through college, I didn't even look at any other boy because … because I loved Luqman. What will I do now?'

Tehzeeb sighed. 'You have to let him go, Maira. If you really love him, you want him to be happy, right? That's one of the rules of love,' she said, wincing, wishing she didn't sound so idiotic.

Maira sobbed in silence. She turned around and squeezed Tehzeeb's hand.

'Thank you so much for everything Bhabhi,' she said. 'I don't know what I'd have done without you.' She was hiccuping now and Tehzeeb felt a sharp stab of guilt for deceiving her.

'Listen, this is all for the best you know. Some things are just not meant to happen,' she said.

Maira wiped her tears and sat up. Tehzeeb sat up as well on the bed. She put her arms around Maira and hugged her.

'I know it hurts right now. I can't even imagine how you must be feeling,' Tehzeeb said.

Maira took a deep breath. She took Tehzeeb's phone and looked at the photo once more. 'I hope this girl never finds any happiness in her life. I hope she suffers too. I want her to feel this pain,' she said fervently.

'Maira!' Tehzeeb said, anguished at her words. She was not one to be superstitious but Maira was cursing her sister.

'Sorry Bhabhi, but you don't know how much it hurts to see him looking at her like that. That look in his eyes ... how much I had hoped he would look at me like that one day,' she said, bursting into tears once more.

Tehzeeb consoled her again. 'Listen. Promise me you won't do anything silly over him. Think of this as turning over a new leaf. You have your life ahead of you with someone who deserves you. Not someone who never saw you for what you were,' she said.

Maira nodded. 'You're so right. I read somewhere that the best revenge is to have a good life and I intend to do just that,' she said.

Relieved, Tehzeeb took her phone back, intending to delete the photos as soon as she could. She had taken leave today to do this task for Maira and she'd made Ana also bunk her classes. She hadn't expected Luqman to actually be happy that Maira was getting married. Everything had been downhill from there.

'Listen, I … I'm not too happy hiding this from Ayub,' she said. 'I didn't like doing this behind his back and … especially since he's Luqman's friend …'

Maira looked thoughtful but she shook her head. 'No, Bhabhi. Bhai won't like that I got you involved in this. Please just let it be. I'm sure Bhai must have known about this girl. I wish he'd told me before. I wouldn't have … I wouldn't have sent you,' she said.

Tehzeeb didn't know what to say, but inside, she was deeply uncomfortable at the thought of hiding anything from Ayub. Maira wiped the tear tracks from her face and sniffled.

'Tell me what will make you feel better. I'll do it for you. Should we order chocolate fudge ice cream? Shall we watch something on Netflix? Shall I make fun of someone you hate?'

Maira looked at her, surprised. 'Make fun of her? This girl?'

'Err … I don't know her. I need to talk to people or listen to them speak and then I can mimic them really, really well,' Tehzeeb said with a smile.

'Oh! Like you can mimic movie stars?' Maira asked, straightening up in bed.

Tehzeeb looked thoughtful and broke out into her favourite Hema Malini act, the one that used to make everyone at home laugh. Maira stared at her, open-mouthed.

From there Tehzeeb switched to Katrina Kaif, and then Rani Mukherjee and then a number of others that soon had Maira laughing so much, she had tears in her eyes.

'Oh my god! You are amazing! Why didn't I know about this? You should totally do this at one of the parties!' Maira said.

Tehzeeb shook her head, alarmed. 'No way! You can't make me do this at those parties. Please,' she said, eyes wide.

'But ...'

'This is just between you and me. Please. I do this only for my sisters and you're my sister too,' Tehzeeb said.

Maira looked conflicted but she nodded and she embraced Tehzeeb. 'I'm SO glad Bhai married you,' she said. 'You're the best Bhabhi anyone could have hoped to get.'

Tehzeeb patted her back guiltily.

'Listen,' she said, sitting back, and Maira looked at her.

'Hmm?'

'Will you go along with what your parents ask?' Tehzeeb asked.

Maira looked thoughtful and then she shrugged. 'There's nothing else to do, right? And I've already been unsuccessful in love. I don't think I'll feel this way about anyone else. The only thing to do is to hope I can feel something at least for the person I marry,' she said softly.

'That's very wise of you, Maira. This is really the best thing for you,' Tehzeeb said, stroking her hair gently. She thought of how lucky she had been, to have fallen in love with Ayub so completely. She wished the same happiness for all her sisters, including Maira. But first, she knew that she had to tell Ayub how she felt.

Where earlier she had stopped herself from saying it to

him because she wanted him to say it first, now she knew she was just waiting for the right opportunity to tell it to him. But screw opportunity. She decided that she would tell Ayub how she felt that very night. She was not going to waste any more time or leave him wondering why she couldn't say the words back yet.

'About that chocolate fudge ice cream? And Netflix?' Maira asked, pulling her back to the present.

'Yes! Bring it on!' Tehzeeb said with a smile.

FORTY

Ayub saw her, standing in the balcony of their room, watching the thunderstorm. She flinched every time the thunder roared but she didn't move from there. She hadn't heard him enter the room and he dropped his laptop case on the sofa and walked up to her softly. Luckily, he hadn't gotten drenched in the sudden downpour that had caught everyone in Bangalore unawares. It was certainly an odd time to rain, he thought. Why would it rain in December?

She stood at the railing and he walked up to her. She still hadn't heard him over the sound of the pounding rain. Rain sprayed all over them and he slid his arms around her waist and pulled her back. Startled, she turned to him, her face pink and wet with raindrops.

'What are you doing out here?' he asked, kissing her soft pink lips lightly. She tasted of rain and jasmine and everything that he had wanted in his life but didn't know until he met her. She threw her arms around his neck and pressed her body to his. He ran his hands over her delicious curves and pulled her closer, growing hard instantly.

'You're all wet,' he murmured against her neck. Her light green kurta was completely drenched and wet splotches were growing on his shirt after contact with her body.

To his shock, she brought her hand between their bodies and rested her palm lightly on his erection. 'And you're hard,' she whispered against his lips. 'Perfect combination.'

He reared his head back to look at her, his mouth dry and pulse beating in hunger. 'You are the most ...'

He didn't complete his sentence because she had pressed her lips to his and kissed him, there on the balcony as the rain fell around them, thunder clapped loudly in the distance and streaks of lightning lit up the sky. Their lips clung to each other, tongues tracing outlines, hands roaming over bodies. He loved how she was no longer shy about touching him. He loved how she initiated things between them. He loved her.

She stepped back and looked up at him. She was breathing hard and her wet kurta outlined her breasts perfectly. He tore his gaze from them and looked at her and he was glad he did, because the words she said made his world spin.

'I love you, Ayub,' she said softly. His eyes wide, he picked her up and carried her inside the room.

'Say it again,' he said gruffly, looking at her. The sky lit up once more with a flash of lightning and the thunder that followed it had her tightening her hold on his arm.

'I love you and I have loved you for a long time. Even before you told me how you felt,' she said, pushing his hair back from his forehead. He let her down gently and pulled her to him once more. The rain was now lashing so hard that a spray followed them inside. But his entire being was focused on this beautiful girl who stood before him, baring her feelings for him.

They kissed and he walked her back, shoving her onto the bed.

'Ayub,' she said breathlessly as he worked on removing her clothes.

'Hmm?' he asked, as he kissed the skin that he uncovered. She was wet, cold and on fire for him at the same time.

'Shut the balcony door,' she said, with a lazy smile.

The outside world receded as he closed the balcony door and hurried back to her. He peeled off his own clothes, left the sodden heap on the carpet and joined her on the bed, covering her face with kisses.

Their lovemaking was different that night – slower, tender, unhurried. He took her again and again and she let him. Exhausted, they lay in each other's arms. Just as she was falling asleep, he pulled her against him and she protested.

'I have work tomorrow,' she murmured.

'I have work too,' he said, his hands resting on her breast possessively.

'Um, then you have to stop doing that,' she said, trying to pull his hand away but he only tightened his grip and pinched her nipple. She gasped.

'You're mine,' he said, against her neck.

'Yours,' she agreed.

'Why today? If you felt this way about me for a long time, what prompted you to say it today?' he asked. He sensed her stiffen and she turned around slowly. He couldn't see her face clearly because the room was dark. But she touched his face and kissed the tip of his nose.

'I don't know. I just didn't want to wait for even one more day,' she said.

'Right. So you didn't plan all the thunder and rain and the lightning while you told me?' he asked, keeping a straight face.

She stared back at him. 'I'd actually wished for a hailstorm,' she said.

'Why?' he asked, frowning.

'So that when the hail fell on you, it would knock some sense into your head.'

'Really? I thought I was quite sensible.'

'If you were, you would have known already how much I loved you,' she said, tracing the hair on his chest with her fingers.

'Maybe I knew it, but hearing you say the words …' he trailed off. She smiled and he traced her smile with his finger.

'Walking into that café was the best decision I ever made,' she said, kissing his chest.

He frowned a little, thinking of the secret that lay between them. But even now that he knew she loved him, he couldn't bring himself to tell her the truth. He was sure it would ruin what they had. Maybe when they were old and tottering, he'd tell her about the history between their fathers and how it had led her to him. Maybe then she would just smack him with her walking stick and forget about it.

The thought of them growing old together made him smile. He pulled her close and rested his chin on top of her head. She pressed herself to him and they fell asleep that way, happy and satisfied.

When things would go alarmingly wrong for them in just the next few days, both would think of this perfect moment, this bright shining moment where there was nothing between them except love.

FORTY-ONE

'Can't you take a day off for this party?' Aafreen asked Tehzeeb over dinner a few days later. Tehzeeb looked up at her, surprised. Aafreen barely spoke to her these days so the direct question caught her off guard. Ayub nudged her, and she realised she was expected to answer.

'Err, when is it Auntie?' she asked with a smile.

'It's this Thursday,' she said. Tehzeeb glanced at Maira, who looked down. Maira had made her take leave just last week to talk to Luqman. And there was an office Christmas party on Thursday. It would look really bad if she didn't go for it.

'I ... actually, there's an office party on Thursday,' she said.

'Office party?' Aafreen frowned.

Tehzeeb nodded. 'It's ... we're doing a small celebration at a restaurant nearby. It's a lunch party so I can't miss it,' she said apologetically.

'I'm hosting a party here after a long time,' Aafreen said.

'We hosted here just last month, Ammi,' Maira reminded her. 'Remember I did the quiz and everything?'

Aafreen's face flushed at the reminder. Tehzeeb didn't

need any reminding, especially about the quiz.

'Yes, but this is going to be different. We are having a discussion about Maira's wedding at this party and I would like you to be present,' she said stiffly.

Tehzeeb glanced at Maira who looked at her a little sadly. If Ayub caught the look between them, he didn't say anything, or maybe he was distracted himself. But he did straighten up. He looked at his father who was eating quietly. Abba rarely got into any sort of discussion at the dining table. But when they sat down to watch TV in the living room, he would sometimes discuss the news with her. The three of them—Ayub, she and her father-in-law—discussed current events and Maira and Aafreen would often begin yawning.

'So have you decided on the right proposal for Maira?' he addressed the question to his father. Abba looked up and nodded.

'There are a couple of families who look promising,' he said slowly. Maira pushed her chair back and got up. Tehzeeb felt compelled to follow her into the living room where Maira sat down on the sofa.

'Are you all right?' she asked.

Maira shook her head and nibbled the edge of her fingernail. Tehzeeb resisted the urge to smack her hand away like she would have done if it had been Ana or Athiya.

'It hurts. So bad. But you were right. I have to just move on,' she said quietly.

'Listen, it will be fine,' Tehzeeb said, although she was feeling guilty. 'Um, look at me and your brother. Ours was also an arranged marriage.'

Maira looked at her sceptically. 'But, Bhabhi,' she sighed.

'But what? I … I'm very happy with him and he's happy with me,' Tehzeeb spoke softly. She looked down at her lap and felt herself redden as she spoke further.

'I … It's possible to fall in love after marriage too, you know,' she said, looking up quickly to glance at Maira.

'Oh my god, you are so adorable. You love Bhai! Did you tell him?' Maira asked, momentarily forgetting her own misery. She was beaming.

Tehzeeb nodded, still unable to stop smiling when she remembered the look on Ayub's face when she had told him.

'And what about him?' she asked, eagerly. 'But … spare me the details. I mean, yuck, gross, he's my brother but … I also want to know!'

Tehzeeb rolled her eyes. 'Well, he said it to me a while ago actually,' she said.

'What? And you made him wait all these days?' Maira asked, eyes wide.

Tehzeeb nodded. She shrugged. 'I … I think I fell in love with him much before he told me. I just … told him the night of the thunderstorm,' she said softly. Maira clapped her hands on her mouth, shaking her head in delight.

'Listen, I said all this to you to give you hope. What you felt for Luqman may not even have been love. Sure, he's good-looking and maybe that had you all confused,' Tehzeeb said. Maira looked at her thoughtfully.

'But to really love someone is to look at their faults and accept those as well. You have to look beyond the faults and mistakes. But you haven't even spent any real time with him. How would it have worked out with Luqman?' she asked.

'You know what. You're right. I never realised all that there is to love,' she said.

'That's all right. I didn't think about love at all. It blindsided me completely when I was least expecting it,' Tehzeeb said. Maira leaned forward and squeezed her hand.

'Thanks, Bhabhi,' she said. They sat together in silence, aware of Ayub and her in-laws in the dining room still discussing Maira's marriage.

'Listen, I have a favour to ask,' Tehzeeb said.

'Anything for you,' Maira said fervently.

Tehzeeb smiled. 'Please convince your mother that it's okay if I'm not at home for this lunch?' she said.

'Oh!' Maira looked down. She nodded.

'Okay. I'll tell her not to force you. I understand. Your job is important too.'

'Thank you for understanding, Maira,' she said.

'Of course, only one professional would know the difficulties of another professional,' Maira said matter-of-factly. Tehzeeb merely nodded.

FORTY-TWO

On the day of the party, both at home and in office, Tehzeeb was surprised to come downstairs and see that preparations were in full swing. Aafreen was busy overseeing the cleaning of the living room and dining room when usually she would be asleep when Tehzeeb and Ayub left for work. Normally, Tehzeeb helped Haleema Auntie in the kitchen with setting the table for the two of them but today she sat down at the table with Ayub, looking around expectantly.

Aafreen came in, muttering something to herself. She wasn't dressed yet in her sophisticated clothes but she was wearing a trailing kaftan nightgown that strangely made her look even more elegant. Her hair was up in a knot and she walked around, telling the servants to clean everything.

'We better get going,' Ayub whispered and she nodded.

'Maybe we should have breakfast outside?' she suggested. But before they could get up, Haleema Auntie brought a plate of kheema samosas and kept them on the table.

'Have some and go,' Aafreen said.

Ayub and Tehzeeb looked at each other and then picked up one each. It was crispy, delicious and quite free of oil.

'Ammi, we're leaving,' Ayub said after he finished eating a samosa. Tehzeeb got up too. Aafreen looked at them and sighed.

'Ayub, tell her to stay, no? I've invited some people over today and there are two women who might be interested in Maira,' she said, addressing Ayub and ignoring Tehzeeb once more.

'I ...' Ayub looked caught between them. Tehzeeb felt her anger grow at her mother-in-law's repeated refusal to understand why she had to go to work today.

'Auntie, I'll try and come back early. Before everyone leaves,' she said suddenly, thinking that would be the best compromise. A part of her was adamant but she also didn't want any tension at home.

'But what will I tell everyone when they ask where my daughter-in-law is?' she asked, looking distraught. Here was the root of the problem, Tehzeeb realised.

'You don't want to tell them I'm working?' she asked softly.

Aafreen straightened up. 'No one in my family has ever *worked* anywhere,' she said. She said the word as if merely speaking it gave her a bad taste in the mouth.

'That's ridiculous, Ammi. Times have changed now and Tehzeeb is talented and brilliant. Why shouldn't she put her education to use?' Ayub said. Aafreen turned to him, a pout on her face.

Tehzeeb didn't want to linger there because she was sure she would say something mean or rude so she walked outside after saying a quick bye. Ayub followed her and they drove away in silence. He didn't speak until they were nearly at her office.

'I'm sorry about that. I didn't realise Ammi felt this way,' he said.

'I wish she wouldn't do that thing ... where she ignores me while I'm there and asks you to talk to me,' Tehzeeb said. The resentment and anger had been stewing inside since she left home. She glanced at Ayub and saw him frown.

'She …'

'Doesn't like me,' Tehzeeb completed.

'That's not true,' he refuted quickly. Tehzeeb shook her head.

'No need to sugarcoat it, Ayub. She's never liked me. Right from the beginning,' she said, looking down unhappily. She'd never had this experience before in her life and maybe that was why it was rubbing her the wrong way. People *always* liked her. From school, college, work, relatives – no matter where she went, she won hearts. It was her thing. Even now, she had suggested coming back early so that eventually, Aafreen would like her.

'Listen, you're wrong about Ammi. She's … it's the way she is. Maybe it would help if you had compromised a little too,' he said, looking straight ahead. She felt a flash of anger but tried to slow down her thoughts.

'I *did* suggest a compromise. I told her I'd come back early,' she said.

'You could have taken leave today,' he said flatly. 'Obviously, it means a lot to her.'

The car stopped in front of her office and she got down without saying goodbye. She was seething and she was sure she would say something horrible to him, so she slammed the door shut and walked off without looking back. She knew he was waiting for her because she didn't hear the car drive away and the fact that he was still there, instead of driving off furiously, neutralised her displeasure.

She turned around and walked back to the car. He was looking ahead, gripping the steering wheel tightly. She opened the door and sat back inside.

'I just came back to say goodbye. I'm going to work now and I'll try to get back home early so I can meet your mother's friends,' she said.

His jaw tightened. 'Fine,' he said but still didn't look at her. She got down from the car, once again furious and this time he drove away.

She walked inside the office, feeling cheated and it just worsened her mood. She shouldn't have returned to the car, she thought. She pushed open the door to the office, taking in the Christmas decorations that they had done the previous evening. Slowly, forcibly, she pushed the rage into a corner of her mind and focused on the day ahead.

*

The restaurant was bright and airy, completely the opposite of Tehzeeb's dark mood that hadn't dispelled all morning. She was angry with Aafreen but more so with Ayub for his sudden about-turn in asking her to compromise. She debated calling up Ana or Athiya and although they were both at home since they had Christmas holidays in college, she wasn't sure she would be able to explain.

She looked down at the table they had commandeered since they got here – everyone was talking excitedly and discussing either work or personal matters. Chandni looked at her astutely as she was the only one not talking.

'All okay?' she asked.

Tehzeeb shrugged.

'Had a fight with your husband?' she persisted. Tehzeeb looked up and bit her lower lip anxiously. She nodded.

'It's part of married life. You won't always see eye to eye on everything,' she said softly. Tehzeeb nodded. She knew that but … it still made her feel shitty.

Chaya, their intern, was taking photos for their Facebook page and Tehzeeb smiled half-heartedly. Chaya was in charge of managing their social media and although they rarely got work from there, she knew it was important to have a social media presence.

Sneha Akka looked around awkwardly. She had refused to come for the lunch repeatedly, only relenting when everyone insisted that she join them. She sipped on her lime juice and looked down, feeling conscious of being in a trendy restaurant.

Lisa, the young designer who worked for them, was talking animatedly to Malini, explaining the new project while the other intern, Deepti, listened. Deepti was quiet and didn't really mingle much although she always smiled at everyone.

Chandni, however, was still on her case. 'Tell me what's wrong. I've been married for bloody seven years now and I think I know everything there is to know,' she said. Malini overheard her and glanced at her, shaking her head and she smiled.

'Married for ten years, okay? I know better,' she said, turning to them. Tehzeeb didn't want to discuss her problems with her bosses. But they were looking at her expectantly.

'There's a party. At home. My mother-in-law wanted me to take a day off today and be there,' she explained briefly.

'So you should have done that!' Malini said, surprised. 'This is no big deal. You know that!'

Tehzeeb knew that but she didn't want to miss out on office lunches, which was where people bonded. She was already on the outside at the parties at home. She didn't want that to happen here.

'I preferred this party,' she said.

'Why? What's wrong with those parties?' Chaya asked. Great. Everyone was listening now.

Deepti smiled at her reassuringly. Taking a deep breath, Tehzeeb described the parties she had attended since she got married. The looks of incredulity on their faces made her forget her bad mood momentarily. In fact, she got very involved in it, as she started to mimic her mother-in-law perfectly.

The women at the table were stunned and speechless by her acting and when she paused for breath to take a sip of water, they broke into applause and laughter.

'Oh my god! You are brilliant! How do you do this?' Malini asked, her eyes bright with laughter. Even Sneha Akka seemed to be enjoying it and that got Tehzeeb into her entertainer mode completely.

'It comes naturally to me. No one in my family has ever *worked* anywhere,' Tehzeeb said, adopting Aafreen's haughty mannerisms perfectly. She went on to mimic Maira then.

'My sister-in-law is a social media influencer,' she said. She lifted her phone and pouted, taking a selfie in an exaggerated show of Maira's behaviour. Soon, everyone was laughing so hard, some of them were even clutching their stomachs.

'Isn't it time we ordered lunch?' she asked, wiping tears from her eyes, Chandni called the bemused waiter to their table.

FORTY-THREE

Ayub stared at Tehzeeb's photo on his desk and contemplated calling her. Then he stopped himself. He didn't know why they had fought today and it was messing him up from the time he had got to work. He had meetings as usual and he had to check an onsite project as well as complete a design that he had been working on for the past month. But his mind kept going back to this morning when Tehzeeb had gotten down from the car and stalked off.

It didn't matter that she came back to say goodbye. He was still pissed at her behaviour. He had met her work colleagues one day when they'd insisted he come inside one morning and he was sure they wouldn't have minded if Tehzeeb had taken the day off. That was what irked him. Her refusal to bend even a little for his mother.

Her compromise about coming in early wasn't really a compromise. Maybe Ammi needed her to be with them at the lunch today. If Maira's prospective in-laws would be at the lunch, then having Tehzeeb there would have looked good for his mother.

For a moment, he forgot about his fight with Tehzeeb and thought of his sister. He had thought she would put up a fight because of her feelings for Luqman but she had acquiesced so quietly, it didn't make sense. Had she finally given up on him?

On impulse, he picked up his phone and dialled Luqman's number. He knew he was in India at the moment and soon enough, Luqman answered the phone. They chatted about this and that but Ayub could immediately sense that something was off. Their easy familiarity was missing.

'So, I've got good news for you,' Ayub said, hoping that would ease this strange tension between them.

'Hmm?' Luqman sounded distracted.

'My parents have started looking for prospective boys for Maira. They're getting her married,' he said. He waited for the sigh of relief but instead, there was silence.

'Oh, good,' Luqman said after a while.

'Dude, I thought you'd be relieved,' he said.

'I am,' Luqman said quickly. Ayub frowned. Something was definitely off here.

'You knew about this already, right? Did she call and tell you?' he asked, knowing he wouldn't put it past Maira. It suddenly made sense to him.

'No actually, she didn't. And this is the first I'm hearing of this,' he said.

'Listen, you sucked at lying right from school. So don't begin now,' Ayub said.

'Fuck. Why did you have to call today?' Luqman groaned.

'What do you mean?'

'Okay, yeah I knew about Maira. Can we just leave it at that?' he asked.

'No. We can't. If she didn't tell you, who did?' Ayub asked, sitting up straight in his chair. This was strange.

'Why do you go around in circles man? Ugh. Fine. I'll tell you everything,' he said.

When Ayub ended the call, he didn't know what to think anymore. Tehzeeb had hidden such a big thing from him? Not only had she met Luqman without his knowledge, but she'd conspired with him to trick Maira?

He got up suddenly, knowing that he couldn't get any work done that day. He was going home and when his wife came back from the office, they were going to talk.

He reached home an hour later, and when he was stuck in traffic, he contemplated calling home to see if she had come back yet. But he stopped himself. He would see soon enough. It was well after lunch when he reached home and he stopped in the foyer, wondering if all the ladies had left. But he could see their footwear neatly arranged in rows and groaned inwardly.

He didn't stop at the living room and went straight upstairs for a quick shower. It was odd being back home early and especially not having Tehzeeb waiting for him. He didn't want to think of her at the moment. He wanted to pinpoint his anger and disappointment towards her when she was here. But at the same time, he couldn't help feeling betrayed when he thought about the events with Luqman, as he towelled himself dry and walked downstairs, hoping to grab a quick bite.

He glanced at the living room and to his shock, he saw that all the ladies were sitting quietly. Usually, they would be chattering away non-stop, in pairs, in groups, but today, they were all silent. He would have walked on to the kitchen to ask Haleema Auntie to serve him some food if his mother hadn't looked up and seen him.

'Ayub!' she said, getting up from the sofa, looking distraught. Immediately, the ladies started murmuring to each other. He felt panic for some strange reason. Something was wrong.

'What is it, Ammi?' he asked, holding her shoulders.

To his surprise, Maira, stood up. Her eyes were rimmed red and she cleared her throat and spoke loudly. 'Ladies, I think it's best if you left,' she said. She looked away as she said the words, and Ayub could see that she was trying hard not to cry.

'What happened?' he asked. It wasn't Abba. He knew that. Abba had still been in office when he left, chatting with an old friend.

Ammi restrained her emotions and took a deep breath. 'Wait,' she said softly. The women started filing past him and they looked at him strangely as they left. He could hear their whispering and he thought he heard Tehzeeb's name. His heart raced. Had something happened to Tehzeeb? Where was she? Why hadn't she called him? Was she okay? Why had he been so stupidly proud about not calling her?

He couldn't wait till the women left and he pulled out his phone and dialled her number. Ammi narrowed her eyes but he turned away, unable to focus on anything. His heart pounded painfully. She answered the phone and she sounded okay. He exhaled in relief.

'Thank god you're okay. Where are you?' he asked.

'Um, in the cab on my way back,' she said softly. 'Is everything all right?'

He looked up at Ammi then, at the grim expression on her face.

'We'll talk when you get home,' he said.

'You're already home?' she asked but before he could answer her, Ammi had taken the phone from him and ended the call.

'What's going on Ammi?' he asked.

Ammi led him inside the living room where Maira was

sitting on one of the sofas. She handed him her iPad. It was open to a Facebook page. He saw the logo—it was Tehzeeb's office—Niche Space.

'I liked their Facebook page when Bhabhi started work there,' Maira spoke softly. Her face crumpled a little and she took a deep breath. 'And I get a notification whenever they post a live video.'

'What video?' Ayub asked, confused.

'This one,' Maira said, tapping the play button in the middle.

FORTY-FOUR

Tehzeeb reached home late. She was exhausted and the traffic had been awful. She let herself in after unlocking the door with the digital lock code and looked around, frowning at how silent the house was. She knew that the ladies would have left by now. She was supposed to have left early because she had told Aafreen she would come back for the party. But she hadn't counted on how long lunch would take, especially after her mimicry had everyone in splits. She took a cab directly from the restaurant and even then reached home quite late.

She heard sounds of conversation as she neared the living room. She contemplated going upstairs to her room for a shower but felt obliged to explain that traffic had made her late. She peeped inside the living room and saw everyone sitting there, even Abba. Aafreen was talking, muttering, holding her head. Abba spotted her, and stiffened. He looked away and that surprised her because she was used to his warm and effusive behaviour towards her.

'Um, hello,' she said. Everyone stopped and looked at her. She smiled. No one smiled back. Ayub's expressionless face worried her. She stepped inside. Aafreen almost recoiled and she stopped in her tracks. She glanced at Maira whose face and nose were red. Maira wiped away tears from her eyes.

'How *could* you, Bhabhi?' she asked.

'What?' she asked. Her stomach felt like it had dropped all the way down to the floor.

Maira got up and walked towards her angrily. She looked like she would knock Tehzeeb down and she stepped back, a little scared.

'What is this?' she asked, showing her iPad to her. Her heart was beating very fast, as she took it from Maira's hands and sat down without realising what she was doing. She tapped play and the moment the video began, she felt like she had stepped on a missing stair, that dream she had of falling sometimes, where she would jerk awake just before she splattered, was now in full force. She was falling and falling and there was no stopping it.

This was a nightmare.

How had she not seen what Chaya had been doing? She had livestreamed her entire act at the restaurant on Niche Space's Facebook page.

She pressed pause, unable to see herself act scathingly like her mother-in-law as she ordered the servants about or like flighty Maira who was posing with her phone for a selfie.

She pressed her lips together but couldn't bring herself to meet anyone's gaze. Her heart was knocking so loudly in her chest that she was afraid it would jump right out.

'This is what she thinks of us. She mocks us. Makes fun of us. In front of her colleagues and now the entire world,' Aafreen spoke softly.

Tears collected in Tehzeeb's eyes but she didn't move to wipe them away. She wanted to look at Ayub, wanted to draw strength from him but she couldn't bring herself to look at him.

She handed the iPad back to Maira without looking at her. Aafreen continued her tirade.

'Now I understood why you didn't want to invite your sisters for our lunches. You think you're superior to us because you people are all about education and you can talk politics with Ayub and Bakhtiyar? You've shown us just what you think of us,' she said.

Tehzeeb continued to sit silently, not knowing when or how this nightmare would end. It was obviously going to get worse.

'I thought you were my friend, Bhabhi! I … I thought you were my sister,' Maira said, sounding anguished.

Tehzeeb shut her eyes, and tears fell. Maira was right. But what could she say? She had no excuse to give, nothing to tell them. She thought less of them because they were shallow and today, they and the many people who saw that video had seen it too.

She still couldn't look up.

'Look at her. Sitting quietly without saying anything now. Why don't you talk now, Tehzeeb? Why don't you imitate me *now*?' Aafreen asked, her voice rising.

'Aafreen …' Bakhtiyar spoke finally and she turned to him viciously.

'This is all your fault. If I had got Ayub married to Shireen's daughter, Nadia, none of this would have happened!' she said. Tehzeeb pursed her lips. She was right.

'Aafreen,' this time, Abba's voice was louder, chiding her.

'Everyone saw that video!' Aafreen snapped.

'Everyone! Maira played it and before she could understand what was happening, before she could shut it down, everyone saw it. The ladies were all so shocked.

How much fun this girl has made of us!' Aafreen was now breathing heavily.

Tehzeeb tried to take a deep breath but found that she couldn't. Was she having a panic attack? She was sweating and she was not able to breathe. She felt like she was frozen in place. She wanted to speak, to ask for a glass of water but she couldn't open her mouth. She couldn't look up.

'This girl,' Aafreen went on slowly, her voice taking on a nasty tone, 'this girl you picked up from the ditch and brought into my house because you felt guilty over what you did to her father!'

'Aafreen! I told you to shut up!' Bakhtiyar's voice thundered but Tehzeeb felt like she had been splashed with cold water. All the noise had receded. She felt like she was in a vacuum.

'Why should I shut up? Did you consult me even once before you brought this low-class girl into my house, into my son's life? Did you ask me what I thought, how I would feel? What has she brought with her? NOTHING. She has nothing to her name but her education. What use is her education if she can't respect her in-laws? I wonder how she thinks she got so lucky. How many times I've wanted to tell her the truth! She's here because you pitied her father. Because you wanted to make reparations. But you ruined my son's life in the process!' Aafreen ranted.

Tehzeeb found that she could move again. The thundering in her chest hadn't lessened. She was still unable to speak and she was still sweating but she stood up. Her face had paled and she felt faint but she looked at every one of them.

Bakhtiyar, who looked panicked and angry. Aafreen, who looked incensed. Maira, who was staring at her in confused shock. And lastly, Ayub. He was still looking at her without any expression on his face. She was breathing hard. Her mouth was dry. Her heart ached. So much.

'I'm sorry,' she managed to get the words out and walked away from there. She couldn't think. She needed to get away from the house. She walked towards the door, half afraid Ayub would stop her, half afraid he wouldn't. But as she opened the door and stepped outside, no one came out of the living room.

She had her handbag with her and her phone. She walked down the stately steps and ran up the driveway. The guard at the gate looked at her, surprised.

'Madam ...' he said, standing up. She shook her head, trying to maintain her composure as she walked out of the gate. She couldn't break down here. She stepped out of the gate and hailed an auto and sat inside the moment one stopped. She needed to go home.

FORTY-FIVE

When Tehzeeb reached home, thankfully Abbu was not there. She unlocked the main door and went inside, just as Ana stepped out of their room to see who had come in.

'Abbu?' she called out.

'No, it's me,' Tehzeeb said with a voice choked with tears.

'Api?' Athiya said, frowning as she looked up from the sofa where she had been lying down. Tehzeeb hadn't seen her sitting there.

Breathing heavily, she walked swiftly to her old room and sat on the bed, while her worried sisters followed her in. She looked up at them, her face anguished.

'What happened? You're scaring me,' Athiya said in a small voice.

She burst into tears then, crying loudly, sobbing hard as she hugged her sisters.

'What happened?' Ana asked, crying with her. 'Please tell us. What happened? Why are you crying?'

'Did someone say something?' Athiya asked, drying her tears and getting angry.

Taking deep shuddering breaths, she told her sisters everything. Both of them were stunned beyond words.

'I n-need you to do one thing,' she said, trying to breathe but still not able to do it comfortably enough. Who knew that leaving the man she loved would make her feel like a fist was squeezing her chest until everything imploded? Who knew that the pain would be physical and excruciating?

'What? Tell me,' Athiya said, straightening up. She held Tehzeeb's shoulders. 'Anything for you, Api.'

Still shuddering in pain, Tehzeeb told her to call Malini and tell them about the video, to take it down. And to tell them that she was quitting.

'What?' Ana asked, eyes narrowed.

'I can't go back there. I can't. I have to figure out what to do now,' Tehzeeb said. She put her head on the pillow, on the faint smell of jasmine that clung to the sheets and she fell into a dreamless sleep.

It was dark when she woke up.

Disoriented, she patted her hand around for the bedside light and then everything came rushing back to her. She wasn't in her room in Ayub's house. The stark horror of what had happened upended her once more. She remembered Ayub's shuttered face and she wanted to cry again. But there were no tears left.

She was incredibly thirsty, and winced as a headache pounded her skull. She walked outside slowly, feeling like everything alive inside her had been wiped away in an instant. She was just the husk now.

Abbu was sitting outside with Ana and Athiya and he looked up when she stepped outside. He stood up and embraced her, tears in his eyes. He patted her and held her against him and she found that she could cry once more.

The four of them sat in the living room in silence. No one wanted to talk about what she should do next.

Tehzeeb's headache made her wince again and noticing her expression, Athiya made tea for her while Ana gave her a headache tablet.

Even breathing hurt. What she had done was reprehensible—made fun of her in-laws—but then she hadn't known that it was going to go on social media. She knew what her mother would have said if she were alive. Ammi had never liked it when she mimicked people and made others laugh.

'You think mocking people is funny? One day you'll be crying because of it,' she had told her, and here she was, unable to stop the tears from rolling down her face.

Despite her mortification, her embarrassment, her shock at Aafreen and Maira seeing her video, in some corner of her heart, she had hoped if she could apologise to them enough, if she could grovel enough, then they would forgive her. She would have done it if Ayub had been with her, if he had supported her, instead of sitting stone-faced through her entire ordeal.

But when Aafreen had started talking, telling her everything, the real reason Bakhtiyar Ahmed had chosen her for his son, she knew she couldn't stay there for even a minute. She had to get out of there.

She looked at her father's worried face. 'Abbu, I'm sorry about everything,' she said softly.

He shook his head and chuckled bitterly. 'No, you don't have to be sorry about anything. What you did in the restaurant … that was just a childish prank. But what Bakhtiyar did … maybe this was his ultimate plan. Humiliate my daughter and cause me pain,' he said.

Tehzeeb shut her eyes to stop the images from replaying in her mind but that just made it worse.

'But why? What happened between the two of you Abbu?' Ana asked. Tehzeeb clutched the sofa arm, wishing for some sort of oblivion. Something that would take away her pain and embarrassment.

'We were classmates in college, beta,' he explained. 'I was better at everything and always got more marks than him. He hated me for that and he made my life miserable. I tried my best to ignore him but he kept getting bolder. One day, he planted some chits on me during an exam. I got caught and I lost a year because of him.'

'What?' Athiya asked, outraged. 'How could he do such a thing? Why didn't you do anything?'

Abbu shook his head. 'What could I do? Even if I complained to someone, would they believe me over him? No. And I thought that maybe all this was meant to happen. Maybe I was meant to finish my studies a year later,' he said.

'But Abbu …' Ana said, looking angry.

'He sought me out then, apologised to me. Told me he had made a grave mistake but I told him to move on. I didn't see him until all those years later in the masjid,' Abbu said. He looked at Tehzeeb who was staring at the mug in her hand. Athiya's tea had failed to revive her. It seemed like nothing could ever make her feel better.

'What are you going to do, beta?' he asked Tehzeeb.

She shook her head and tears formed in her eyes once more. 'I don't know. I … just left without thinking. I've quit my job. Maybe I'll try to find another one sometime later,' she said.

Abbu was silent but she knew the unasked question. What about her marriage? What about Ayub? Was she planning to stay back here forever?

She wished she knew.

FORTY-SIX

What the hell had just happened? Ayub rubbed his eyes in fatigue. They were all sitting in the living room, Ammi was still ranting but he could take it no longer. Abba was standing at his favourite spot near the bookshelf and he walked up there to join him.

'Abba,' he spoke softly. Bakhtiyar turned around and shook his head.

'I messed everything up again,' Bakhtiyar said. He looked pained and older for some reason.

Ayub was still unable to believe the events of the afternoon. He could not for the life of him understand what that video was. He had never seen Tehzeeb mimic anyone, so to see her act coy, then foolish, then vapid and then flutter her eyelashes, telling her audience that this was how her mother-in-law and sister-in-law simpered and cooed, was beyond his understanding. He felt anger and shame and combined with the loaded knowledge that she had met Luqman and tricked Maira, he had been furious with her.

When she walked inside, he still hadn't figured out how he would deal with her. Would he punish her by not talking to her for a few days? Would he insist she apologise to his family? He felt that same lurch in the region of his chest when he saw her, and when she sat down and watched the video unfold, her reaction had heartened him. He wanted her to be embarrassed and sorry and he wanted her to apologise to his family.

But then … Ammi had started speaking. And she didn't stop. He still remembered the look of horror on Tehzeeb's face when she had stood up. She said sorry and went away. He stiffened when he heard the front door open and he stifled the urge to go to her. To stop her from going. He knew where she was headed. Her father's place. Where else would she go?

'If Ayub had married Nadia, we would have all got along so well. But this girl from the gutter thinks she's better than us. What a joke!' Ammi said. Ayub turned to her.

'Ammi. You've spoken enough,' he said firmly. Ammi glared at him.

'Just because she's beautiful doesn't mean she can get away with saying nonsense about us. She's a rat. She's …'

'Aafreen! Enough!' Abba thundered, turning around from the bookshelf. But Ammi only got angrier.

'You dare shout at me?' she screeched. 'Me? Your wife of thirty years!'

'You have to stop this,' Abba said, shaking his head.

'Why? Why should I stop? That girl made us the laughing stock of our entire community. All the important people were here today. I had invited them to make an impression about our family for Maira. Imagine the sort of impression they must have had of us! That girl …'

'Is my wife,' Ayub completed. Ammi turned to him and glared.

'After all she did …'

'I still love her,' Ayub said. Ammi's eyes became wide. Maira looked at him tearfully and she stood up.

'She's always been so nice to me, so I don't know why she did what she did!' she burst out.

'She did that because she's a low-class, honourless ...'

'Ammi,' Ayub said in a warning tone. 'You are talking about my wife. I really think you need to keep quiet now. You've said enough!'

'He tells me to keep quiet!' Ammi screeched. Without a word, Ayub walked out and went out of the house. He got into his car, unable to believe that just this morning they had had their first fight and now ... their first ... what was this? His heart constricted painfully.

He started the car and drove away. At the gate, he stopped and rolled down the window. 'Where did madam go?' he asked.

'I don't know, saab. She took an auto and left,' he said. Ayub knew she had gone to her father's house and he didn't want to go there. He didn't want to face her now. He needed to think. He needed to vent to someone. He called Luqman and told him he needed to talk. Luqman asked him to come over to his office.

The two of them sat in Luqman's cabin an hour later, not talking.

'Shit. I can't believe this,' Luqman said.

Ayub was weary. He had opened the Facebook page to show the video to Luqman but it had been taken down by then. The damage had been done though.

'I don't know what to do anymore,' Ayub admitted after some time.

'I don't know what advice to give you man. What's the scene at home?' Luqman asked. Ayub winced.

'It's bad. Ammi is livid, Maira is crying and Abba is tired of everything that's happened,' he said. 'Everything was going perfectly. Why did this have to happen?'

Luqman was silent for a bit. He seemed lost in thought. 'I have no idea. But I think your mother has been resentful towards her from the beginning,' he said.

Ayub nodded slowly. It was true. But he hadn't known that his mother was capable of such venom and hate. The hurtful names she was calling Tehzeeb were getting too much for him to bear.

'Also, I want to apologise about Maira,' Luqman said. Ayub turned to him. Had it been just this morning that he had spoken to Luqman? It seemed like ages ago. When life had been different. When the fight between him and Tehzeeb had been a mere wrinkle in the fabric of their relationship, not a tear.

'Why did you do it?' he asked. Luqman shrugged.

'I didn't tell you all the details earlier today. Tehzeeb came here with her sister to ask me to reconsider my feelings towards Maira. I had to convince them that I had no feelings. And then I realised I had to convince Maira of that as well and I remembered what you told me during your engagement. To get married or get a girlfriend.'

Ayub exhaled. He wished he hadn't given up smoking two years ago. He wanted nothing more than a fag to light up, not that it would help in any way. But it would give him something to do. It would lessen this crowding in his heart, this numbness that refused to go away.

'Tehzeeb wasn't out to trick Maira. She was doing this to help her move on,' Luqman continued.

'Yes, but she showed today what she really thought of my family,' Ayub said, with a bitter laugh. If it hadn't been such a nightmare, if it hadn't been his family, he might have laughed too. She was that good.

'Dude, you know what your family is like,' Luqman

began uncertainly. Ayub flashed him a look but didn't say anything. Luqman was right. He had never had the patience for any of the women in his family and extended relatives. He had been relieved that Tehzeeb was nothing like them. But to make fun of everyone on a public platform? He realised that she hadn't known that the video had been livestreamed. The shock on her face made it evident enough.

Ayub got up from there wearily. He waved at Luqman without turning to look at him and walked away from there, out to the parking lot where he got into his car. It was evening now. He checked his phone, knowing that she wouldn't text him or call him but he still hoped.

At home, the atmosphere was mournful. The living room was dark and no one was in the dining room. He assumed they were all upstairs in their rooms. He was in no mood to eat but Haleema Auntie had dragged him to the kitchen table and made him sit. She looked like she had been crying too.

'Why are you crying?' he asked her, his heart feeling heavy.

She shook her head, sniffling, and spoke in a rush. 'Tehzeeb bibi is very funny. She cannot help it. She likes to imitate everyone. She can imitate Hema Malini and Amrish Puri and she can imitate me also. I like it when she imitates the way I walk and how I cook. She imitates Naaz too,' Haleema Auntie said, nodding to one of the servant girls. 'We all laugh with her when she does it. It's just that Aafreen Apa saw it today for the first time.'

Why hadn't she shown this side of her to him, he wondered. Why had she kept it hidden?

'All that is fine. Why are you crying though?' he asked her irritably as he ate.

'Don't divorce her, please. Don't marry Nadia!' Haleema Auntie burst out, looking around fearfully. The food in his mouth turned to ash.

'What?' he asked quietly.

She nodded. 'Aafreen Apa was talking to someone on the phone. She was saying that you will divorce Tehzeeb bibi and marry Nadia.'

He pushed the plate away angrily and stalked upstairs to talk to his parents.

FORTY-SEVEN

A week had passed. How the days went by, she didn't know. The world around her celebrated New Year's Day with firecrackers; singing and shouting but she stayed inside her house, lying in her bed, staring at the ceiling. After that, she progressed to sitting outside in the living room, or outside the door, on the small steps, trying to breathe. Trying to come to terms with her life now. She kept her phone by her side, hoping he would call or text but he didn't. She knew she wouldn't answer if he called but he hadn't.

She had heard Abbu talk to his father on the phone once. She didn't know what they discussed. She didn't stick around to listen because thinking of even the vaguest connection to Ayub hurt. She tried to stop herself from looking at his photos on her phone, but she couldn't resist it. The longer he stayed away from her, the more the pain grew. Would it ever stop hurting, she wondered when she woke up in the middle of the night once, thinking of him, dreaming of him.

Maira had called her one day and uncertainly, Tehzeeb answered, not sure of what she could tell her.

'I'm so sorry, Maira,' she told her.

'Are you sorry you did it or are you sorry we saw it?'

Maira asked, surprising Tehzeeb with her wise insight.

Her mouth went dry. 'Both,' she admitted. Maira didn't say anything for a few seconds and Tehzeeb wondered if she had hung up. She wanted to ask her about Ayub but she couldn't bring herself to say his name without bawling, so she didn't say anything.

Maira sighed. 'Bhabhi, this is such a mess,' she said. Tehzeeb wondered if her actions meant Aafreen and Maira would be treated like pariahs in their community. Would they never be invited for events again?

She tentatively voiced the question to Maira, even as her heart constricted. Maira was confused.

'No, in fact, everyone will want me and Ammi to attend so they can gossip about you and get more details,' Maira said. Oh. When Tehzeeb didn't say anything, Maira continued. 'Bhabhi, when are you coming back?'

Was that even an option anymore, she wondered. Aafreen had made it clear what she thought of her.

'I … your mother …' she began.

'Oh, Ammi is mad at you. But I am horrified at the things she told you that day,' Maira said. Momentarily, Tehzeeb was taken aback.

'Will you forgive me?' she asked her quietly.

'I have. I mean, it was hurtful when I first saw it but then you did such an uncanny impression of me. It almost seems funny, you know,' Maira said.

Tehzeeb shut her eyes. Maira had such a big heart. She felt ashamed to think of how she had mercilessly made fun of her.

'Thank you, Maira. I don't know if I deserve your forgiveness though,' she said.

'That's okay. But when are you coming back? Bhai is …'

Tehzeeb's face paled. She didn't want to hear anything about Ayub and at the same time, she did. How was Ayub? Where was he? Why hadn't he called her?

'I have to go now,' she said and ended the call quickly, breathing heavily.

When it was one week to the day since she had walked out of his house, she came to a decision, one that made her feel tremulous inside. Ana's college was due to begin in a couple of days. Athiya's had already begun; she was in college and would be coming home soon. She called her sister outside, to the steps where they sat together, watching dusk roll across the sky. The scent of jasmine no longer comforted her. It reminded her acutely of him, of her wedding night, of his touch and if she thought about it too much, she didn't know how much more her heart could break.

'I need you to do something,' she said to her sister softly.

Ana rubbed her elbow comfortingly.

'Anything for you, Api,' she said, leaning her head against Tehzeeb's shoulder. Tehzeeb took a deep breath.

'I … I'll give you a few things that I have with me, that belong to Ayub, to his family. Things that I was wearing that day. Can you please go and return it to him?' she asked.

Ana looked at her quizzically. 'But …'

'Go to his office. It will be better there. Don't go to the house,' Tehzeeb said quickly. Just talking about Ayub hurt her physically.

'Api, but why?' Ana asked.

'How can you ask me that?' Tehzeeb said, looking at the darkening sky. 'He doesn't want me any longer. He hasn't texted even once, not even to offer an explanation for what his father did. I know I messed up big time but …'

'But you love him so much!'

'And I hate it,' Tehzeeb said softly. 'I hate not having control over my own emotions. I hate this feeling of dark despair inside me.'

'How will this help? Returning these things?' Ana asked. 'And why should I do it? Why can't you go and throw it all back in his face?'

Tehzeeb shook her head. 'I can't. I don't think I can see his face and not burst into tears. I'm very emotional right now and I'm not the right person to do this.'

'Have you spoken to Abbu? Does he know?' Ana asked, looking worried.

Tehzeeb shook her head. 'I'll deal with Abbu later,' she said. 'Please do this for me? I don't want anything that belongs to him with me any longer. I don't want a single thing of his.'

'Really? And what about the thing you can't return to him? Or won't?' Ana said quietly. Tehzeeb stared at her sister's face in silence, heat blooming across her cheeks. How had she known?

'How? What … I mean … how?' she asked, flustered. She had found out only a couple of days after coming back here.

'I keep telling you guys, I'm very observant,' Ana said with a sigh. 'You think if you hide in the bathroom with the taps open at 6.30 a.m., I won't know you're retching inside there?'

Tehzeeb worried her lower lip with her teeth. Her situation had become more complicated now. She knew when this had happened. The night of the thunderstorm when she told him she loved him. He'd been too overcome with emotion to think about protection and she hadn't either. They had made love that night, several times, and ... now she was going to have his baby. She didn't have any confirmation yet but she had missed her period and the morning sickness had already begun. She noted the changes in her body miserably, and had thought her secret was safe with her. Apparently not.

'I can't tell him about the baby right now,' she said to Ana.

'Why not? It's his baby too,' she said.

'Yes, but ... I don't want him to try and convince me to come back because of the baby,' Tehzeeb said softly. 'I'm afraid that if he asks me to go with him, I will agree readily. And I will never know if he wanted me or the baby.'

'He'll come to know eventually,' Ana said. Tehzeeb nodded.

'I'll worry about that when it happens,' she said. She turned to Ana and put her head on her sister's shoulder. 'Let this remain between us for now? Don't tell anyone yet?'

Ana sighed. 'Not even Athiya?' she asked.

'Especially not her. She'll fly into a rage, walk into his office and do something rash. You know how she is.'

'That's true,' Ana agreed. She squeezed her sister's hand. 'It will get better, Api.'

Tehzeeb shook her head. 'Nothing will get better. How can it, Ana? His mother hates me. His father tricked us ...'

'But Ayub Bhai loves you,' Ana reminded her. 'And Maira already forgave you.'

Tehzeeb stayed silent. 'I don't know anything anymore. Maybe he stopped loving me when he saw that video. When he saw how vicious I can be,' she said after a minute. Ana was already shaking her head.

'First of all, you weren't vicious. It's just something

you do. You make fun of people to make others laugh and you're so good at it, you should probably have your own YouTube channel. You'd be a star. But you're SO foolish, Api. Do you think love is like a switch that can be turned on and off at will?' Ana asked.

Tehzeeb looked at her but then her gaze was drawn to the gate that creaked as it was opened. That stupid burst of hope inside her bloomed and was crushed immediately. It was Athiya, returning from college. She saw the two of them sitting on the steps and she smiled as she walked up there and joined them.

'What do you know, Ana? What do you know?' Tehzeeb said softly.

FORTY-EIGHT

Luqman wished there was something he could do to his ease his friend's pain but he didn't know what he could do apart from showing up and offering moral support. Ayub wasn't even pretending that he wasn't devastated that his wife had left him and gone away. He stayed in the office beyond his normal working hours which is where Luqman found him, staring into space when he walked in one day.

He made himself comfortable on the chair on the opposite side of the desk and sat there, wishing he knew the right thing to say. He and Ayub went back a long time. They had been friends in school, then in college and even after they opted for different streams, they had remained firm friends. They knew each other's shit and they didn't need to provide any context. Whenever he was in India, Luqman made it a point to spend every other Saturday or Friday evening with him.

Since Ayub had gotten married, things had changed though. He had been reluctant to spend time away from his wife. Luqman realised Ayub wasn't staring into space as he thought earlier, but was looking at Tehzeeb's photo that had been framed and kept on his desk.

'Listen, why don't you just call and talk to her?' Luqman

asked. He hadn't suggested this the past few days because he didn't know if it was the right approach. But if Ayub was so miserable without her, he should contact her and not wait for her to contact him.

'And say what?' Ayub asked, his eyes still not moving from the frame.

'Tell her to come back,' Luqman said, as though it was very obvious.

'She went on her own. She can come back on her own,' he said.

'Yes, but … you said your mother said a lot of things to her. About the history between your father and hers and …'

'I never wanted her to know that. In fact, even I was shocked when Abba told me. But I think I fell in love with her when I saw her in the café that day and nothing else mattered. I just wanted to be with her,' Ayub said, his voice low and pained.

'So be with her now,' Luqman insisted.

'How? She hurt my mother and my mother hurt her back. I can't go to her when the situation at home is like this!'

'Then speak to your parents and tell them that you love her and want her back,' Luqman said, as though it was obvious.

'My mother knows I love her,' Ayub said, shifting his gaze from the frame and staring down at him. 'In fact, I made it clear to her many times over because she had this strange notion that I would be divorcing her and marrying someone else.'

'What?' Luqman asked, shocked. Ayub nodded.

'She knows I won't do that now. I've told her that she has to stop making such plans because I have no intentions of doing that.'

'And?'

'Ammi's not talking to me at the moment. She's angry that I would still love Tehzeeb after what she did. But seriously, how can I *stop* loving her?' Ayub asked, looking anguished. 'If she hadn't ranted that day about … Abba trying to help Tehzeeb's father, things wouldn't have gone this far. I wish Abba had never told her the truth.'

'How's Maira?' Luqman asked warily. Ayub raised an eyebrow and Luqman put his hands up in front of him defensively. 'Just asking. No ulterior motives.'

'She's better, actually. She came and spoke to me some days ago, saying that she has forgiven Tehzeeb already. She said that Tehzeeb really helped her when she was going through some shit because of you,' Ayub said, making a face.

Luqman looked down, shamefaced. 'So she doesn't know …'

'That you tricked her into thinking you have a girlfriend? No,' Ayub said flatly. Luqman winced but he sat back in his chair, wondering how his friend's life could have gone from hundred to zero in just a matter of hours. He thought of her sometimes, the girl with the strange name. Ana. But he reined his thoughts in. Marriage wasn't on the cards for him for the next few years and someone like Ana would be getting married soon.

Almost as if he had conjured her by thinking of her, she stood at the door to Ayub's office and knocked. His mouth dropped open in shock. How had she come here? Was Tehzeeb with her? But there was no one standing beside her.

Images of her crowded his head, the ones that he had tried to dispel ever since Tehzeeb had helped him out by taking his photo with her. Her beautiful almond shaped eyes, her dewy lips, her soft skin. She'd flinched when he held her hand and gazed into her eyes as though he was in love with her. And now she was taking firm strides inside Ayub's office, holding a bag.

Ayub stood up, stunned. 'Ana! Is everything all right? Is Tehzeeb fine?' he asked, his voice strangled. She stared at him and only then, turned to see that he was sitting there and she looked startled. He could see that she'd lost her composure for a few seconds but then she nodded.

'She's fine,' Ana said firmly. Luqman couldn't stop staring at her. She was dressed in a salwar kameez, a deep blue outfit that set off her complexion perfectly. Her hair was tied loosely in a ponytail and her light blue dupatta was slung around her shoulders carelessly.

'She wanted me to return this to you,' she said, handing over the bag to Ayub. He took it from her, confused.

'What's this?' he asked slowly, still looking at Ana as though she had all the answers.

'She … she's returning whatever jewellery and things she was wearing the day she left your house,' Ana said.

Ayub's face blanched and he rounded his desk and came up to her. 'What is going on?' he asked, his voice low and worried.

'How can you ask that?' she asked him softly. 'She sits with her phone by her side, looking at your photos and waiting for a call or even a text from you. And you have just ignored her all these days. She's …'

Ana stopped speaking as though she had already spoken too much.

'She's waiting for me to call her?' Ayub asked.

Ana shook her head. 'Maybe if you'd called up and spoken to her after she came back home, maybe even the next day. But now …'

Ana indicated the bag and she turned around to walk away.

'Ana, wait!' Ayub said, following her. 'I don't know what to do.'

'I …'

'Do you still love her?' she asked him.

'Yes, I do,' Ayub said fervently.

'She's sorry about the video and …'

'I don't care about that anymore,' he said. 'Luqman even told me about how they used you to make Maira believe he has a girlfriend. I was angry that she had hidden it from me but not anymore.'

Ana blushed as she glanced at Luqman who stared back at her evenly. She acknowledged him with a slight nod but then turned back to Ayub.

She took a deep breath. 'When you are poor like us, self-respect is the only thing that matters to us. And your mother slashed Api's self-respect that day.'

Ayub's throat worked but he couldn't get any words out. Ana looked at him expectantly, but when he didn't say anything, she shook her head and left. Luqman kept looking at her as she walked away, when she turned around and sighed. 'She still loves you too,' she said and left the office.

Ayub let out a breath but his face paled when he pulled out whatever was inside the bag. There was a set of clothes that had been neatly ironed but he crumpled them as he lifted them to his nose to sniff. Along with the clothes, there was a watch, a pair of diamond studs and a slim bangle. He stared at these things and when he lifted his head, Luqman saw that there were tears in his eyes.

FORTY-NINE

Tehzeeb was waiting for Ana to return home after meeting Ayub. She was sitting on the steps outside the house, her heart thumping as she wondered what Ayub would tell her. She couldn't bring herself to look at his face on her phone again but she kept her phone next to her anyway. What if he called?

Athiya had returned from college and came outside looking for her.

'What are you doing here?' she asked as she sat down beside her.

'Nothing. Just sitting,' Tehzeeb said. Athiya put her arm around Tehzeeb's shoulders, forcing her to rest her head on her shoulder.

'You miss him, right?' she asked.

Tehzeeb nodded and then straightened when an auto sputtered to a stop outside their gate and Ana stepped out. She saw the two of them sitting and she waved at them.

'Where were you?' Athiya asked her. Ana looked at her as though asking for permission to tell her what had happened. Tehzeeb nodded.

'Api wanted me to return a few things to Ayub Bhai so I went to his office,' she said.

'Oh!' Athiya looked at Tehzeeb.

'What did he say? How was he?' she asked.

Ana bit her lower lip thoughtfully. 'You two should talk,' she said. Tehzeeb shook her head but Ana persisted.

'He said he loves you. And you love him too. Why are you unnecessarily creating drama?' Ana beseeched her.

'Unnecessarily?' Athiya asked, eyes wide in anger. 'How can you say that? After what his parents did!'

'How's he?' Tehzeeb asked. He still loved her. The knowledge should have given her hope but it only made her sad. Why hadn't he reached out to her then?

'Not good. At least from what I could see. He looked sad and heartbroken already but when I gave him the things, he was ...'

'He was?'

'He was devastated, Api. You have to do something. You know what I mean, right?' Ana said. Tehzeeb looked away. Devastated.

'I don't care. Let him be devastated. What does it matter?' Athiya said.

'It matters because Api still loves him,' Ana said. Tehzeeb rose and went inside. Her sisters followed her, still talking to each other about the best course of action. Abbu, who had been in his room, emerged from there, frowning.

'What's going on?' he asked. He had his mobile phone in his hand. Tehzeeb wondered who he had been talking to.

'Nothing,' Tehzeeb assured him. His gaze softened when he turned to her.

'Tehzeeb beta, we have to decide something about your future,' he said.

'Abbu, not now,' Tehzeeb replied, turning away from there.

'Relatives are calling me, asking me why you have come back here,' he said.

'Who told them? Jobless fools,' Athiya said angrily. Abbu shrugged helplessly.

'Word gets around,' he said, looking at them. Tehzeeb realised why Abbu was worried. He had two more unmarried daughters and it would not look good if the first daughter came back from her in-laws indefinitely.

'We'll figure something out. As long as you tell me what you want,' he said, turning to Tehzeeb. Nodding, she walked away to her room.

*

Dinner was a quiet affair, as it had become these days. Even Ana and Athiya ate in silence and Tehzeeb longed for the banter and the bickering that had been the norm before she got married. She had missed them when she lived in Ayub's house but now she ached to see his face, longed to touch him, to feel him curled up behind her when they slept.

They had just finished eating and were clearing the table when they heard the creak of the gates. Tehzeeb forced her heart to stop reacting. It wouldn't be him. He hadn't called her. He wouldn't. But the doorbell rang, and Abbu went to answer the door.

Tehzeeb froze when she saw it was Bakhtiyar and Aafreen. Even Abbu was shocked. What were they doing here? Tehzeeb turned to go to her room. She was no longer ashamed of her draughty, rundown house but she couldn't face them now.

'Tehzeeb, wait,' Bakhtiyar called out. Abbu stepped aside and Aafreen and Bakhtiyar walked in uncertainly.

Tehzeeb stopped in her tracks and turned around. Looking at Aafreen was very difficult. The last time she had seen her, she had been seething in anger and with good reason too, but she had also said such awful things to her. What were they doing here?

Abbu led them to the living room in silence and they sat down. Ana nudged her forward.

Tehzeeb walked forward, looking down, unable to meet their gaze. Why had they come here? Where was Ayub?

'Tehzeeb beta, come and sit here,' Bakhtiyar Ahmed said. Tehzeeb sat down next to her father and finally looked at Aafreen and Bakhtiyar.

'Will you have some tea?' Abbu asked. Tehzeeb got up immediately.

'I'll make tea,' she said.

'No, you sit. I'll get tea,' Ana said and she took Athiya with her inside the kitchen. Tehzeeb sat back on the sofa reluctantly. Pining alone for Ayub all these days, wondering what was going to happen to them was different but with his parents sitting across her in her house, she had to face the reality now. What was it going to be?

Bakhtiyar Ahmed spoke first. 'Tehzeeb, I am so sorry about what happened the other day in our house. I really am,' he said.

Tehzeeb felt her face flush in embarrassment.

'Actually, I'm sorry about … about that video,' she managed to get the words out, unable to look at Aafreen.

Bakhtiyar Ahmed shook his head. 'Forget that. We have forgotten it,' he said. Really? Had they? She found that hard to believe.

'I want to tell you why I did what I did,' he continued, turning to Abbu slightly. Abbu was shaking his head.

'We know why you did it. There's no need for an explanation,' he said flatly.

'Hear me out, please,' Bakhtiyar said.

Abbu crossed his arms and sat back. Tehzeeb focused her gaze on the floor before them. She kept wondering where Ayub was.

'I was so ashamed of what I did to you all those years ago,' Bakhtiyar Ahmed began. Abbu's face remained expressionless.

'I already forgave you,' he said.

Ayub's father shook his head. 'Yes, but I didn't forgive myself. I have never been able to put away the thoughts of the kind of person I had become during that brief time in college.'

He looked at them and sat forward, clasping his hands together. 'I saw you once before I met you in the masjid. I saw you with your daughters and ...'

'And?' Abbu asked. He didn't look very pleased.

'You looked content, Yusuf. You didn't look like you had accomplished much in your life. And yet, you looked happy. In that brief moment, I understood what I didn't have with all my money and everything. I'm not saying I wasn't happy. But there was always something missing, a part of me that remembered what I had done. And I knew that this was a sign from Allah, that I had to make reparations.'

Abbu's jaw worked. He wanted to say something but Bakhtiyar Ahmed continued speaking. 'Hear me out. Please. I didn't know which one was Tehzeeb. I didn't know if you would even be willing to marry one of your daughters to my son. I just knew that I had to try. I hoped that your daughters were the source of your contentment and I wanted that happiness, a part of it at least, for my son. You were rich beyond what I could imagine, Yusuf. I was just hoping you would let me borrow some of it,' he said.

Tehzeeb was speechless. She looked at Aafreen who lifted her head and met her gaze just then. Tehzeeb didn't look away even though she was embarrassed. Aafreen smiled then.

'Come back home, Tehzeeb,' Aafreen said quietly. 'Ayub is miserable without you. I have not seen him like this ever in my life. I'm sorry for the horrid things I said to you. I was angry and … I lashed out.'

Tehzeeb didn't know what to say. 'I'm sorry if I haven't behaved properly with you since you got married to Ayub. I … I felt alienated by my husband's actions. I said some horrible things to you and I'm sorry about that. After you left, we had a discussion. We …' she winced. 'I thought I knew what was best for Ayub. But he set me right. He told me he would always love you.'

'Then why didn't he come?' Tehzeeb asked, unable to stop herself.

'You need to ask him yourself,' she said, looking down.

'Why?'

'He … he's been staying late at work all these days. Today, he came back and we knew things were different. He was … broken. You sent back your things today, with your sister?' she said softly. Tehzeeb looked down and she knew Abbu was looking at her in shock.

'He thought … he thinks you're done with him,' she said.

Tehzeeb felt herself growing hot and cold. 'He told me that we had to go to your house and apologise to you and your father. He said that your happiness matters most and if you were happy without him, then so be it,' Aafreen continued.

'But you just asked me to come back?' Tehzeeb asked, her face turning red. Aafreen shook her head.

'That's on me. *I'm* asking you to come back to your home. He told me to tell you that you were free to do what you want. But I can't bear to see him like this. None of us can,' she said.

Tehzeeb turned to her father. Just then, Ana emerged from inside the kitchen holding a tray of tea. She brought it to the living room and served them all. Abbu patted her shoulder thoughtfully.

'You decide what's best for you both,' he said. Tehzeeb frowned. Both? He glanced down at her still-flat abdomen and she realised that Abbu also knew. Her in-laws hadn't noticed the exchange and she was glad. She wanted to tell Ayub first.

She thought of him, the man she loved, and the idea of spending her lifetime without him seemed preposterous. In the larger scheme of things, nothing else mattered except that they loved each other. Why should she stay away from him because of pride? Bakhtiyar and Aafreen had come here to her house to apologise to her after all.

She cleared her throat.

'Abba,' she said, turning to Bakhtiyar and then turning to Aafreen, she spoke, 'Ammi. Thank you for coming here. I want to apologise once more about what happened in the restaurant and the video.'

Aafreen nodded. 'It's okay. Everyone is over the shock now. The video is no longer there and I'm waiting to see how well you mimic Raheema Apa,' she said with a smile.

Tehzeeb stared at her in surprised shock. 'Really?' she asked softly. Aafreen smiled and nodded.

'Wait for me,' she said, getting up to go inside her room to talk to her sisters.

FIFTY

Ayub stood in the balcony outside his room, waiting for his father's car to come into the driveway. He had been standing there ever since they left two hours ago. He hadn't been able to move away. After Ana left his office, he came back home and told his parents that enough was enough, they had to go and apologise to Tehzeeb.

His mother had been worried for him but she maintained that what Tehzeeb did was wrong, so why should she apologise?

'So what?' Ayub said, his voice rising. 'So what if she made fun of you and Maira? It's all right. Learn to lighten up. It's not just you. She mimics everyone else too, even Haleema Auntie.'

'But …'

'But what Ammi? So she did something silly and she didn't know it would get broadcast to the world like that. It's no longer on the Facebook page. They've taken it down. But what Abba did and the things you told her …' he shook his head. He showed them the things she had sent back to him, trying hard to keep his composure.

'She's sent back everything. She's no gold digger, if that's what you thought she is,' he said slowly. Ammi shook her head.

'No, I never implied she was one but ...'

'No buts, Ammi. You and Abbu need to go now,' he said.

'But then why aren't you coming with us? You should go and get her back,' Ammi protested. He shook his head firmly.

'The two of you wronged her so you should go and apologise. If I go ... I will probably beg her to come back with me and she'll hate me even more. If she doesn't want to be with me, then she should be free to do what she wants,' he said, even though his throat felt choked at saying the words. He turned around and walked away to his room and went to the balcony. He watched them leave and muttered a prayer.

The air was still and the night sky was hazy as usual. For a while, as he stood there, the sky cleared a bit and he could spot a single star shining in the sky. The star gave him a spurt of foolish hope.

Maira had come to his room, asking him to come back inside but he had refused. He was going to wait for her here, in the spot where she told him she loved him.

His legs cramped from standing still for so long and he knew it was silly to just wait here endlessly. When the gates opened and the car purred inside, his heart jumped and then started racing. He was waiting to see if she would emerge from inside the car. Abba stepped out and shut the door and then Ammi did the same. Tehzeeb was not with them.

The disappointment he felt was acute and strong and made his legs a little shaky. She hadn't come back to him. What would he do now? Should he go to her and beg her to come back? Holding the balustrade, he leaned forward, his mind crowding with thoughts. He had hoped against hope that she would return. Ana had said that she loved him. He had told his mother to tell her that she was free to do what she wanted but he hadn't meant it entirely. He couldn't imagine spending another day, let alone a week or a month or a lifetime without her by his side.

When soft hands went around his waist and pulled him back, he turned around with a start, unable to believe what he saw. She stood before him, shadows under her eyes, her skin pale with a smile on her lips. She was still the most beautiful woman he had seen. And she was wearing the same dress she had worn when she met him for the first time. When he had fallen in love with her.

'You came back,' he whispered, holding her to him and hugging her. She held him tightly as well and then stepped back.

She nodded and then leaned forward, standing on tiptoe and she kissed him. He held the back of her head, as though afraid she would disappear and he kissed her back.

He couldn't speak. He was choked with emotion. He picked her up in his arms and went inside the room.

'You came back,' he repeated the words as though unable to believe it. 'How? Where? I didn't see you get down from the car.'

She smiled as he put her down. 'Maira let me in through the kitchen door. She told me you hadn't moved from the balcony for the past two hours.'

He tugged her hand and held it to his chest. 'I love you Tehzeeb. I … I wanted to come and meet you the very day you left but I was hurting and I was sure I would have no self-respect or control if I saw you. I would have begged you to come back with me but I thought we both needed time to cool down and think.'

She looked sad, he thought, as she touched his cheek lightly. 'I waited every day, every moment for you to call,' she said softly.

'I'm an idiot,' he said fervently, pulling her close to him. 'I'm sorry for everything.' He held her close, inhaling deeply as he buried his face in her neck.

'Ayub,' she said softly. He looked up. He still couldn't believe she was back with him. A week without her had driven him to despair. She pushed the hair back from his forehead.

'I'm sorry too,' she said. 'For everything.'

He held her hand. 'You have a lot to answer for, by the way,' he said.

She looked at him warily. 'About the video?' she asked, looking down.

'No. About your crazy talent for mimicry. We've been married for nearly three months now. Why haven't I seen any of it yet?' he asked.

She looked unsure and then she shrugged. 'It's not such a fantastic talent you know. My mother hated it. She kept telling me it would come back and bite me in the ass.'

He pulled her close and brought his hand to her rear, bringing her flush against him. Her eyes widened.

'Your mother said that it would come and bite you in the ass?'

She rolled her eyes. 'Obviously I'm paraphrasing,' she said, as he still held her firmly.

'Well, it's not fair. You've done it for everyone but me,' he said.

'You saw the video, didn't you?' she protested, shutting her eyes tightly.

'Are you still embarrassed about it?' he asked. She opened her eyes and nodded.

'Don't be. Let's not think about it now,' he said as he pushed her backwards.

'Okay, I won't but there's something I need to tell you first,' she gasped as she fell back on the bed.

'First, I want to know why you look like this,' he asked, bringing his hand under her back and pushing her up on the bed.

'Like what?' she asked.

'Tired. Pale,' he said, pushing her hair back. He traced her full lips with his finger and leaned down to kiss her again.

'That's because I'm pregnant,' she said softly. He froze and lifted his head to see her. He couldn't believe what he'd just heard. She nodded.

'What?'

She smiled. 'Are you, Mr Ayub Ahmed, ready to bear with me for the next three months as I hurl everything in my stomach, first thing in the morning?' she asked him, like an interviewer pressing on with a question holding a mike.

He still couldn't believe it. 'How? When ... we always used prot ...' he trailed off. Her eyes went up and then down and she nodded.

'Yup. That night,' she said.

He blew out a breath. 'Wow. I mean ... just wow,' he said. She sat up, worried.

'You're happy right?' she asked, cautiously. He cursed himself for making her doubt his feelings.

'Deliriously happy, actually,' he said and her face brightened. 'How long have you known?'

'Just three days or so,' she said.

'You weren't going to tell me?' he asked, the thought sending a shaft of pain through his heart. His child. Their child. Would she have kept him away from his own child?

'Not right away. I didn't want to muddy your feelings for me with feelings for the baby,' she said. 'I wanted to come back because you wanted me, not just the baby.'

He listened to her in silence. He knew she wouldn't have come back only because she was pregnant. He knew first-hand how her self-respect worked. If she hadn't wanted to come back, she wouldn't have, whether or not she was pregnant.

He pulled up beside her and touched her belly lightly. 'Our baby,' he whispered. She turned to him and kissed him.

'I missed you so much, Ayub,' she said. 'I cried myself to sleep every night because you weren't with me, holding me, loving me.'

'I couldn't bear to be in this room without you either,' he said. 'Too many memories.'

She tugged off her clothes, taking them off one by one. 'What are you doing?' he asked her warily.

'What you should be doing,' she said, going to work on the buttons of his shirt.

'But …'

'But?'

'The baby?'

'What about the baby?' she asked, pressing a kiss to his chest and pushing away his shirt from his shoulders and getting to work on his pants. She was panting lightly and the sight of her rosy body, covered with a sheen of sweat, turned him on like nothing else.

'What if we hurt the baby?' he asked.

She sat back and kicked off the bed covers and shoved their clothes off the bed.

'So you're saying we shouldn't … shouldn't have sex until the baby is born?' she asked innocently as she removed her bra and handed it to him. His eyes widened and his breath quickened as he took it from her hands.

'No, I'm not saying that,' he said, throwing her bra somewhere behind him.

'Then? Unless you plan to be rough with me, I don't think there should be any problem,' she said.

He pushed her back down on the bed and kissed up from her stomach, placing gentle kisses near her navel and then moving up slowly.

'Ayub,' she groaned as his mouth found her nipple and he drew circles around the tip with his tongue.

'I'll be gentle. Very, very gentle,' he promised as he pushed inside her. They both gasped and he held her hands above her head as they found their rhythm.

He kissed her slowly. 'Tehzeeb,' he panted.

'Hmm?' she asked, squirming under him, wrapping her legs around his waist.

'I'm happy you came back,' he said.

'I can see that,' she said, gurgling with laughter. 'Although I'm regretting missing the chance to make you beg.'

His eyes became serious and he stilled. 'What? What are you doing?' she asked.

'I'll beg now if you want,' he said.

'What I want is for you to keep moving,' she hissed.

'Yes, but I'll beg you any time, any day. Never leave me and go away like that.'

Her gaze softened and she swallowed her protest. 'Never,' she whispered.

EPILOGUE

Eight months later

The party at Api's house was probably like one of the many she made fun of, Ana thought, as she and Athiya got down from the auto outside the big house and walked inside. But since it was her baby shower, it could also be different.

Much had changed in the past few months since Api had returned to her husband. She had started working again in the same office because they'd wanted her to come back and they had been very apologetic about the video incident. She had started her maternity leave just last week and the baby shower had been finalised for today.

From what Api spoke about the situation at home, her mother-in-law was none too pleased that she was continuing to work despite being pregnant but it hadn't become an issue between them. Things were almost great between them. Well, almost, because no matter what Tehzeeb told her, she knew that a mother-in-law could never replace a mother and there would always be some friction between them. Nevertheless, Api's one week of estrangement from her family had seemed like it had been a trial by fire for all of them, from which they had all emerged, scarred but stronger.

As for her, she had completed her studies and was trying to get a job as a behavioural counsellor but had been unsuccessful so far. She still hoped to get a job in a hospital soon though.

'Do you think there will be a quiz?' Athiya asked. 'I'd love to get hold of some prizes.'

Shrugging, Ana walked up the steps and rang the doorbell. Maira opened the door, looking excited.

'Come, come!' she said, pulling them inside by grabbing their wrists. Maira was dressed in a classy outfit – light pink tiered sharara pants with a matching top and Ana wished she and Athiya had dressed up too instead of wearing their regular outfits.

'Where's Api?' Athiya wondered out aloud as they walked past the sumptuously decorated foyer and then the living room where everyone was seated, talking among themselves.

'There she is,' Ana whispered as Tehzeeb saw them and got up with a great deal of difficulty. Her due date was the following month. Tehzeeb was wearing a chocolate brown kurta and palazzo pants and a dupatta that rested lightly over her bulging stomach. She was glowing and her hair was loose and she wore no makeup.

'Ana! Athiya!' she said, holding out her arms. The two of them went to her and embraced her lightly. The baby decided to kick just then and Tehzeeb winced.

'Wow,' Ana said, shaking her head. 'Wow. Did that just happen? Did your baby just kick his aunts?'

Tehzeeb grinned. 'Taking after Ayub already,' she said, looking down at her belly and rubbing lightly.

'Meaning, being very possessive of you and not letting you out of his sight,' Athiya said wryly. Tehzeeb shrugged.

'Could also be a she, you know,' Ana said. Tehzeeb smiled.

'Where's Ayub Bhai by the way?' Ana asked, looking around curiously.

'Um, it's a baby shower. Only for women. Men aren't allowed,' Tehzeeb reminded her. 'But if you must know, he's upstairs in my room, waiting for me. Come, sit. I'll get you something to eat.'

'No, you sit. I'll get us something to eat. If that's all right,' Ana said, looking for some indication of protocol. Tehzeeb nodded and smiled.

'Go ahead,' she said with a smile.

Ana walked outside, leaving Tehzeeb talking with Athiya and she bumped into Maira, who was laughing at something another young girl was saying.

'Ana! Where are you going?' Maira asked.

'Err, to get something to eat,' Ana said. She was still awkward around Maira because of Luqman. Sometimes she still thought of him, without any reason, and she would blush. Maira nodded and walked on back to the living room.

As Ana fixed a plate for herself and Athiya, talking to Haleema Auntie, the cook who seemed to love Api like everyone else, an older lady walked inside. She looked around and Haleema instructed one of the servant girls to take the guest to the living room.

'No, it's all right. I want to sit here for some time,' the woman said. Ana and Haleema Auntie exchanged a look as the woman sat down at the kitchen table.

'You're Tehzeeb's sister, right?' the woman asked. Ana nodded perfunctorily.

'How old are you? Have you finished your education?' she asked. Ana realised this was a rishta moment. Shit. She quickly filled up the plates and nodding to the lady, she walked back to the living room.

'What took you so long?' Athiya asked, taking the plate from her. Tehzeeb stole a kabab from Ana's plate as she settled down beside her, breathing heavily.

'What's going on?' Ana asked.

'I don't know. Maira said she had some announcement to make,' Tehzeeb said.

The lady from the kitchen ambled into the living room then and Tehzeeb's mother-in-law stood up and welcomed her warmly.

'Welcome to my house, Salma Apa,' she said, hugging the woman whose gaze somehow managed to find Ana in the living room once more.

Ana shifted in her seat uncomfortably.

'Luqman keeps telling me I should attend more of your parties. But you know how it is in my house ...' the woman said. Ana felt a lurch inside her chest. This was Luqman's mother.

Maira saw the woman and for a second, she lost her focus but then found her composure once more.

'Is she going to conduct a quiz?' Athiya asked. The room was silent at just that moment and everybody heard her. Ana rolled her eyes as Maira smiled and shook her head.

'No more quizzes. They were dumb anyway. And why should we have a quiz when we have an entertainer in our house? Please welcome my Bhabhi, Tehzeeb!' she announced.

Tehzeeb's eyes grew round. 'What? No! You didn't say anything until now,' she hissed to Maira.

'Obviously I didn't. Or you would have bunked your own baby shower,' Maira said.

Her mother-in-law was leading Luqman's mother towards one of the sofas and she turned to Tehzeeb and winked.

'Go, do your best, Tehzeeb. No one is going take any videos!' she said in a hushed tone.

Tehzeeb looked shocked. 'Ammi! Don't joke about that!' she whispered. Her mother-in-law shrugged.

Ana grinned. 'Listen to your mother-in-law, Api. Do your best,' she said. Athiya and she high-fived her behind Tehzeeb's back. She glared at them both as she got up.

'I'll get my revenge. Just you wait,' she promised them.

'Do the Raakhi one. Mere Karan Arjun aayenge!' Athiya shouted.

Everyone laughed. Tehzeeb reached the centre of the room where Maira had thoughtfully kept a chair and she sat down on it carefully. She lifted her head, raised her eyebrows dramatically and smiled.

ALSO IN THE JASMINE VILLA SERIES
BY ANDALEEB WAJID

ALSO IN THE JASMINE VILLA SERIES
BY ANDALEEB WAJID